"21"

"21"

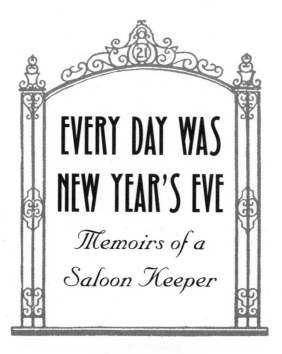

EVERY DAY WAS NEW YEAR'S EVE

Memoirs of a Saloon Keeper

H. PETER KRIENDLER
WITH
H. PAUL JEFFERS

Taylor Publishing Company
Dallas, Texas

Photographs, drawings, and excerpts of material from *The Iron Gate of Jack and Charlie's '21'* (1936, 1950) are used with permission of the Kriendler '21' collection. Photos also provided by Karen Kriendler Nelson and Jan F. Constantine.

Floor-plan drawing and contemporary photography by Kevin Gordon.

Published by Taylor Publishing Company
1550 West Mockingbird Lane
Dallas, Texas 75235
www.taylorpub.com

Library of Congress Cataloging-in-Publication Data

Kriendler, H. Peter.
"21" : every day was New Year's Eve : memoirs of a saloon keeper /
H. Peter Kriendler, with H. Paul Jeffers.
p.   cm.
Includes index.
ISBN 0-87833-229-4
1. Cookery. 2. Restaurants—New York (State)—New York. 3. 21
(Restaurant : New York)—History. I. Jeffers, H. Paul (Harry
Paul), 1934–   . II. Title.
TX715.K894   1999
647.95747'1—DC21   99-12046
CIP

Printed in the United States of America
10 9 8 7 6 5 4 3 2 1

CONTENTS

INTRODUCTION

So how did a nice Jewish fella with a law degree wind up as a saloon keeper?

By chance. And with a little luck thrown in. But most of all by being born at the right time, in the right family, and having a big brother with the smarts to recognize a good thing. The good thing was Prohibition.

It had been a long time arriving. The first liquor law in the New World went on the books in Virginia in 1619, a year before the Pilgrims set foot on Plymouth Rock. The edict outlawed "the drunkard" and laid out punishments. Eleven years later in Massachusetts, Governor John Winthrop encouraged abandonment of the practice of "drinking healths," and this was soon formalized by outlawing getting drunk. The law limited imbibing more than a half-pint at a time and banned tippling "above ye space of half an hour."

In 1697 New York outlawed patronizing saloons on Sundays, a ban that would remain in effect for more than two centuries. In 1777, in the midst of our war for freedom, the Continental Congress adopted a resolution recommending immediate passage of state laws "putting an immediate stop to the pernicious practice of distilling grain, by which the most extensive evils are likely to be derived if not quickly prevented."

Although efforts were mounted during the Civil War to stem drinking in the ranks of the Union army, liquor continued to be smuggled to troops by enterprising merchants who concealed the bottles in the tops of boots, giving the American language the term "bootlegger." But it was after the Civil War that a national "Temperance" movement got into the prohibitionist spirit, led by such self-righteous characters as Frances Willard of the National Women's Christian Temperance Union, Susan B. Anthony, and Carry Nation, who wielded an axe to bust up saloons.

With the dawn of the twentieth century, prohibition laws were pending before virtually every state legislature. By 1917 more than half the states and four territories had embraced the banning of the sale of alcoholic drinks. Then all forty-six were asked by Congress to extend the ban nationwide.

When the Eighteenth Amendment to the Constitution of the United States of America went into effect on January 17, 1920, I was fourteen and a half years old.

My parents, Kieve (Carl) and Sadie Kriendler, had been brought to America by her brother Sam Brenner in 1896. I was born in Brooklyn on July 8, 1905. My father became a metalworker at the Brooklyn Navy Yard. After he died at the age of forty-four in the flu epidemic of 1917, Mama was left the responsibility for raising four daughters (Augusta, Anna, Eunice, and Beatrice) and four sons: John Carl (Jack), Maxwell (Mac), Robert (Bob), and me.

We lived on the Lower East Side of New York City in a five-room, fifth-floor tenement walk-up at 167 Norfolk Street. To get warm, we had to stand by the kitchen stove. To be cool in summer, we went "on vacation" on the roof or fire escape. Opposite our home was the neighborhood synagogue. Our school was P.S. 160. We got haircuts for two cents from an Italian barber who went around with a portable chair made from a fruitbox. The local movie house was the Odeon at Clinton and Houston Streets. Admission was three cents. At the corner of Avenue A stood the 10th Street Boys Club, site of numerous fistfights featuring Italians versus Poles, Russians versus Lithuanians, and frequently everyone versus Jews.

Mama held the family together by working as a midwife and driving into us the value of getting an education. She'd studied at the University of Kraków, Poland. One of her favorite sayings was, "They can't take away what you have in your head." She made it clear that she expected her sons to go to college and her daughters to make good marriages and families.

Doing his best to follow Mama's advice concerning education, Jack enrolled at Fordham University with plans to become a pharmacist, while his best friend, our cousin Charles A. Berns, was attending New York University's School of Commerce with plans to go into law. Both earned night school tuition by working days as salesmen and handymen in Uncle Sam's shoe store. Sam was also a partner in a small saloon in the heart of the Jewish ghetto at Essex and Rivington Streets. With Sam's name spelled in silver dollars cemented into the floor just inside the front door, the place was like all such establishments at the time, a beehive of politics. One of my jobs when I was ten years old was to teach immigrants how to fill out paper ballots so they'd be able to vote for candidates of the local Democratic Club.

While Uncle Sam did a thriving business in shoes, the saloon was the bigger moneymaker by far. This was due in large part to Uncle Sam's recognition that the only way to keep the customers coming back was to take care of them and provide them with good quality. He served the finest beer and charged accordingly—ten cents a glass, rather than the nickel tariff at other bars. Food was likewise top-notch, consisting primarily of Wiener schnitzel and Hungarian goulash.

But the main draw of the place was Sam. One historian of New York drinking establishments described him as the most fastidious saloon keeper on the Lower East Side. In his well-tailored suits, showing impeccable taste and elegant manners, and sporting a large diamond ring, he was without a doubt the spiffiest purveyor of food and drink anywhere in town.

None of this was lost on Jack.

Then came the triumph the prohibitionists had agitated for—the banning of the manufacture and sale of alcoholic drinks under the Eighteenth Amendment and its empowering legislation known as the National Prohibition Enforcement Act (Volstead Act). Passed by Congress in 1919 over the veto of President Woodrow Wilson, it defined as intoxicating liquor any beverage containing more than one-half of one percent alcohol. Establishing a commissioner to enforce it under the Bureau of Internal Revenue, the act was to go into effect at midnight on January 16, 1920. With great expectations on the day before, the Anti-Saloon League issued a statement saying, "It is here at last—dry America's first birthday. Now for an era of clear thinking and clean living."

The first Prohibition commissioner, John F. Kramer,

vowed, "This law will be obeyed in cities, large and small, and in villages, and where it is not obeyed it will be enforced. The law says that liquor to be used as a beverage must not be manufactured. Nor sold, nor given away, nor hauled in anything on the surface of the earth or under the earth or in the air."

History records not only how wrong Kramer was, but also that in going dry the country created a fertile field for bootleggers, rumrunners, and gangsters. Almost instantly, the speakeasy took the place of saloons, and in far greater numbers. Another result was, as Frederick Lewis Allen noted in *Only Yesterday*, "the general transformation of drinking from a masculine prerogative to one shared by both sexes together."

Observing these illicit drinking spots springing up all over town, Jack suggested to Charlie that they might earn enough money to finance their educations by opening one of their own. What he had in mind was a partnership with a friend by the name of Edward Irving. As a result of a bad investment, Irving had come into possession of a small tearoom in the heart of Greenwich Village and close to New York University on Sixth Avenue between Washington Place and Fourth Street.

Although Charlie was dubious, Jack persuaded our sister Anna and her husband, Henry Tannenbaum, to lend him part of the money needed to buy into Eddie's business. The remainder was obtained when Uncle Sam hocked his diamond ring.

As the saying goes—and as you will read in this book—the rest is history. It's the story of a family business delivering to the public what it wanted—excellent-quality liquor and good food served in a pleasant setting. Born during one of the most colorful periods in the country's history, the Roaring Twenties, the Kriendler family enterprise would continue over the span of eight decades at four locations, the last being the one with an iron gate and jockey figures in front, and whose name is its address.

Brimming with anecdotes and crowded with the person-alities of twentieth-century America's social, cultural, political, business, and entertainment worlds, my tale presents the inside story of our nation's most legendary restaurant, providing not only a unique memoir of '21', but also a chronicle of America, its premier city, and the fascinating people who dropped in for a drink or a meal, from the giddy days and nights of the Jazz Age to yesterday.

"Mr. Pete" Kriendler

One

CONGENIAL HOSPITALITY

The speakeasy that Jack opened in 1922 was called the Red Head. It offered booze served in teacups and quickly caught on as a hangout for a college crowd very much like the youths described by a patron of the place, F. Scott Fitzgerald, in his 1920 novel *This Side of Paradise*. Its protagonist, Amory Blaine, saw the girls "doing things that even in his memory would have been impossible: eating three-o'clock after-dance suppers in impossible cafes, talking of every side of life with an air of half-earnestness, half of mockery, yet with a furtive excitement," while the young men sipped liquor from silver hip flasks filled with "hooch" and everyone danced wildly to the musical rage of the day—jazz.

In addition to Fitzgeraldian collegiates, the Red Head drew the attention of artists, musicians, writers, and other bohemian types of the Village. It was not the usual "speak" where the men sat silently downing drinks. It offered the cozy atmosphere of a fraternity room. Patrons discovered a jivey place where, when the band took a break, they could take over on the club's piano and drums.

At age sixteen, all I could do was sip a soft drink and hang around trying to act like a big cheese while hoping to catch a dance with one of the "flappers" who came downtown from uptown boarding schools. They came in the belief that it was the cat's meow to paint their faces with makeup and take the El or a double-deck Fifth Avenue bus to *the Village*, without guys escorting them.

A painting of the time by Joseph Golinken entitled *Speako Deluxe* portrays the interior of a speakeasy in bright colors with beautiful people crowded around an elliptical bar and being served by suave-looking waiters. Certainly, there were such spots, but the Red Head wasn't among them. Small and a little on the cramped side, it had embossed-tin walls, a revolving ceiling fan, a few wooden tables, and straight-backed wooden chairs. A tiny kitchen was separated from this room by a curtain. Light came from wall sconces with paper shades bearing the silhouette of a redheaded woman.

As the customers flocked to the Red Head and money poured into the cash drawer, Charlie Berns tossed aside his misgivings and joined the firm as a much-needed accountant and keeper of the till. When Eddie Irving decided he would rather be a full-time Wall Street broker, Charlie came in as Jack's full partner. Serving as cashier under this new management was a man with dreams of becoming a newspaperman but with no inkling that he would go on to give New York the nickname "Naked City," produce movies, and have a Broadway theater named for him—Mark Hellinger.

Years later, Mark recalled the first time he met Jack and Charlie. "I hadn't been sitting in their place more than fourteen hours when the house bought a drink," he wrote. "I cannot forget that occasion, because it has never happened since. Charlie was a plump youth with plenty of hair on his head. Jack was a wide-eyed lad with lots of suits that always fitted him perfectly."

Mark later said his time at the Red Head was the happiest period of his life because he just sat and raked in the fifty-cent cover charges and pocketed as much as he wanted. The booze was sold in dollar-an-ounce flasks that were kept in coat pockets until it was necessary to fill a teacup. Such drinking spots were soon known as "cup joints."

The source of the liquor was Uncle Sam Brenner, with more than a little help from Mama. Living on East Fourth Street, she took delivery from Uncle Sam's bootleggers and stored the supply until an urgent call came from the Red Head for replenishment. This was usually handled by me and brothers Mac and Bob by way of a little red wagon camouflaged with groceries.

Because gangsters quickly recognized a promising future in the illicit booze business, a couple of mugs showed up one day to express an interest in what was going on at the Red Head. Members of the notorious Hudson Dusters gang—cradle for all the gangsters of the time—led by Linkey "the Killer" Mitchell, decided to cut themselves in as partners.

As Charlie Berns remembered it, "Being innocent college boys, Jack and I refused to discuss the matter. A couple of weeks later they came around again. They told us unless we paid for certain protective services, they would wreck the joint. Jack and I remained unimpressed. A few nights later, as we were walking home, a couple of them jumped us. We gave a pretty good account of ourselves, and they took quite a licking."

The next time Charlie wasn't so lucky. Jack survived in one piece, but Charlie's attacker had a razor. Charlie wound up at St. Vincent's Hospital with a dozen stitches in his neck.

A few well-placed "gifts" to the Charles Street Police Precinct assured that the Red Head wouldn't have to worry about the thugs anymore. Charlie recalled, "We would slip the captain a $50 bill from time to time and a box of cigars to the cops on the beat. They could always count on us for free meals and drinks, and at Christmas time, of course, we had a gift for everybody."

While the local gendarmes were taken care of in cold hard cash, the removal of the threat of federal raiders was the result of the sentimentality of a pair of revenue agents. One was a bulbous little man who owned a cigar store and ran a boxing club on the Lower East Side before the country dried up. At age forty, five-foot-five, 250-pound Isadore "Izzy" Einstein pictured a bright and probably prosperous future as an agent in pursuit of Prohibition lawbreakers. But after one look at the portly figure, James Shevlin, chief enforcement agent for the Southern District of New York, expressed grave doubts. "I must say, Mr. Einstein," he remarked, "you don't look much like a detective."

This was exactly Izzy's point. Because he looked like anything *but* a detective, he would never be suspected of being one, enabling him to nab bootleggers and speakeasy owners red-handed. Teamed with another unlikely cop, Moe Smith, who'd also been a Lower East Side cigar salesman and fight club manager, he and Moe quickly became famous by masquerading as everything from parched gravediggers bellying up to a bar to a couple of jazz musicians carrying trombone and clarinet cases. So good was this duo at closing down speakeasies that O. O. McIntyre wrote in his syndicated newspaper column that Izzy was "as famous as the Woolworth Building." And the *New York*

Tribune hailed him as "mastermind of the Federal rum ferrets." Soon the pair were donning disguises to carry out raids in Pittsburgh and points west, including Chicago. Sixty-some years later, Izzy and Moe were portrayed by Jackie Gleason and Art Carney in a television movie.

Yet Izzy and Moe never raided the Red Head. Indeed, they became Jack and Charlie's steadiest customers. They'd both known all "the little Kriendler boys" from the old neighborhood. While the Red Head thrived without having to fork over payoffs to gangsters or worry about cops and Prohibition raids, it operated under the rules laid down by the police, which required an open-door policy, meaning anyone who came in had to be served. The club also had to close at one o'clock in the morning, while clubs in other precincts could stay open as long as they wished. Unhappy about these strictures, Jack began looking around for a spot where he could open a fancier place and feel free to operate with better hours. He found it not far away in the cellar of 88 Washington Place.

Named the Fronton, the new club was much more like the kind of spot associated in the popular imagination with a speakeasy. One large room had a dozen banquette seats and several tables with high-backed chairs that accommodated about sixty people. A pair of wooden sawhorses held up heavy planks to form the bar. Under this was a floor drain to catch the liquor that might have to be hurriedly ditched in case of a raid. The booze itself was kept on top of the bar in four large pitchers, one for each type—scotch, bourbon, rye, and gin. And yes, before anyone was let in, Charlie Berns's cousin Bill Hardey checked them out by looking through a peephole in the door. In case the person who approached the door looked suspiciously like a revenue agent, there was a button that set off a buzzer signaling the occupants of the club to beat a hasty exit.

Bill Hardey also took charge of hiring entertainers. As an exhibition dancer himself, he had an eye for talented women who could dance and sing but also act as hostesses. A five-piece band provided music. The star attraction was the great jazz pianist Al Segal, who was later to coach Ethel Merman.

Most of the Fronton customers came from the Red Head, but to solicit new customers Jack and Charlie distributed business cards that read:

Congenial Hospitality
Jack and Charlie
Call SPR 0007.

Among the new clients were poet Edna St. Vincent Millay, Herbert Bayard Swope of the *New York World*, and the dapper mayor of New York, James J. Walker. Known affectionately on the East Side, West Side, and all around town as Jimmy and "Beau James," he was introduced to the club by businessman Billy Seeman, himself a well-known man-about-town, party-giver, pal of Walker, and occupant of the apartment above the club. Claiming that "whiskey kills all germs," Billy had a reputation for starting his day with a glass of gin and keeping a drink of some kind in his hand until bedtime. Because the action at the Fronton never really got started before eleven o'clock at night, it was not only Billy's kind of place, but right up fun-loving Mayor Walker's alley.

While the Red Head had offered a menu with two choices in sandwiches—ham and cheese or cheese and ham—the Fronton became a genuine restaurant with an Italian chef who cooked up steaks, chops, sauced meats, and a variety of sandwiches. And the club surpassed other speaks by providing a wine list. The goods came from an Italian bootlegger with the right connections on the Hudson River docks.

In keeping with the classier tone of the Fronton, Jack began to dress the part of natty restaurateur, a role he would carry on until his dying day. Once when he walked into the Fronton with a flower on the lapel of his well-tailored suit, a customer looked him up and down incredulously, then turned to Charlie and asked, "What's he, a floorwalker?"

Jack and Charlie also broke ground by being particular as to who was allowed in, with special attention to seeing that gangsters did not cross the threshold. When word reached Charlie that one of the thugs was talking about muscling himself in, Charlie turned to a boyhood friend, Jimmy Kerrigan, who just happened to be a revenue agent. "The minute I got word from these hoodlums that they were planning to visit us on a certain night," Charlie recalled, "I got in touch with Jimmy. He arrived in a car with five of his fellow agents, parked across the street, and waited. When the gangsters showed, the agents swarmed all over them. They held a long conversation out there on the sidewalk, and that's the last we heard from that group."

Two events that friendly federal agents could not prevent were a flood and a fire. The former was the result of a few days of rain and a backed-up sewer. Because the club was below street level, the result was potential disaster. Rescue came in the form of the nearby firehouse, whose chief was a regular patron. When he learned of the crisis, he sent a truck with pumps to stem the rising tide. The fire, of undetermined origin, was also handled by the chief's men, but this time they had to use axes to get at the source of the flames, leaving the premises a wreck.

"Cheer up, fellas," the chief said to the glum-looking partners. "Think of all the money you're going to get from the insurance."

Charlie groaned. "We're not insured."

"Never mind," said the surprised fire chief. "I'll see that my boys fix it all up."

Because the firemen were also customers, they lost no time in getting the place back into shape.

With business thriving and requiring his total attention, Jack recognized that he was not going to realize his plan of selling booze to earn money to pay for the completion of his college education. He was in the drink and food business, and that was that. Not so with Charlie. Even while he worked full-time at the Fronton he kept up his studies. He got his law degree and passed the bar exam in 1926.

The following year, thanks to the city's starting condemnation proceedings to clear the area around Washington Place for construction of a subway station, Jack and Charlie again had to look around for a new spot. It had to have all the appeal of the Fronton and attract a greater number of even more sophisticated customers.

They decided to head uptown.

Two

JACK AND CHARLIE'S

"It was understood and agreed that the big thing in life was liquor," wrote John O'Hara in describing the tragic main character of his 1935 novel *Butterfield 8*. Among the places where Gloria Wandrous did her heaviest drinking between 1926 and 1930, becoming "known by name and sight" as she "awed the bartenders by the amount she drank," were gangster Legs Diamond's Hotsy-Totsy; the Dizzy Club and the Bandbox, a pair of speakeasies operated by Tony Roma; the Clamhouse; Tommy Guinan's Chez Florence; and a popular spot at Forty-two West Forty-ninth Street.

At that location was a townhouse standing on leased land that was owned by Columbia University. The building had belonged to Albert H. Wiggin, later chairman of the board of the Chase National Bank. He in turn had rented the house to Benjamin Quinn Sr., a Yale man and head of the stock exchange firm E.C. Benedict & Co. But when the block was rezoned for commercial use Mr. Quinn joined other homeowners in moving out of their residences and leasing them to men interested in opening speakeasies.

Setting up shop at No. 42 in 1925, Caesar Betti and Peter Mossi opened a restaurant and also "ran a little liquor." When their enterprise failed to catch on they looked for someone to take the place off their hands. Jack and Charlie called it the Puncheon, but the new bistro would also be known by other names (partly to confuse the federal tax men)—the Grotto, No. 42, and Jack and Charlie's.

I don't know whether O'Hara's real-life inspiration for Gloria ever entered the speakeasy in a fashionable townhouse in the heart of the carriage-trade residential neighborhood a stone's throw from the Bergdorf Goodman store. But O'Hara came into the club often. He would remain a familiar face in Jack and Charlie's clubs for the remainder of his life.

When this was going on I was in my twenties and a college student with my heart set on a career in law. While I admired the success of Jack as a saloon keeper, the farthest thing from my mind was following him into the business of providing food and drink to people who considered themselves the Smart Set.

One of the stars of that group of style-setters, wits, and self-promoters was a roly-poly fellow with a toothbrush mustache and a wry sense of humor. Discovering Jack and Charlie's new boîte, Robert Benchley was soon extolling its glories to a giddy band of sophisticates who lunched each day at the nearby Algonquin Hotel. Among the pals Benchley temporarily lured away from the famous Algonquin Round Table were theater critic Alexander Woollcott, novelist Edna Ferber, columnist Franklin P. Adams, playwright George S. Kaufman, ex-reporters Ben Hecht and Charles MacArthur, humorous essayist Donald Ogden Stewart, and a clever woman named Dorothy Parker.

So much has been written about the wits of the Algonquin Round Table, some of which is probably true, that there's little I can contribute to that story except to say that as a twenty-one-year-old college kid hanging around the Puncheon, I was as impressed with them as everybody else was at that time. Donald Ogden Stewart best described the tenor of those years. "The speakeasy was a kind of club," he wrote, "where what counted was not social position but whether the people one met were fun to be with."

The man I recall as most fun to be with was Robert Benchley. Having read quite a few of his humorous essays in magazines, I'd been an admirer of his witty way with words. One of the first essays I recalled had appeared in 1923. Entitled "The Lure of the Rod," it dealt with one of my interests: fishing. "Fishing is one of my favorite sports," Benchley wrote, "and one of these days I expect to catch a fish. I have been at it fourteen years now and have caught everything else, including hell from my wife, a cold in the head, and up on my drinking."

Not only did Benchley not give me short shrift, as other famous people might have done, but one afternoon he delighted in taking a deck of cards from his pocket and spending hours teaching me all the ways to play solitaire. I also became an admirer of his ability to drink all day and into the evening with not a hint of inebriation. Years later, in an introduction to a book of Bob's funny essays, Frank Sullivan captured the Benchley essence with these words: "To be in his company made you feel happy; he had a faculty for making you feel that you were far more brilliant and personable than you really were."

Certainly, Bob Benchley was precisely the kind of patron who would receive a hearty welcome at the Puncheon. Jack's goal was to make the club a place where people of letters, social status, and wealth could feel comfortable. This required tight control over who was allowed to pass through the iron front gate. No one was admitted who was not known, unless introduced by a regular.

The guardian of the portal was Gus Lux. Shortly after Gus was hired, he heard a pounding on the gate. Opening the door a crack, he found a man in work clothes. When the man demanded admittance, Gus retorted, "You can't come in here dressed like that."

The man asked, "Do you expect a tinsmith to wear a top hat?"

Closing the door, Gus said, "We don't need any tinsmiths."

"But my son said it was an emergency."

Gus opened the door a little. "And who's your son?"

Cracking a smile, the tinsmith replied, "Charlie Berns."

Among those for whom the gate swung open was a group of Yale men who immediately adopted the club and dubbed it "Ben Quinn's Kitchen." This name was bestowed in honor of the son of the man who had abandoned the townhouse. Upon looking around the room on his first visit, Ben realized that he was in the cellar of his former home. "This is my old house," he shouted. "Martinis for everyone."

In leaving us a word picture of Jack and Charlie's new spot on West Forty-ninth Street, Ben Quinn Jr. recalled "an attractive new speakeasy with good liquor" that was reached by going through an iron gate, down three steps and up two, then being admitted by a doorman into a room with small tables covered with red-and-white tablecloths. A bar stood to the right at the far end of the room.

Of these Yalies, John O'Hara wrote in *Butterfield 8*, "The young men were happiest when they could arrive at '42,' stewed and in cutaways, glad to be back with decent people.

"'Down with Princeton,' Gloria would say.

"'Down with Princeton,' the Yalies echoed.

"'To hell with Harvard,' she said, a little louder, and the Yale boys shouted in reply, 'The hell with Harvard.'"

In the November 1932 issue of *College Humor*, the Yale humor magazine, Robert Cruise McManus described the club in 1927: "On its renovated ground floor was a dressy little bar with small tables fringing the walls, while upstairs were two more elaborate dining rooms and, on the third story, accommodation for private parties. The liquors are of the best quality and widest variety so far obtainable in Manhattan. Cuisine and service were Parisian; the checks added up right."

What really put the place over with Yale men and kept them coming was the *Yale Record*. Under the banner "Brownstones and Bottles," it said of Jack and Charlie's Puncheon Club:

> A Yale man made this place a habit of Yale men—and quite a good habit it was. It has remained that ever since. The ordinary run of speakeasy is a necessary evil of Prohibition. Thus it is a genuine pleasure to find such a place as the Puncheon, combining as it does the connoisseur's ultimate in wining and dining. This has long been the watering place of particular epicures—you may mingle with them here in the expensive aroma of good cigars.
>
> Jack makes it a pleasure to stop singing and be quietly respectable, while Charlie compels you to remain in a good humor—greatly aided by a most reasonable check when

you leave. Cuisine comes first to both of them—you are
expected to enjoy eating and you may drink if you wish.
Familiar faces will always be present—and all those faces
familiar in the best places.

Although a Harvard man, Robert Benchley certainly
found no cause to challenge the assessment of the *Yale Record*.
Nor did any of his friends, nor any of the upscale customers who
flocked to the door hoping to pass muster and be admitted. By
now one of the gate guardians was my brother Mac, fresh out of
law school. A would-be patron discovered it was easier to join
a private club than to gain admittance to the Puncheon. And
being rich did not help. If a man was preceded by a reputation
for being a rowdy or unruly drinker, how well-heeled he was
would cut no ice with Jack and Charlie, Mac, or Gus. What
mattered more than ability to pay was manners and appearance.

One well-dressed customer who dropped in at the club in
1927 was millionaire Gilbert Kahn. Just back from two years in
Britain, he arrived wearing the hat the English call a bowler.
After a couple of cocktails, he left without the black topper,
which had somehow managed to disappear. Later that evening,
one of the Puncheon's waiters arrived at Kahn's home carrying
a silver tray with a cover. With a courteous bow, the waiter lifted the lid to reveal the hat topped with a sprig of parsley. Kahn
got Jack's message: "You are welcome in our club, but you look
ridiculous in this thing, so please don't wear it when you come
in." Kahn never donned that bowler again, *anywhere*.

Women were allowed inside the Puncheon only if escorted by a gentleman approved by the proprietors. But one woman
who never tried to set a dainty foot in the place dispatched a
group of men to give the place a once-over for her. They arrived

one day in 1927, sent by Mabel Walker Willebrandt, federal assistant attorney general in charge of Prohibition enforcement.

"Two things put her on our trail," Charlie Berns recalled for John Kobler's history of Prohibition, *Ardent Spirits*. "First, the rumor going around that we were the only New York speakeasy in continuous operation that had never been bothered by the city police or the feds. Secondly, a valued customer, a Southern gentleman, who didn't trust his local brew, telephoned to ask us to send him some whiskey. The employee who took the call stupidly sent it through the mail with the return address on the package. The post office spotted it, reported it to the prohibition authorities and made Mrs. Willebrandt doubly determined to get us."

When the feds burst in, they found liquor out in the open everywhere. After working out a compromise with the prosecution to plead guilty to possession of liquor and to pay a fine, Jack and Charlie vowed not to repeat the mistake of leaving the booze in plain sight. Instead, the cache was stowed in vacant rooms at the top of the house next door. When the supply ran low in the club someone crawled out on the roof and down through the skylight to fetch reinforcements.

Among those who delighted in the quality of the liquor at the Puncheon was the acerbic muckraking journalist H. L. Mencken, who enjoyed bantering at the bar with Frank Crowninshield, editor of *Vanity Fair*; Will Rogers; George Jean Nathan; and the author who turned the Jazz Age into literature, F. Scott Fitzgerald. Offended by the raid, Mencken railed in print, "Why raid a place that is serving good liquor and not poisoning anybody?"

The selection of both food and drink was Jack's domain. The chef who prepared the choices on the menu was Henri

Geib. Originally from Alsace-Lorraine, he was encouraged by Jack to add his own flourishes to standard French fare. One of his creations was a kind of relish (we called it sauce maison) composed of mustard and other highly seasoned ingredients. The recipe would become a zealously guarded secret of the Puncheon and its successor, '21'.

Hungry New Yorkers with sufficient dough to pay the tab had a choice of superb French wines, champagnes, and cognacs to wash down fresh crab, brook trout, prosciutto, petite marmite Henry IV, saddle of lamb, roast veal, filet mignon, an omelette with pureed mushrooms, and hamburger raised to high art.

For all this good eating and fine drink a Puncheon customer was handed a bill that would have rendered the average American breathless. But these were the giddy 1920s, when a booming stock market put fortunes into pockets of the big spenders in a city that Jimmy Walker quipped "will be a really great place if they ever finish it."

Everybody seemed to be making money, and none more so than Jack and Charlie. Poor no more, Jack shared his success with the family, including moving our mother into a roomy apartment on fashionable Riverside Drive, paying for Mac to train an operatic-quality singing voice, and buying a seat for me on the New York Curb Exchange (later the American Stock Exchange), which enabled me to cash in on the general prosperity as well.

While becoming a wealthy man, Jack was refining his reputation as an affable restaurateur and host. Putting in sixteen hours a day, he worked to develop the character of the club as a place in which patrons could expect their comforts, wants, and whims to be served. But he also worked on his personal image, evolving into what one writer characterized as "a dandy despot, a Napoleon of the restaurant business."

By contrast, Charlie Berns was all business: moderate, slow, and deliberate as he made sure the books balanced. "Jack supplied all the looks and charm," Charlie would recall, "while I supplied only brains."

As all this was going on, I was studying law with a sharp-minded guy named Irving Lazar, from whom much would be heard in the years ahead, and I was making a few bucks through my seat on the New York Curb Exchange. Mac was learning the ropes as a doorman at the club. Brother Bob was in high school and planning to attend Rutgers University. And our four sisters —Augusta, Anna, Eunice, and Beatrice—were doing well in the paths they'd chosen and raising families of their own.

And the rest of America? Well, the country was doing great. It was in the midst of a binge that is now looked back on fondly as the Roaring Twenties. In more ways than one the 1920s offered everyone a high old time.

One bootlegger interviewed in the 1970s by author Marilyn Kaytor thought back on those days and with a nostalgic glint in his eyes saw it as an adventurous, romantic, and exciting era:

"From the outside No. 42 was anything but imposing," author Marilyn Kaytor wrote, "but inside Jack and Charlie's speakeasy the famous and picturesque of New York were drinking barrels and barrels of spirits, mixed into gin rickeys, Bronxes, orange blossoms, daiquiries, Bacardis, pink ladies, whisky sours, martinis, and side cars—the drinks destined to go down in history as the cocktails of the twenties."

Marching at the forefront of that legion of "the famous and picturesque" was the gaggle of free spirits who put the

Algonquin Hotel on the map through their much-reported and quoted lunches at the large round table in the middle of the hotel's Rose Room. All journalists when they began their careers, this group had gained fame as writers for *Vanity Fair* (Robert Benchley, Dorothy Parker, Robert Sherwood, and Heywood Broun), in the theater (Marc Connelly, George S. Kaufman), as authors and poets (Edna Ferber, Alice Duer Miller, and Donald Ogden Stewart), and as newspapermen (Ring Lardner, as well as Ben Hecht and Charles MacArthur, who would turn their journalistic experiences into the hit play *The Front Page*).

The acknowledged drum major of this colorful band of witty literary lights was a fat, bespectacled drama critic who claimed to be the inventor of the Brandy Alexander— Alexander Woollcott. Because the Algonquin Hotel was near-by on West Forty-fourth Street, once Bob Benchley had discovered the Puncheon, little coaxing was needed to get Woollcott and his fellow Round Tablers to follow him to the iron gate and into the club. Like Bob, Aleck had an amazing ability to down drinks without getting (or at least appearing) drunk. As for the legendary Dorothy Parker, despite her saucy tongue I found her a very likeable gal. Along with everyone else who ever laid eyes on the constantly rumpled Heywood Broun, I could not disagree with a George Kaufman crack that Broun always looked like an unmade bed. He also had a habit of walk-ing with his head down, as if he were hoping to discover a dropped nickel or dime. Because all of these luminaries knew how to behave properly in a respectable speakeasy, they were greeted with heartfelt welcomes.

Although I was charmed and amused by all the Round Tablers, I believe I remained most attracted to Bob Benchley, because he seemed to me to be unaffected by his fame and the power that came with being a New York theater critic. When I got up the courage to ask him why his reviews were so personal and sympathetic to actors, he answered, "I'm a pushover for a rising curtain."

Reading many of his critiques, I discovered myself learning more about Bob's behavior in the theater than I learned about the production on stage. In June 1928, summing up the theatrical season, he claimed to have caught up on his sleep, "owing chiefly to there being fewer pistols fired in the drama of 1927–28." He also boasted that he had found a way to fold an overcoat so that small change didn't drop from the pockets.

What I hadn't known about Bob, but learned in January 1928, was that he had a talent not only as a humorist and drama critic, but also as a performer of his own writings. As he sipped a drink in the Puncheon, he told me quite matter-of-factly that he'd been persuaded by Thomas Chalmers of the Fox Picture Corporation to make a movie version of a piece he had written and presented on Broadway in 1922 as part of a revue called *No Sirree* which the Round Tablers took onto the stage. Bob's contribution was "The Treasurer's Report." The film was made at the Fox studios in Astoria, Long Island, and became such a hit that many movie theaters billed it on their marquees above the feature being shown. Produced for $16,000, it earned ten times that figure at the box office, making Bob a hot ticket in the movie business. The success of "The Treasurer's Report" was quickly followed by a ten-minute laugh riot, "The Sex Life of the Polyp," released in July 1928.

When these triumphs and a string of others took Bob out to Hollywood, I resigned myself to losing not only a regular patron at Jack and Charlie's but also a good friend. Happily, this

"21"

did not prove to be the case. In the autumn of the next year he was back in town, hired as a drama critic for the *New Yorker*.

Unfortunately, that was the season when the good times came crashing down, not only on Wall Street, but on Forty-ninth.

Three

SWING STREET

In 1928 Alexander Woollcott mused that New York, meaning the isle of Manhattan, was a place with no yesterdays, no reminders from one day's dawn to the next that others had walked streets we now walked and had lived where we now lived. On that cramped but enchanted patch of granite bedrock, Aleck pointed out, everyone's address was temporary.

In an essay entitled "No Yesterdays" he wrote, "In the fly-by-night flats where we hang our hats and try to sleep, there is no space for the chance memorabilia. None of us mounts a dubious ladder to hang a picture in October without a gray foreboding that it will have to come down in May, perhaps because the rent leaped beyond our reach, perhaps because the house itself is to make room for a new steel thrust at the amused stars."

For Jack and Charlie in that same year, that's exactly what happened. It was not that the rent was hiked; they could easily have afforded that. A notice arrived informing them that when their lease expired they would have to clear out of No. 42 so it could be torn down to make room for John D. Rockefeller Jr.'s grand scheme to build a huge commercial center with blocks of skyscrapers, stores, restaurants, gardens, and a grand plaza whose keystone and centerpiece would be a new home for the Metropolitan Opera, which was then situated at Broadway and Thirty-ninth.

With the lease on the old opera house due to expire in a few years, and noting that changes in the neighborhood had rendered the hundred-year-old site a noisy, congested, confining, and all-in-all inelegant location, the Metropolitan Opera and Real Estate Company directors had voted on January 21, 1926, to build a new home. The property they had in mind was the land owned by Columbia University from Forty-eighth to Fifty-first Streets between Fifth and Sixth Avenues. The way to obtain it, they proposed to Rockefeller, was for him to acquire the leases and then transfer them to the opera company. The plan, as Rockefeller later said, "commended itself" to him "as a highly important civic improvement." But as it turned out, the opera house didn't materialize. The Met remained where it was until the 1960s, when it moved to Lincoln Center. What rose on the property was the RCA Building, so that what stands approximately where No. 42 was in the 1920s is 30 Rockefeller Plaza, home of the NBC television network and its local station.

Paid eleven thousand dollars to vacate No. 42, and given six months to do so, Jack and Charlie remembered having been forced out of the Red Head and the Fronton and vowed that once they found a new address they would never again be made to move. This time they would *own* not only the building, but also the land beneath it.

The selection of a property was not just a matter of getting a good real estate deal. Also to be considered in choosing the new address was the clientele that they had spent years in building. In Woollcott's city of no yesterdays, people were known to switch loyalties to restaurants as readily as they changed apartments, and in Manhattan (then and now) anything more than a couple of blocks away might as well be in New Jersey.

For Jack and Charlie there was also the crucial issue of a move's causing them to lose the protection they had courted and won from the enforcers of Prohibition. What was needed for their new club, they agreed, was a spot that was in the jurisdiction of their old friends among the city's police and easygoing feds. Charlie recalled, "We didn't want to leave the neighborhood, not after the good relations we'd established there."

After considering a building on East Fifty-fourth between Park and Lexington Avenues, which was on the market for a very reasonable $40,000, they learned of another available property that better met their concerns about not having to cultivate fresh friends in law enforcement. It was a five-story brownstone on Fifty-second Street, a little west of Fifth Avenue. Owned by the Hochstadter family, its asking price was a hefty $130,000. But the lower price of the Fifty-fourth Street property did not figure in the cash that would probably be required to persuade Prohibition enforcers to look the other way. The house on Fifty-second was not only already on the turf of friendlies, but a walk of only three blocks was not too much to ask of their old customers.

Consequently, the deal on the house at 21 West Fifty-second Street was closed in early 1928 (because the Fifty-fourth Street property was such a bargain, it was also purchased), and plans were set in motion to convert No. 21 into a speakeasy and restaurant in the expectation that it would open for business on January 1, 1930.

"21"

As history sadly records, a calamity occurred on Tuesday, October 29, 1929, that left more than a few of the habitués of Jack and Charlie's Forty-ninth Street club eager to follow them up to 21 West Fifty-second. "Black Tuesday" was the day the bottom dropped out of the stock market, and patrons who had never given a thought to paying steep bills at the Puncheon suddenly found themselves asking for drinks and meals on the cuff.

After huddling to assess their finances, Jack and Charlie adopted a bold policy of not flinching in the face of economic disaster. They decided both to hold the line on prices and, if a regular couldn't afford to pay right now, to extend him credit. Further, the partners advanced money to those who had been left broke. As the Wall Street collapse led to the Great Depression, they printed scrip "redeemable for full value" in the club. They accepted customers' bank checks and held them until they were good. And they offered long-term loans. Thus they could boast that they were "bankers to the royal families of New York." It was a jest, but also true. On the same day in 1933 when the federal government closed banks, Jack and Charlie handed out fifty-dollar bills to customers who'd been caught high and dry.

"We work for the long haul," Charlie asserted, "not for the short profit." It was smart business, but it was also a demonstration of friendship. Both paid off handsomely.

Two months after the show-business newspaper *Variety* carried the headline "Wall Street Lays an Egg," Jack and Charlie invited loyal patrons to a private party to celebrate New Year's Eve and the last night of business at 42 West Forty-ninth. On the list of "trustee members" asked to participate in what Jack and Charlie dubbed "a demolition party" were Bob

Benchley, Gilbert Kahn (sans bowler), British comic actress Beatrice Lillie, Irish poet Ernest Boyd, Broadway producer Alex Aarons, silent-film stars Doris Kenyon and Milton Sills, and Billy Seeman, among others. As Jack and Charlie greeted them at the door they handed them shovels, crowbars, and pickaxes and encouraged them to "take the place apart."

There were Hawaiian guitarists strolling about as entertainment. Rare drinks "on the house" consisted of Major Baileys (mint juleps with gin), planter's punch, and sours. For "good luck," eggs were distributed. They were supposed to be hardboiled, but Bill Hardey decided it would be a good joke to hand out raw ones, giving new meaning to "having egg on your face."

At some point a friendly cop from the mounted unit (Vlav Wieghorst, who later became an accomplished painter of Western motifs and scenes) rode his horse through the place, which by then was mostly rubble. Doris Kenyon assigned herself the job of demolishing the ladies' room, then proudly wore the toilet seat around her neck as if it were a Tiffany necklace. Much champagne was poured over heads. And there was a raucous choral rendering of "Auld Lang Syne."

At one point Mac looked at the dusty, melancholy faces around us and asked of me, "Why is everybody so sad? We're only moving three blocks uptown!" As we all trudged out of the wreckage and rubble that had been the Puncheon, in a burst of sentimentality someone shouted, "Let's take the gate!" And so the wrought iron that had been the portal to the Puncheon was unhinged and toted off. The next day it was installed at 21 West Fifty-second Street and all the Kriendlers gathered around a table for the first of what would be seven decades of innumerable luncheons, dinners, suppers, and countless drinks served to the (carefully screened) public.

To convert the former Hochstadter residence into an eating and drinking establishment, Jack and Charlie had enlisted a bon vivant architectural engineer, Frank Applegate Buchanan, whose claim to fame was, in his words, as a "consultant and designer to clubs and hotels of distinction." Among his clients were the West Palm Beach Hotel in Florida and the Sleepy Hollow Country Club in New York's Westchester County.

Electing to retain the homey character of the building, Buchanan created a cozy, woody decor of an English tavern or men's club. In the rear of the ground floor he installed a library-sized room with space for only eight tables. The bar was nine feet long. The floor was bare wood, the ceiling beamed, and painted walls were decorated with plaques and drinking signs. In sharp contrast to this informal style, a second-floor front dining room featured crystal chandeliers, velvet banquettes, white linen–draped tables, and wall tapestries. A room at the back was similarly furnished, but with library-style wood paneling on the walls.

Whether upstairs or down, steep prices ensured that the person seated next to you or standing beside you at the bar was someone you would not mind having as a guest in your own home.

This was not always the case in the other establishments that soon followed '21' into Fifty-second Street between Fifth and Sixth. Scooped up at depression prices, other vacated former residences were turned into small clubs such as the Onyx, Tony's, and Famous Door. They offered drinks and entertainment by jazz musicians. Other swank nightclubs had comedians, dancers, and singers. One which opened next door became famous as Leon & Eddie's. Before long, the block was nicknamed "Swing Street."

Just how many places were selling booze along Fifty-second Street interested Robert Benchley, who of course had lost no time in following Jack and Charlie to their new location. Deciding to conduct a census of speakeasies, he insisted that Jack go along. Beginning at Sixth Avenue and proceeding east on the even-numbered south side of the block, the pair investigated the interior of each club and sampled the booze. Reaching Fifth Avenue, they crossed to the odd-numbered side and returned westward. Bypassing '21', they logged thirty-eight increasingly illegible names in Benchley's record book.

Broadway columnist Louis Sobol observed that, because of Prohibition, dark and guarded doors along the drab side streets of New York opened into a spreading world of soft lights, seductive scents, silken music, adroit entertainment, smoke, and laughter, of perfection of food and services, of wines and liquors of the finest quality. According to another newsman of the period, Quentin Reynolds, the difference between a club and a saloon was that in a club you had to keep your coat on even in the summer, but in a saloon you didn't.

Because '21' offered a broad spectrum of food but nothing in the way of entertainment, it was not a nightclub. Decor and decorum placed Jack and Charlie's far above the level of saloon. But you could drink there, which was illegal. It was a speakeasy—a really high-class one, but a speakeasy nonetheless.

"Of all the 'unlawful' establishments on 52d, none could vie in elegance or snob appeal with Jack and Charlie's '21'," wrote Arnold Shaw in 1971 in *The Street That Never Slept*. "And no one joined in the national game of 'beat the booze hunters' with more zest than its owners, or displayed greater ingenuity in the apparatus they devised to outwit them."

Charlie Berns described it this way: "We had Frank Buchanan install a series of contraptions for us that worked on different mechanical or electrical impulses. For example, the shelves behind the bar rested on tongue blocks. In case of a raid the bartender could press a button that released the blocks and let the shelves fall backward and drop the bottles down a chute. As they fell, they hit against angle irons and were smashed. At the bottom were rocks and a sandpile through which the liquor seeped, leaving not a drop as evidence."

When Prohibition Commissioner Roy A. Haynes published *Prohibition Inside Out* in 1923 on the subject of "the great experiment," he cited three links in "the chain that connects the illicit liquor industry with our social and commercial life." First was "the man who makes the forbidden beverage." Second was the man who distributed it. And third was the person who bought it. It was the last individual in the chain who most riled up Haynes. He lamented, "It is surprising to me how many high class citizens are doing this very thing, men who are respectable in their communities, who are otherwise above reproach, but who go out and buy liquor that has been sold in violation of the law and think they have a perfect right to do it."

But that was exactly the point. "The big thrill," said our loyal patron Louis Sobol, "was that we were all doing something unlawful."

Among the respectable citizens I greeted as they poured through the iron gate in 1930 were not only former patrons of the Puncheon, but an array of fresh faces including Doris Duke Cromwell, Prince Serge Obolensky, Barbara Hutton, Billy Rose, Gypsy Rose Lee, financier Bernard Baruch, Mary

Pickford, Charles Laughton, and the writers who had followed the lead of Bob Benchley to Jack and Charlie's new club.

One customer I definitely didn't mind having around was the city's most respected arbiter of fine food and good drink, Lucius Beebe. Along with heaping praise on turtle soup that "ceased to be merely a bath of hot sherry floating miniscule cubes of India rubber," he joyfully pointed out that train oil or some other corrosive were "no longer the essential ingredient of a martini." Lucius also indirectly noted that the club appeared to be immune to raids. "It was no longer necessary," he said, "to carry bail money when one dined out for fear of being tossed in the poky just after the fish and Chablis."

Such published bouquets, plus word-of-mouth recommendations from regular customers, drummed up a good deal of interest, yet Jack and Charlie clung to a strict policy of carefully sifting the wheat from the chaff. One of the surefire means of gaining access was to show a yellow club business card that bore Jack's handwritten "OK." If a situation arose in which Jack could not avoid giving one of the cards to someone he really did not want admitted, he omitted the OK and inscribed the number 34. The recipient assumed the digit referred to a table. What it meant to a doorman was "Keep this bum out."

One famous New Yorker who found himself banned from the club was the gossip columnist Walter Winchell. A former song-and-dance man, he strutted around town like a bantam rooster. Acting as if he were cock of the roost of Manhattan nightlife, he crammed his columns with tantalizing tidbits and claimed that a mention in a column could make or break any person or any business. His being barred was not meant as a personal snub. Jack's policy was to keep out any columnist or reporter whose only purpose in coming in was to snoop around and eavesdrop in order to publish titillating tales of newsworthy clientele. A newspaperman who was not in the tattletale trade, such as Mark Hellinger, Heywood Broun, or Broadway reporter Louis Sobol, was allowed in. But Winchell's intent in touring clubs was to dig up and dish dirt, which made him persona non grata to Jack.

Obviously miffed at being excluded, Winchell ran an item in his *Daily Mirror* column with the provocative headline "A Place Never Raided, Jack & Charlie's at 21 West Fifty-second Street."

What happened next showed that Assistant Secretary of the Treasury Frederick Lohman had read the Winchell blurb. He picked up his telephone and ordered a man named John Calhoun to rescue the Prohibition bureau's reputation, and Calhoun went to a federal judge in New York. Claiming Jack and Charlie's was a liquor-selling nightclub that featured hostesses and dancing on the third floor (untrue), he obtained a warrant to search 21 West Fifty-second from attic to cellar.

How they searched! After barging in, agents swarmed all over to wreak havoc not only in the public areas but also in private rooms upstairs, including a small apartment where Jack frequently stayed the night. Breaking open bureau drawers and trunks, the feds confiscated Jack's coin and stamp collections and other personal items. Rummaging around in the club's office, they gathered up Charlie's meticulously kept financial records. And of course they hauled away a huge quantity of stockpiled liquor.

Jack and Charlie were arrested, along with Mac and Bill Hardey and other employees. The charge was conspiracy to import and traffic in liquor and spirits. Their bond was set at one hundred thousand dollars. Our lawyer, Julius Hallheimer, immediately challenged the validity of the search warrant, pointing out its baseless claim that '21' was a nightclub. When newspapers reported how the feds had invaded and trashed Jack's bedroom and carted off his stamps and coins, a *seriously* embarrassed Assistant Secretary of the Treasury Lohman rushed up from Washington in a vain attempt to save face. What he got was an order invalidating the search warrant, meaning the case had to be thrown out, and a directive from an irate Judge Francis J. Coleman to the feds to return all the seized property, except the liquor, of course. For possession of that, Jack and Charlie were each fined fifty dollars. (They were later granted pardons.)

Having come through a very close scrape in which they might have been put out of business and sentenced to prison, Jack and Charlie realized a few changes would have to be made: not in their line of work, but in how and where they stored their liquor. Once again they called in Frank Applegate Buchanan, along with builder Sol Lustbader. The purpose of their meetings was to design a security system as "raid-proof" as humanly possible.

The first device was simple and already in place. This was an iron grille covering the front door, which was equipped with a peephole. By looking through it, doorman Jimmie Coslove literally kept an eye on anyone on the other side. When admitted, the customer found himself in a vestibule and facing a second door that opened into the lobby of the club itself. If Jimmie suspected that an approaching figure might be the leader of a raiding party, he had a set of four buttons placed at different locations so that no matter where he stood at a particular moment he was able to reach one of them and set off alarm bells on every floor of the building. When the bells sounded, whoever was manning the bar would activate the previously described system of collapsing shelves as waiters rushed from table to table scooping up drinks and taking them behind the bar for disposal down the chutes.

Secret spaces also had to be created. One of them appeared to be a closet. Open the door and you saw several metal hooks with waiters' uniforms hanging from them. But if you took a table knife and placed it between two of the hooks with each end touching a hook, an electric circuit was completed and the back wall of the closet swung open to reveal a narrow room with shelves of wine.

Entry to a storage space concealed behind another closet on the fourth floor was gained by manipulating a metal pole that supported more waiters' outfits. This opened a door to a small empty room with empty hangers. But pick up a small piece of metal from the floor and place it against one of the wall fixtures and you closed another circuit, which opened another wall to reveal a treasure trove of temperature-controlled vintage wines. A second secret room on the fourth floor was ten feet long and six feet wide. Built over a stairway, it was opened with the touch of a wire coat hanger to a pair of coat hooks. Controlling the electric current to all of these devices was a master switch behind the ground-floor bar.

But the masterpiece of this elaborate system of deception would be in the cellar. Designed and built by architect Soll Roehner, assisted by his brother Ernie and two friends and artisans, Ben Crow and Joe Whitney, it was a huge room for storing thousands of bottles of liquor and wine.

As Soll recalled, "It was necessary to construct a warehouse that could not be found by conventional measuring, and a concealed entrance was needed with a secret door of exquisite design and workmanship."

He decided to create a door in the brick foundation of 21 West Fifty-second Street that would provide access to the vacant house next door (No. 19). The door would be made invisible by making it "of materials and construction similar to the adjacent wall." It also had to be thick enough so that it would not sound hollow if tapped. It had to be strong enough to resist conventional tools if its secret location were somehow discovered by "pirates, enterprising hoods, or the law." Preventing such a discovery meant the door and surrounding walls had to mesh so snugly that a test for air flowing between the cracks—such as blowing cigarette smoke—would fail.

Because the door would have to be built of—or at least be covered with—brick, Soll estimated the weight at more than two tons. This presented another problem: how to mount something that heavy so that brick merely kissed brick as it swung open and shut? Other challenges included making a locking mechanism that would not jam, would work from both sides of the immense door, and would be invisible on the outside.

The answer was a plate on the inside of the door that was activated by inserting a long thin rod through a tiny hole near the bottom. When the rod met the plate, a click could be heard as the roller mechanism released the lock and freed the door so it could be pushed open. To make the small hole even less obvious, dozens of other holes were cut into the brick, although they did not go all the way through.

So impenetrable was the door to the secret room that if its lock ever broke the only way to get through it would be to tear down the building. Fortunately, in almost seventy years of operation, lock and door have never failed.

Although very few people knew of the existence of the room behind the brick door, one who was let in on the secret was the irrepressible mayor of New York, James "Gentleman Jimmy" Walker. In the words of a contemporary patron of Jack and Charlie's, Stanley Walker (no relation), "the great James was the paradox of American politics." He was esteemed as a wit and called the best-dressed man in public life, and as mayor "he could have been as good as he wanted to be." Was Jimmy seen with a woman who was not his wife at prizefights? Yes. But for a huge part of the public, the attitude was, "Very well. Good for Jimmy. Many a man would rather be at a prizefight with a woman other than his wife."

The other woman was an actress/showgirl, Betty Compton. And after Walker was shown the secret room below Jack and Charlie's, he persuaded them to set up a booth in it so he could wine and dine Betty without being constantly interrupted by admirers or others who might grab the opportunity to implore a favor from a man with a reputation (and the calamitous flaw) of not being able to say no.

Of all the famous faces of the Roaring Twenties and the early 1930s who gained admittance to Jack and Charlie's, none was so closely identified with New York City as the mayor. "For many dizzy and splendiferous years," observed Stanley Walker, Gentleman Jimmy was "immune to the more serious forms of criticism, which, in other times, would have ruined any man in public life."

Like nearly everyone in New York at the time, I liked Jimmy Walker and was saddened when scandals involving his administration brought his political downfall through forced resignation. Evidence of just how well liked he had been by everyone at 21 West Fifty-second Street since the years he'd been a patron of the Fronton, Puncheon, and '21' can be found in the cellar room. Preserved in a corner is the booth where he'd passed many a clandestine evening, confident that even if there happened to be a raid on the joint, no one would find him.

Another personality indelibly impressed in the public's mind as a symbol of New York during Walker's tenure was the gangster Legs Diamond. And like Walker, Diamond had also followed Jack and Charlie's success in the food-and-drink game with a good deal of interest. Soon after the iron gate swung open on Fifty-second, Legs Diamond made another try at cutting himself in.

Before his first, and unsuccessful, attempt back when Jack and Charlie were testing their wings at running a speakeasy in the Fronton, John Thomas Diamond had begun his criminal career as a teenage member of the Hudson Dusters. As a co-owner with Hymie Cohen of the Hotsy Totsy Club on Broadway between Fifty-fourth and Fifty-fifth, he had garnered a reputation as not only the flashiest gangster in town, but also as one of the most vicious, ranking right up there with Lucky Luciano, Dutch Schultz, Louis Lepke, and Owney Madden. Having been a dancer, and because he'd proved he had a talent for eluding arrest by being fleet of foot, he had picked up the moniker "Legs." He'd been shot at and wounded so often that he earned another underworld nickname: "the Clay Pigeon." But his frequent brushes with death also left him feeling so invulnerable that he once boasted, "The bullet hasn't been made that can kill me."

To deliver the message that Legs expected to be let in on the action at Jack and Charlie's, a trio of "dese, dem, and doze" characters showed up looking and talking as if they'd just come from a movie and were trying to emulate Edward G. Robinson's role as gangster Rico in *Little Caesar*. Because Jack was not in the club at the time, it was Charlie who dealt with them.

"It reminded me of our Village days," Charlie recalled. "I guess the adrenaline just got up and my reaction was automatic." With an assist from Jimmie Coslove, Charlie gave Legs's thugs the bum's rush. Word soon came back that Legs was putting out contracts on both Charlie's and Jack's lives. But Jack and Charlie weren't the only ones who had made it onto Legs's hit list. A '21' customer who had been introduced to them at the Puncheon by Bob Benchley soon found reason to worry.

In his late twenties, the big raw-boned, red-haired former reporter for the *Kansas City Star* had been wounded while serving as an ambulance driver attached to the Italian infantry during World War I. This had been followed by a stint as foreign correspondent for the *Toronto Star* in Paris, where he'd met and hung out with James Joyce and other writers who flocked to the literary salon of Gertrude Stein. His name was Ernest Hemingway, and by the time he was brought to the Puncheon by Benchley in 1928 he was viewed as a promising new talent on the strength of a 1925 collection of short stories featuring a character named Nick Adams. His highly praised 1926 novel about American expatriates in Paris, *The Sun Also Rises*, was followed in 1929 by *A Farewell to Arms*.

Despite these publishing successes, there were times between royalty checks when Hemingway found himself short of cash. Having taken Bob Benchley's lead in following Jack and Charlie up to Fifty-second Street, he found he could rely on Jack to tip him off to whatever private party was going on in one of the upstairs rooms.

In late 1931, after crashing one of these posh affairs, he was introduced to an Italian girl he later described as the most beautiful female—face and body—he'd ever seen, before or since, any country, any time. Ernie told his biographer A. E. Hotchner that "she had that pure Renaissance beauty, black hair straight, eyes round at the bottoms, Botticelli skin, breasts of Venus Rising."

Relating the encounter to Hotchner in 1949, Hemingway continued, "After the joint closed and everyone started to leave, she and I took our drinks into the kitchen. Jack said it was okay, since there were two or three hours of cleaning up to be done downstairs. So we talked and drank and suddenly we were making love there in the kitchen and never has a promise been better fulfilled."

By now it was five in the morning, and the young woman said they'd better be leaving. Hemingway reluctantly agreed. They got as far as a landing on the stairs and started making love again. It was, he said, "like being at sea in the most tempestuous storm that ever boiled up."

The young woman would not let Hemingway take her home. Unable to get her out of his mind the next day, and realizing that he didn't know her name, he hurried back to '21' to ask Jack who she was. But as he barreled into the club Jack pulled him aside and blurted, "Listen, Ernie, you better lay low for a while. I should've warned you—that was Legs Diamond's girl, and he's due back in town at five o'clock."

Luckily for Jack, Charlie, and Hemingway, on Saturday, December 19, 1931, in Albany, New York, Legs at last found himself unable to outrun a barrage of bullets. Two gunmen tiptoed up the stairs of a shabby hotel where he was asleep and pumped seventeen slugs into him.

One of the sure signs of success in 1931—whether as a gangster, actor, actress, business leader, or politician—was to come to the attention of the editors of Henry Luce's enormously popular and influential *Life* magazine. So it was with a lot of pride that we Kriendlers picked up the issue of June 12 and found on the cover a cartoon poking fun at the exclusivity of the club. It depicted President Herbert Hoover being interrupted at a meeting in the White House. Holding a note, an aide is saying, "A Mr. Peebles phoning from New York, Mr. President. He wants to know if you can push a button and open a place at 21 West 52nd Street?"

I presume that Mr. Hoover was not as amused as I was. Nor do I suppose the president of the United States found to his liking a George Jean Nathan opinion published in the *New York World-Telegram* on June 26, 1932. With the presidential election in the offing, Nathan wrote, "Jack and Charlie, of my favorite speakeasy, would make the best President and Vice President. And I am quite serious. The speakeasy makes money, and the customers and owners are happy. In what other business is that true? The speakeasy is the most efficiently run enterprise in America today. It is an independent unit except when the government horns in."

Other than the big raid that had been prompted by Winchell's sour grapes, the only dark cloud to appear on the '21' horizon in 1931 was a strike called by a union of waiters. Although the men who worked for us expressed no grievances over the wages we paid, nor about working conditions, the walkout had been called against all the city's restaurants and hotels. Its most immediate effect was to put all my brothers, cousins, and me into waiters' aprons as we took a quick course from Jack on how to handle the trays of food and drinks without bumping into one another or spilling everything into a customer's lap.

Patrons were affected by the strike to the extent that they sympathized with the labor movement. Was a picket line sacrosanct? Or did the desire for a decent drink and a good meal override the stigma of crossing it? Indeed, was there in fact a stigma attached to such an act of defiance?

These were questions that soon confronted the wags and wits of the famed (but rapidly dissolving) gatherings at the Round Table of the Algonquin. Overwhelmingly liberal in their politics as well as their views on all aspects of moral behavior, they'd been outspoken in suppport for the causes of organized labor, especially regarding the formation of the Newspaper Guild. And no one was more militant in that endeavor than Heywood Broun. On fire with a zeal to bolster striking waiters picketing the Waldorf-Astoria, he got Dorothy Parker and Alexander Woollcott to join him in a march of solidarity in front of the hotel.

However, once they had shown their "Union forever" colors, I detected no sign of embarrassment as they breezed past picketers in front of '21'; that is, until Bob Benchley walked in and spotted them skulking at a corner table. Feeling no guilt at having crossed a picket line himself, but clearly outraged at what he deemed the greater sin of hypocrisy, he railed indignation at Broun. Then, turning to Dorothy Parker in her signature floppy-brimmed black hat, and wagging an admonishing finger, he declared, "And don't you blink those ingenue eyes at me."

Broun and Parker ought to have known they'd never get away unnoticed by Bob, who was nearly as ubiquitous a figure in '21' as Jack. The things that Benchley is renowned for having uttered in the club may or may not have been said there, or even by him, but quips such as "I must get out of this wet coat and into a dry martini" nevertheless enhanced both his and the club's reputation.

One possibly apocryphal story has Bob leaving his table (No. 3), exiting the club, and encountering at the curbside an impressive figure in an ornate uniform.

"My good man," said Bob, tapping a braid-bedecked shoulder, "please hail me a cab."

With a "Harumph," the man wheeled around, fixed Bob with an icy glare, and snapped, "Sir, I am an admiral in the navy."

"Very well," said Bob, "then hail me a battleship."

Despite all his loyalty and his seemingly continual presence, Bob somehow missed being in attendance during the 1930 raid, as well as one pulled in June 1932 that put to the test all of Jack's new and elaborate security arrangements.

It was just past noon on Friday, June 24, when Jimmie Coslove peeped through the hole in the gate, glimpsed a pair of men he didn't know, closed the peep, walked into the club, and said to Jack, "I have a hunch we're about to be raided."

Jimmie's instinct was enough for Jack. Clinking two glasses together, he got the attention of the patrons in the barroom and said quietly, "Ladies and gentlemen, please finish your drinks and keep calm, we might have a few visitors." He cracked a smile and added, "In other words, it's a raid, so bottoms up."

As Gus Lux triggered the mechanism to set shelves awhirl, waiters collected emptied glasses and delivered them to the bar while muted sounds of smashing bottles and the aroma of excellent liquor wafted up from the chute.

Back at the gate, Jimmie let the callers in. But when Benjamin La Rosa and Benjamin Lippi rushed into the restaurant they found a bare bar and tables, bemused people doing nothing illegal, and the powerful odor of an illicit substance which had been in plain sight just moments before. A lone agent had initiated the raid after visiting the club on June 20 and 22 on orders from New York's Prohibition administrator, Andrew McCampbell. When agent Montrose Rice reported to United States Commissioner Francis A. Duffy what he had seen at 21 West Fifty-second on both occasions, Duffy signed a search warrant that allowed the two Benjamins to lead a squad of eight raiders into the suddenly dry premises.

Observing a raid for the first time, I was simultaneously fascinated by the agents' diligence, infuriated that Prohibition still existed after more than a dozen years of evidence that it was a disaster for the country, tickled pink at the agents' vain efforts to locate what they were looking for, and proud of my brother's brilliance in having found so many ingenious tricks to thwart them. Observing one of the agents tapping on the brick wall in the cellar and listening for anything to suggest a room behind it, I had to bite my lip to keep from laughing.

Undaunted by the lack of evidence and customers' giggles, the feds roamed all over the building for twelve hours—rapping knuckles against the walls, using measuring tapes, examining the interiors of closets, thumping their feet on the floors, and even plunging arms elbow deep into pots of meat sauce and soups in the kitchen.

Trying the button that activated the shelves above the chutes, they were met with a gust of air from below that was so rich with the smell of dumped liquor that I wondered if a man could get drunk just by inhaling the fumes.

Finally the wearied and stymied posse departed to report their findings—that is, what they'd *sniffed*—to a brash and bold United States attorney by the name of Thomas E. Dewey. I imagine that the man who a few years later would send Lucky Luciano up the river, get elected governor of New York, and run three times for president of the United States shook his head gravely, stroked his bristled mustache, and ruled that the smell of liquor was insufficient evidence to make a case.

On Sunday the *New York Times* headline read:

WET SPOT GOES DRY

AS RAIDERS ARRIVE

Agents Armed With a Warrant

Get a Cordial Welcome at

Speakeasy, but No Liquor

. . . . . .

TRICK SHELVES REVEAL WHY

. . . . . .

Push Button Had Dumped Bottles

Into Chutes and Only Odor

Remained, Federal Men Complain.

As if this failure had not provided enough embarrassment for the raiders, when they gave up their searching and left the club they found that their cars had been ticketed for illegal parking. As the raid was in progress, Charlie Berns had phoned our friends in our neighborhood police station to request a small favor.

As fate and a long-overdue return of common sense among the American people would have it, the fiasco of the big raid turned out to be the last we had to endure. After a dozen years, the end of "the great experiment" of Prohibition was in sight.

Four

LEGIT!

The nationwide prohibition of alcoholic drinks had been three centuries in the birthing. When Franklin Delano Roosevelt won election as president of the United States in November 1932 with a pledge to end the failed experiment, Prohibition had been the law of the land for almost thirteen years. A month after FDR's landslide victory over Herbert Hoover, Republican senator John J. Blaine of Wisconsin offered a resolution calling for submission to the states of an amendment to the Constitution (the Twenty-first) to repeal the Eighteenth. Both houses of Congress quickly adopted it, and on February 21, 1933, submitted it to the states for ratification. At 3:30 P.M. on December 5 in Salt Lake City a delegate to the Utah ratification convention, S. R. Thurman, cast the vote making Utah last of the thirty-five states required to approve it.

Prohibition had gripped the country for thirteen years, ten months, and eighteen days. In that time America had witnessed changes in public attitudes, liberating women to the extent that they felt free to drink and smoke in public, popularizing the cocktail party and the gin martini, giving Americans a taste for Scotch whisky, and making possible the rise of organized crime syndicates.

Prohibition and its repeal had a great effect on the Kriendler family. Wealth which was beyond imagining for any of us back in 1922, when Jack borrowed a little money and hocked Uncle Sam Brenner's diamond ring, was at our fingertips in 1933. And now the Fifty-second Street offspring of the Red Head, Fronton, and Puncheon was "legit."

When the iron gate was flung wide and an enormous shipment of liquor was openly carted in, Charlie Berns declared the event the greatest sight he'd ever seen. There was so much booze that crates were stacked everywhere, including in the men's room. Customers used them as chairs and footrests as they swigged whiskey right from the bottles.

A customer who chose to celebrate the end of Prohibition with a meal at '21' could have started with a plate of bluepoint oysters or a bowl of minestrone for 45 cents, or chosen $2.25 imported Makaroff caviar from the hors d'oeuvres list. If meat were to be the entrée from the a la carte menu, the choices ranged from steak de veau sauté, eggplant orientale ($1.30) to roast prime ribs of beef jardinère ($1.70), with a variety of vegetables and potatoes. The dessert list ranged from berries in season (half a buck) to baked Alaska for two ($2.00). Café kirsh would set a newly liberated imbiber back a dollar and a quarter. Regular coffee with cream was forty cents. In the depths of the Great Depression these were very steep prices. Add to the tab the cost of before-dinner cocktails, wines, and an after-dinner drink and you had an *expensive* meal. But so what? Anyone who had patronized the Red Head, Fronton, and Puncheon knew that being handed a stiff bill had always been the hallmark of clubs owned by Jack and Charlie.

But running '21' was also costly. Wholesale food bills ran to fifty thousand dollars a year. A staff consisted of eight chefs, a sommelier, twenty-nine waiters and a captain, a steward, two maids, hat-check room and cigar-counter attendants, bartenders, doormen, busboys, housekeepers, and porters. Added to these payroll expenses were the costs of services such as laundering staff uniforms and napkins, the club's hallmark red-and-white checkered tablecloths, plus electricity and telephone bills, garbage services, and other overhead.

On the positive side of Charlie Berns's ledgers, however, Repeal meant the elimination of payoffs to the police for protection against raids. But the ending of the long dry spell also brought with it a surge in the number of competitors seeking to lure the patronage of New Yorkers who could afford to venture out for an evening of drinking and dining. The group previously described as "café society" became "nightclub society" as they taxied between El Morocco, Sherman Billingsley's Stork Club, Peacock Alley, the Starlight Roof of the Waldorf, and a good many more. Lucius Beebe called this splurge in legalized drinking an "amiably demented whirl" of "living in a white tie till six of a morning before brushing the teeth in a light Moselle and retiring to bed."

All this competition quickly put '21' in an economic squeeze so tight that I found myself looking forlornly at empty chairs and fewer bellies to the bar. Jack and Charlie were staring into the grim face of bankruptcy. Being legit was not going to be easy. Charlie wondered aloud, "With the clout and spice of the illegal gone, are we destined to survive only in memory as one of those funny places people used to go to?"

Jack reminded Charlie of Charlie's brave words in the stock market crash of 1929: "We're in for the long haul." Rather than save money by letting employees go, and to keep them from defecting to competitors, they raised their salaries. But they neither slashed prices on the menu nor cut back on the service and style that were the bedrock of the '21' reputation for class. Not a moment's thought was given to turning the place into one more "former speakeasy" like our neighbors along Swing Street by converting it into a jazz joint.

By sticking to "the record and reputation we had built up" (in Charlie's words), and by holding on to the support of such loyalists as Bob Benchley and the men from Yale, my brother and cousin not only weathered the storm, but started drawing up a plan to expand operations by creating a company to import and distribute libations to meet the public demand for quality liquor.

If there was one quality of character that Charlie Berns did not lack, it was a steely sort of nerve for which the Yiddish word is *chutzpah*. Determined to tap into a post-Repeal booming demand for booze, he set his cap on cornering the market for a brand of scotch that had become the '21' standard, Ballantine's. But first he had to persuade the distiller to assign '21' exclusive rights to import and distribute the product. This presented a challenge, as neither Charlie nor Jack had ever been in the business of wholesale liquor selling. Brushing aside that technicality, Charlie assembled a crew of salesmen and dispatched them across the country as if they were authorized representatives. The gambit worked. So many orders poured in that an official of the firm happily agreed that henceforth '21' would be Ballantine's sole distributor in the U.S.A. But there quickly appeared a fly in the ointment in the form of a federal law that forbade a liquor retailer from also being a wholesaler.

The solution to this problem took the shape of a new entity, 21 Brands, with Jack and Charlie legally dissolving their partnership and Charlie switching to 21 Brands. (The arrangement also required a shuffling of real estate, the details of which I will discuss later.) Named president of the new company was Frank Hunter, a tennis pro who'd been partnered with Bill Tilden for the World Champion Doubles Team.

With the new company established, a staff of salesmen was organized. One of them was a handsome and debonair young actor who had recently come over from England with hopes of forging a career in the New York theater, which might lead him to movie stardom in Hollywood. I thought he definitely had a name that would fit nicely on a theater marquee and movie screen—David Niven.

I'd first met David a year or so before he joined 21 Brands. It was around Christmas 1932, and he was at the bar having a drink with a few American friends who were hosting him during a brief visit. When Gus Lux explained the system of trick shelves for dumping liquor down a chute in case of a raid, David was fascinated by the device and appalled that such a contraption was necessary. He said he agreed with one of his hosts who'd said, "Damned Prohibition. Takes a man's balls off."

After his introduction to '21' David became a familiar face for a couple of weeks, due entirely to the hospitality of his American pals. In a book of memoirs he entitled *The Moon's a Balloon* (to know why, you will have to read it), he wrote, "The headquarters of the group I was adopted by was Jack & Charlie's 21 Club—the best speakeasy in New York, run by the good-looking Jack Kriendler and the amiable, rotund and folksy

Charlie Berns." He continued, "The price of New York was bloodcurdling, but such was the generosity of my newfound friends that it was just taken for granted that I was never to be allowed to pay for anything. It was even made clear that if I attempted to do so, I would no longer be invited."

After returning to England, David came back to New York the following October (1933). Even more broke than before, he was staying at a downscale Midtown hotel on Lexington Avenue, across from the back side of the Waldorf-Astoria. One evening in November, as he lamented the desperate state of his finances to a friend, newspaper reporter John McClain, who was a '21' regular, John said, "Jack and Charlie are going to become wine merchants—maybe they will give you a job. I'll have a word with them."

John kept his promise, and David left a meeting with Jack as a salesman for 21 Brands on forty dollars a week retainer against ten percent of what he brought in by way of orders. Before David could go to work, however, the law demanded he go downtown to the New York office of the FBI to be finger-printed and photographed with a small numbered card draped around his neck, giving the photo the appearance of a mug shot of a wanted man. Back from being printed and photographed, David was told by Charlie, "Go out now and get orders."

His assigned territory was Lexington Avenue to the East River and between Forty-second and Ninetieth Streets. But his first sale was not to a business. He sold a case of champagne to a man named "Woolly" Donahue, who said he needed it at once. Taking it from the '21' stock, David delivered it by way of a yellow cab just before midnight. The date was December 4, 1933, and it went into Charlie Berns's ledger (and his heart) as 21 Brands's first sale.

Three cold hard facts about being a liquor salesman became immediately evident to David: first, his territory was also the turf of some very nasty ex-bootleggers and gangsters; second, the old-timers who'd been used to patronizing local merchants before the onset of the dry spell preferred to return to their original sources, who'd gone back into the trade; and third, he could not bring himself to try to sell his wares to the very friends who'd staked him to so many drinks and meals.

David was also embarrassed by where he lived. Considering the Montclair Hotel well beneath the status of a salesman for 21 Brands, he made it appear that he lived elsewhere. Carrying his bags of samples each morning, he crossed Lexington to the back entrance of the Waldorf-Astoria, wended his way through the vast gilded lobbies, descended the steps at the front entrance, and with a "Good morning" to the doorman, and the knowing doorman's reply of "Good morning, Mr. Niven," stepped out onto Park Avenue.

The routine of using the Waldorf-Astoria as a front for his true address was reversed at the end of a day's rounds. Many of those days were disappointing, proving that David was not fated to make a fortune—or even a decent living—selling liquor. It's just as well, because not long after he threw in the towel as a 21 Brands employee he made it to—and *in*— Hollywood.

Through a friendly contact with the FBI we managed to get a copy of the picture taken of David on the day he'd been fingerprinted. Prominently hung on a wall in the barroom, it bore the inscription:

OUR FIRST AND WORST SALESMAN

Location further delineated Charlie's activities at 21 Brands from those of the club. The Brands offices were set up in No. 17, bought for eighty thousand dollars. But being two doors east of the iron gate did not mean that Charlie didn't keep his hand in the restaurant. He and Jack had been split apart only on paper. While Charlie was chairman of the board of 21 Brands, the day-by-day, nuts-and-bolts running of the firm was handled by Francis Hunter, who in keeping with his name festooned his office with big-game trophies. All this, along with a bar, couches, and large comfortable chairs, was installed in a penthouse which became famous (some thought notorious) as a bachelor pad.

Soon the scope of 21 Brands was expanded to include other liquors. Selected by Charlie, they included Hine cognac, Tribuno vermouth, Bobadilla sherries, Ezra Brooks bourbon, and an array of California wines. Eventually, 21 Brands also offered delicacies for which the '21' menu was renowned. Under the labels Irongate Products and Fidelis Trading and Fishing Company, these included seasonal game, grouse from Scotland, asparagus from the Baja, and Ecuadorian melons. The catalog would also offer "The famous 'sauce maison' of Jack and Charlie's '21' in jars of convenient sizes for home consumption . . . delivered to any address in any quantity, at any time."

But the 21 Brands property wasn't the only real estate into which Jack and Charlie expanded. Having weathered the period immediately after Repeal when new bistros appeared, Jack and Charlie found that customers who had strayed were returning. The change in administrations in Washington had produced an air of optimism. People reasoned that if the only thing we had to fear was fear itself, as FDR had said in his inaugural address, then why not exhibit some of that fearlessness by having dinner and drinks at the '21' club? For whatever the reason, business was up and "the joint was jumping."

With patrons starting to swarm into '21', something had to go. Jack and Charlie decided that the wall between 21 West Fifty-second and the house next door, No. 19, had to be knocked down. With typical Jack Kriendler panache and Charlie Berns prudence and planning, a new "demolition party" was planned. But it was kept secret from the guests. At the end of 1935 Jack and Charlie sent out a New Year's greeting card which read:

WE ARE BREAKING THRU TO '19' 36.

With amazing cunning and devilish deception, the work on the conversion included secretly removing the masonry wall between the rooms that were to be joined and replacing it with a wooden partition. When everything was ready, the unveiling of the expansion ranked, in my opinion and that of others, as the most unusual grand opening in the history of New York restauranting.

On the appointed night a bunch of regulars was asked to wait in the barroom until the other customers had gone. Then Jack announced the commencement of a "Breaking Thru Party." At two in the morning, led by famed divorce lawyer Dudley Field Malone, the men were told to put their backs against the east wall. On Malone's signal to push, down went the wall.

So moved was Francis Hunter by the occasion that he wrote, "The modern Twenty-One is somehow linked with a sort of historic conservatism which peeps out here and there and affects one like the fragrance of lavender in a drawer that brings back, with sudden magic, the memories of the old days and per-chance forgotten faces."

Francis's sentiments were contained in the introduction to a book published privately to mark the "breaking thru" into No. 19, the sixth anniversary of the '21' opening in 1930, and a bit of the history that had preceded it. Entitled *The Iron Gate of Jack and Charlie's '21'*, and with contributions in the form of essays, poems, and other offerings from writer-customers, as well as drawings, sketches, cartoons, and paintings by famed artist-patrons, the commemorative book's purpose, in Francis Hunter's words, was to provide a means for the contributors to express to Jack and Charlie "the consciousness of their gratitude that what had been known as '21' Atmosphere had been transformed into, and henceforth would be regarded as Tradition!"

It's safe to say that when Jack and Charlie went into the speakeasy business in 1922, neither intended or expected to be remembered for having created either atmosphere or tradition, but that is what those who contributed to *The Iron Gate* claimed and believed.

In "Bar of Our Night" Lucius Beebe harkened back to the dreary dry days of Prohibition. "Jack and Charlie's came into being in the Dark Ages of the American legend," he wrote. "The imperial glories of the early twenties had vanished, and in their place arose a time of ill omen to the gastric juices, of bliz-zards of bad cheques, and the alarming discovery that the two cases you had put aside were not going to last through the Great Foolishness after all. Panic and fear gripped every heart. It began to look as though prohibition might be enforced and we would all be eating at the Horn and Hardart's automat." It was in the midst of this terror, Lucius went on, "that Jack and

Charlie's brought words of encouragement and something resembling the proper service of dinner."

A witty regular named Steve Hanagan joked, "The food's so good at '21' even the waiters eat it."

The attorney who led the crew demolishing the wall between 21 and 19, Dudley Field Malone, wrote, "No mystery attaches itself to the fame, success and popularity of Jack & Charlie's '21.' It is not a bar, not a restaurant—just a friendly club where all of us, men and women, boys and girls, took shelter and happiness from hateful chills of prohibition. And so we come now, and always shall come, in grateful memory of tiresome days, always to find our friends, and also please God to be greeted by *real* friends in the persons of Jack and Mac, and when he is not preoccupied by his present business, by Charlie."

The unexcelled glorifier of Broadway dandies and shady characters, Damon Runyon, poked fun at '21' exclusivity with "Each guest had to present his bank book at the door to prove that he had a worthy balance. The doorman looked him up in the social register before admitting him."

In "An Inn by the Side of the Road," Adela Rogers St. John claimed '21' as "my own" restaurant because:

> When I step across its threshold, I begin to feel elegant. I like myself. If I've had a bad morning on the typewriter, or one of those moods when I feel all hands and feet and tag ends, I forget about it instantly. Here is friendliness. Here is approval. I don't know why—but that always happens to me in '21.' I am quite sure that I am slim, that I look my best.
>
> I like to stand at the bar and suddenly see the face of a friend I have missed for perhaps a year—maybe he's been in Hollywood—or London—or Timbucktoo for that matter. I like

to sit against the wall upstairs and hear the pleasant sound of voices, all a little hushed into intimacy. I do not like music with my meals and may there never be any at '21,' where conversation is still an art and friendship and even romance may find a gentle gaiety.

I like sometimes, if the spirit moves me, to sit all afternoon at the little red-and-white-checkered tables. I like to drift in there late at night after the theater, if restlessness is upon me, and find peace with companionship.

Some of the nicest things in my life have happened to me in '21.' Friendships have ripened there under the good food and wine and soft lights. Ideas have blossomed. Battles have been fought.

And that is why '21' is an inn by the side of the road. It may be on 52nd Street in the heart of noisy, vibrant, hectic New York. It may serve exquisite things to eat and fancy cocktails to drink, instead of bread and cheese. But it's that open door at the roadside that alone makes a restaurant a part of your life. Something you need and love and are a little bit grateful for.

Popular singer Morton Downey, known for his renditions of Irish ballads, wrote a special set of lyrics to be sung to the tune of a sentimental musical valentine to Ireland entitled "A Little Bit of Heaven." It went:

Have you ever heard the story of how Twenty-One was
    named?
I'll tell you so you'll understand from whence the idea came.
No wonder that we warm to that one place we love to be,
For here's the way that Jack and Charlie tell the tale to me:
Well, a little bit of fortune fell from out the sky one day,

And settled on Manhattan in a spot not far away,
And when the boys discovered its good fellowship and cheer
They said, let's patronize this place, we seem so welcome
    here.
Then they spread the tidings of it just to let the others know
'Twas the only place you'd find such food and drinks wher'er
    you'd go.
So we built it up with atmosphere to make it seem like
    home,
And when we had it finished, why we called it Twenty-One.

Charles MacArthur offered his contribution in the form of a letter to Mayor Fiorello La Guardia's tough-as-nails police commissioner, Lewis J. Valentine. Explaining in the manner of a confession to a crime that he (Charles) had gone astray because he had become "A Victim of Circumstances" as the result of meeting the proprietors of '21', he pleaded, "I was a model man until I met Jack Kriendler and Charlie Berns. I had never missed the 5:42 to Nyack, where I was a member of the Parent-Teachers Association, the Sunnyside Avenue Methodist Episcopal Church and a property owner. My family and friends and the people at the Nyack bank all trusted me. I had a great belief in myself and a healthy desire to get somewhere.

"Charlie (the four-eyed fellow whose picture you showed me the other day) started me off on beer. When they had me well on that habit, they switched me over to Ballantine's. I had no reason to distrust them, as they both seemed very friendly, cashing my paychecks every week, even introducing me to people like Gene Fowler and Robert Benchley and Ben Hecht. I will not take up your time about the Hecht matter, as I know that you are a very busy man.

"Well, now I don't know where I stand, excepting that I don't believe I bit George Jean Nathan in the leg the other night. That story comes from Jack. (He is the man with the Shinnecock Hills moustache and the side vents in his coat.) I know that when I asked Benchley how all this could have been prevented, he told me the only danger sign in drinking that *he* knew anything about was when a man has to dog-trot to remain upright going down Fifth Avenue. He had just dog-trotted all the way from the Royalton Hotel.

"This statement is free and voluntary, as your rubber hose left no marks."

In 1928 Charles MacArthur and Ben Hecht had together written and put onstage a successful Broadway play, *The Front Page*, based on their newspapering experiences. They went on to write another Broadway hit, *The Twentieth Century*, and to co-direct several films in the 1930s. Ben's movie career both as screenwriter and director would continue until his death in 1967. Charles had a less prolific Hollywood career, and when he died in 1956 he was best known to the general public for being the husband of Helen Hayes. He'd captured her heart by handing her a bag of peanuts and saying, "I wish they were diamonds."

What I remember about Charles is the unfortunate fact that too frequently his best friend was the bottle. But few men were more adored at '21' during the 1930s. Jack and Charlie thought so highly of his friendship that they gave him a watch engraved with the club's symbol, the iron gate. Such a sentimental moment cried out for a MacArthur quip. He did not disappoint. Gazing at the watch, he said, "I paid for this with my left kidney."

Both Charles and Ben enjoyed sticking the needle in Jack. Keenly aware of Jack's pride in the quality of the offerings on the '21' menu, they showed up one night with four waiters toting trays of food from the Stork Club. As silver covers were lifted from the dinners, Charles explained that only the drinks at '21' were good.

Liquor aplenty—and a lot of food—was consumed and paid for by Charles on St. Patrick's Day in 1936. The party was not just a tribute to the patron saint of Ireland. It was Charles's way of saluting Helen's latest triumph on Broadway. The affair was so glittery that it was reported by the *New York World-Telegram* under the headline "Jolly 21 Club is Crowded by a St. Patrick Day Party." Reporter Helen Worden bubblingly wrote, "Yesterday at Jack and Charlie's 21 Club the star of 'Victoria Regina' looked like a beautiful young Queen Victoria with her straight light-brown hair parted in the middle and slicked down over her ears. A little black taffeta hat that might have been a Victorian bonnet was worn far back on her head."

Of Helen Hayes's adoring husband, Alexander Woollcott said, "What a perfect world this would be if it were full of Charlie MacArthurs." Amen to that.

I can think of no more appropriate title for a biography of Alexander Woollcott than the one chosen by Howard Teichmann for his 1976 book. He called it *Smart Aleck*. Certainly, no one from the Algonquin Round Table group who patronized the Puncheon and '21' possessed a more wicked tongue than Woollcott. After playwrights George S. Kaufman and Moss Hart told Aleck over dinner at '21' one evening in 1938 that they were lagging behind schedule in their work on a play based on him, Aleck excoriated them. "The two of you disgust me," he growled. "Kaufman, you're a second-rate hack with the ethics of a Storm Trooper. Hart, you're a groveling slum gutter with the instincts of Gyp the Blood. Together you have prostituted your little talents in the most cheap and vulgar way imaginable. Collectively, you remind me of a Bruno Hauptmann without charm."

As he sat cringing at this tongue-lashing, George Kaufman was arguably the preeminent satirist working in the theater. He'd triumphed in collaborations with Marc Connelly (*Dulcy* in 1921 and *Merton of the Movies*, 1922), with Edna Ferber (*The Royal Family*, 1928; *Dinner at Eight*, 1932; and *Stage Door*, 1936), and with Moss Hart in *Once in a Lifetime* (1930) and a send-up of President Roosevelt in *I'd Rather Be Right* in 1937.

The play Kaufman and Hart ultimately completed based on the outrageous Woollcott was called *The Man Who Came to Dinner*. It starred a former drama professor at Yale University and occasional actor in movies, Monty Woolley, as Woollcott in the title role of Sheridan Whiteside. Of the production Brooks Atkinson wrote in the *New York Times*, "After doing their bit for democracy last season, Moss Hart and George S. Kaufman have turned to the more relaxing task of doing one of their friends. . . . Taking him (Aleck) in his malicious phase as a spiteful-tongued tyrant with literary overtones, Mr. Hart and Mr. Kaufman have translated him into the first comic phenomenon of the season." Woollcott was so delighted that he eventually starred in the play himself when the hit went on a national tour.

Another famous writer of the 1930s who frequented '21' and found himself under a kind of verbal assault from Woollcott was detective novelist Rex Stout. Woollcott insisted that Rex had to have based the extra-portly, semireclusive, orchid-growing gourmet Nero Wolfe on him. After reading *The League of Frightened Men* (1935), Aleck invited Stout to dinner and laid out his reasoning. First, both men were fat. They were both brilliant and absolutist. Furthermore, Edna Ferber had once described Aleck as "that New Jersey Nero."

Rex denied that Woollcott had been his inspiration, but Aleck did not buy it, insisting until the day he died that he had been the spark behind Nero Wolfe. In one of those ironic twists of life, Rex was participating with Woollcott in a radio program on CBS on Saturday, January 23, 1942, when Aleck slipped Rex a note which read, I AM SICK.

"I knew something was radically wrong with Aleck," Stout recalled. "A healthier Woollcott would have printed I AM ILL."

Stricken with a heart attack, Aleck was rushed by ambulance to Roosevelt Hospital and died that night.

Of all the conversations involving Aleck Woollcott which took place over a lunch or a dinner in '21' in the 1930s, none matched for pure astonishment a luncheon in the summer of 1939 to which Aleck was invited by Heywood Broun. Spread out before Aleck were all his favorite wines and food. The meal was consumed with all the gusto one expected of a pair of fat men. Over the dessert Broun finally got around to explaining the purpose of the repast. Having recently coverted to Roman Catholicism, Broun all but begged Aleck to do the same.

"Not me, my dear old friend," Aleck replied. "One literary fat ass is enough for the Roman Catholic Church."

Broun's own startling conversion a few months earlier had been guided by a man whom many people at that time regarded as the most famous Christian proselytizer since Saint Paul. With burning eyes, magnetic presence, and a mellifluous voice heard by millions on the radio, Monsignor Fulton J. Sheen counted among his more famous converts another '21' regular, Clare Booth Luce.

Barely six months after the lunch with Woollcott, Heywood Broun came down with pneumonia. After receiving last rites from Monsignor Sheen, he died on December 17, 1939. Among mourners at the funeral mass celebrated by Monsignor Sheen were cabinet members, ballplayers, actors, newspapermen, labor leaders, Round Tablers, waiters, doormen and bartenders of '21', Jack and Charlie, Mac, me, and Bob, who'd recently graduated from Rutgers.

Although Bob did well in his university studies, he had not been all that great a student in high school, so getting him admitted to Rutgers required a little persuasion in the office of the dean of admissions. This assignment fell to me. Fortunately, a member of the school's board of trustees had been a regular at '21' for a few years. Fortified with a glowing letter from him, I traveled to New Jersey and made a successful pitch.

In the long run Bob's acceptance proved to be enormously beneficial to the college. It became the repository for many works of art from Jack's collection of paintings (more about this side of Jack later) as well as Bob's collection of first editions and manuscripts of some of the country's greatest writers who found time (often a lot of time) to spend in '21'.

How Bob got the idea to start collecting signed books can be traced to one of his first assignments after coming to work at the club. Jack had received an urgent call from Gene Fowler, who was confined at that moment to a hospital and was in desperate need of a drink. Jack told Gene not to worry, he was sending Bob over with a bottle of Ballantine's scotch.

Because Bob had an interest in writers, he'd persuaded Jack to institute a policy at '21' of stocking the books written by its illustrious author-customers. The books were put on sale at the tobacco counter. Often, a customer who'd seen a book there discovered that the author was in the club, so he could depart not only with a good meal under his belt, but also a signed first edition under his arm. As Bob headed out the door with Gene Fowler's scotch, he noticed Gene's new book, *Salute to Yesterday*, at the counter. Grabbing a copy, Bob delivered it with the booze and asked Gene to autograph it. Gene inscribed, "To Bob Kriendler . . . who rushed into battle with a bottle and thereby saved a life."

Emboldened by this success, Bob got up the courage one day to ask John Steinbeck to sign *The Grapes of Wrath*. Steinbeck was reluctant. Bob persisted. Steinbeck asked, "What shall I say?"

Bob replied, "Something scatological."

Steinbeck boldly wrote, "To Bob Kriendler, Scatologically, John Steinbeck."

Within two years of Bob's graduation he'd donated so many signed first editions and other material to Rutgers that he was invited to become a member of the Administrative Committee of the Friends of the University Library, and the library put on its first "Kriendler Collection" exhibition.

In addition to recruiting Bob and me to help cope with the rapidly expanding patronage, Jack brought in Charlie's younger brother, Jerry. Jerry quit his position as film critic for the *Cincinnati Enquirer* (a choice he never regretted for a second).

So blatant had Jack's nepotism become that Mark Hellinger stuck his tongue firmly in his cheek and wrote: "A brother, Jacques Kriendlere, was imported from France as a chef. Another brother, Jimmy Kriendlerio, was brought in from Italy and placed at the door to take care of the check room, to take care of the customers, and to take. Another brother, Mac Kriendler, was yanked from a musical education and given menus to distribute—thereby spoiling a great career with the Metropolitan Opera, as an usher.

"Encouraged by this success of his theory of relativity, Jack, now known as something of an opportunist, marched boldly onward. He hired squads of men to search for other Kriendlers the world over. Jack and Charlie's Chinese food today is prepared by a Chinese brother from Canton—Chin Down Krien. The head waiter is a sort of half-brother from Russia by the name of Phillip Kriendlowski. The boss bartender, another brother from Ireland, is Sean Kriencasey."

A genuine Kriendler who joined the family business was a son of our sister Gussie (Augusta Kriendler Axelrod). Kermit soon got a sharp taste of Jack's policy regarding relatives learning the ropes. On summer vacation from college and working as a food checker, Kermit was on duty at the service bar one afternoon when a customer ordered a martini. Kermit decided to help out a busy waiter by making and bringing the drink to the customer's table. As Kermit was pouring it out, Jack grabbed the glass and growled, "You don't know enough to make drinks for *my* customers."

The lesson Kermit drew from this, he said later, was that to his Uncle Jack a bartender was a very upper-strata employee, very important. "In his opinion, no college kid like myself could make a good drink. No way. He really roasted me. What a martinet."

That customers ranked first, even ahead of family, was not lost on patrons. I know very well that Marilyn Kaytor was right when she wrote that '21' clientele in the middle years of the 1930s welcomed the attention that accompanied the clubbiness, clannishness, coziness, checkered tablecloths, and the relaxed atmosphere where you were left alone to mingle freely, drink and dine, flirt, play pranks, and even plan love affairs. Chances were good that one day you'd find yourself seated next to some celebrity, perhaps Groucho Marx, who, if he couldn't remember someone's name, addressed that person, man or woman, as "Mr. Benson."

On February 28, 1936, Lucius Beebe's *New York Herald Tribune* column noted a dazzling depression-era Who's Who:

> Seen at lunch at Jack & Charlie's '21': Lawrence Tibbett, very gay [the word back then meant "happy"]; Morris Markey, very professional; the Albert Hinkleys, very Bostonian; Townsend Martin; Dwight Dere Wiman; Ben Hecht and Charley MacArthur; Valerie Ziegler, Mrs. William Randolph Hearst, the Laddie Sanfords, George Marshall, very laundryman; Bill Corum, Dorothy Fell, very severe; Frank Buck, very solvent; and Lord and Lady Cavendish. There isn't quite as much hanky waving at '21' as there is at lunch at the Colony these days, but people go to '21' largely to eat, whereas they go to the Colony mainly to see what sort of hat Elsa Maxwell is wearing.

If anyone could correctly be described as a "phenomenon" at the time, it was Elsa Maxwell. She billed herself as "a society hostess." And she was. But not because she was a member of that elite group by reason of either parentage or wealth. Born poor in San Francisco, she had made up her mind as a little girl to be a partygiver. Before attaining that goal she'd worked as a piano player in silent-movie theaters and vaudeville houses, then discovered a niche as a newspaper columnist. It was her ability to provide publicity to hotels and eateries that afforded her the access to the worlds of society and celebrity she sought. This trajectory eventually landed her regular guest spots on Jack Paar's show.

Plain-looking, short, and plump (I'm being charitable), she based her career on what she saw as an innate human love of silliness, based on her belief that within everyone (especially the rich) was a little voice crying out to feel like a kid again. To fill that need she threw extravagant costume parties, cooking parties, painting parties, and treasure hunts. One she held in the Jade Room of the Waldorf was a "barnyard party" at which guests cavorted around baled hay and other farming motifs. There were two real cows and one made of papier-mâché with udders giving out champagne. Quite a few '21' regulars attended.

When Elsa came to '21' she occupied table 3, which not only gave her a commanding view of who came in and left, but put her in a position to be seen by them. Two of the richest women in America who passed before Elsa's eyes were Doris Duke and Barbara Hutton. The club policy at that time was to admit unescorted women only until 4:00 P.M. and only to the upstairs dining room. Should the lady bring along a poodle, the pooch would be looked after in the lounge. For a few years, if a woman desired to "powder her nose" she had to ask a man to check to be sure that the men's room was unoccupied, then to stand guard for her. Inequality in such facilities was eventually eliminated. And when actress Peggy Joyce Hopkins informed Jack that she hated having to climb the stairs to eat, space for tables in the barroom was expanded and women were let in for lunch. A further whittling away at restrictions imposed on women occurred when Katharine Hepburn was admitted in slacks. Yet it would not be until the war years that the manner in which women were welcomed would change dramatically and forever. As a footnote to the evolving place of women customers, I record here that the first and only patron to become the namesake of a dish was Helen Hayes (boiled tongue, coleslaw, toasted rolls).

Gossip columnist Ed Sullivan, writing in *Silver Screen* magazine in March 1936, noted, "Checking up on the stars at play in New York always leads me to Jack and Charlie's famous '21', which is a favorite rendezvous of the movie colony when it emigrates East. The last night that Joan Crawford and Franchot Tone were in town, I had dinner with them. Near us sat Gene Markey and Joan Bennett, across the room were Ben Hecht and Charlie MacArthur and Gene Fowler. Downstairs were Joe Schenck and Lewis Milestone and other cinema executives. This is a favorite meeting place of Jack Warner, Ann Alvarado Warner, and other couples, for it is exclusive."

The club was such a favorite of Jack L. Warner, boss of the Warner Bros. studio, that his wedding dinner was in one of the upstairs banquet rooms. Invited to the celebration on January 10, 1936, were, among others, Mr. and Mrs. Jack Dempsey, Marilyn Miller, and Ethel Merman, as well as an old and loyal friend and patron of Jack and Charlie's clubs, Billy Seeman. (Now married and no longer the playboy, he was a man-about-town during Jimmy Walker's day.)

On September 25 of that same year the club hosted an even more impressive party on the eve of the George Vanderbilt Cup race at Roosevelt Raceway. Master of ceremonies for the gala was FDR's political "right-hand man," Postmaster General James A. Farley. Obviously tilted toward the sports world, the guest list included sportswriters and broadcasters Bill Corum, Steve Hanagan, Clem McCarthy, Graham McNamee, and Grantland Rice. Also on the roster was department-store mogul Bernard Gimbel, Jack Hearst (of the newspaper and magazine Hearsts), and aviation pioneer and wartime combat ace Eddie Rickenbacker, now general manager of Eastern Airlines.

A particular kind of party became dear to all our hearts. For regulars who couldn't get home for Christmas Jack came up with the "Christmas Lonely Hearts Dinner." Although the club closed on major holidays, regulars with nowhere else to go for Thanksgiving were invited to dine at '21' while being serenaded by the Yale Glee Club. And on New Year's Eve regulars could ring out the old year at their "usual" tables amid old friends.

Parties were also thrown at which the menu was corned beef and cabbage. These bashes were held in private rooms above the club. Nor did Jack forget the Yale men who had put the Puncheon on the map. For the "Sons of Eli" we hosted two annual parties. One was called "Ben Quinn's Kitchen." The head count was usually around twenty-five, led by its namesake, who admitted as years passed that it became such a gala occasion that as they became older "our constitutions could not take such festivities, even once a year," so the custom was discontinued.

Another annual Yale soirée, which continued into the 1990s, was for the "Comanche Club." Guests were members of the Fence Club, a Yale fraternity that produced more than its share of millionaires. One attendee was sports commentator and writer Bob Cooke. In 1936 when he invited classmate Richard E. Moore to the first banquet, the guest was astonished that Jack and Charlie would spend so lavishly on a free dinner "just for a group of New Haven men." He wagered Cooke that the dinner would be a one-time event. Not only did Moore lose, but the Comanche Club continued dining "on the house" for the next sixty years. Moore went on to become a special assistant to President Richard Nixon. Over the years the Comanches produced a large number of movers and shakers in business and finance, politics, and the arts.

One participant in the Comanche dinner since his graduation from Yale in 1958 was Frank Polk, whose family tree includes President James K. Polk. Frank became such a familiar face that he has a table reserved for him (No. 53). It's in a corner near the east end of the bar that some customers consider "Siberia." But it in fact offers a panoramic view and has always been my table of choice. An insurance executive, Frank has been given the rare honor of a seeing a plaque put on the wall behind his spot designating it "Frank Polk's Table." (More about others who were honored with commemorative "table" plaques later.)

One partaker of these Yale annuals believed it was axiomatic that a Yale diploma was an open sesame to '21', as attested by this rewrite of the lyrics of the Yale anthem:

We are poor little sheep
Who have gone far astray
Where's the bar-bar-bar?
But to Twenty One fin'lly

We've found our way
Where's the bar-bar-bar?
Gentlemen songsters out on a spree
Hoping and praying that you, Jim'mee
Will not deny entrance to such as we
Where's the bar-bar-bar?

Of course, the ultimate arbiter of who got in and who didn't was Jack. The impresario for the stellar assemblage of personalities at '21' in the 1930s was described by Francis Hunter as "the ever genial host, connoisseur and restaurateur deluxe, whose outstanding ability enabled him, with the splendid collaboration of his associates, to establish and build a veritable empire in the restaurant world."

I couldn't have agreed more with *New York Sun* columnist Ward Newhouse's opinion that Jack was shrewd and smart, indordinately generous, strict but also deeply considerate, often quick and abrupt, at times aloof and inhospitable, but also the most gracious of men.

Journal-American sportswriter Bill Corum declared, "In my time around N.Y. there have been quite a lot of folks, bless 'em all, who have made the greatest of all cities bright and cheerful. But not many who did it better than Jack Kriendler."

In a town and at a time when there were plenty of colorful characters, why did Jack garner such verbal bouquets? Looking back from the 1970s, Marilyn Kaytor wrote, "No one in the New York restaurant business has ever been able to hold a candle to Jack Kriendler for sheer personality, or for receiving so much newspaper space, including page-one coverage. There have been others equally or more loquacious, opinionated, and tyrannical, but none as calculatedly and obviously eccentric."

As Jack's brother, I agree he was all of the above, but he came to deserve and to glory in these descriptions because when he was working to build a fabulous restaurant he was determined to fashion a unique personality and style for himself that would do '21' justice. It can be argued that '21' was not created, but evolved, with contributions to what it became from many people. That can't be said of Jack.

My big brother was in every way his own invention. The personality Jack created, in Louis Sobol's analysis, was dual in nature. He observed one side of Jack as "haughty, aloof, social-minded," with his box at the opera, his sable-lined overcoat, as "addicted to cutaways and dinner suits and tails" as he was "to rare vintage wines and Corots and Rembrandts, to say nothing of costly Havana cigars." The other Jack was a gay, congenial, hail-fellow-well-met, quick on the draw when it came to grabbing a tab or shelling out for any cause, major or minor. "Yes, indeedy," Sobol wrote for the "Saturday Home Magazine" of the *New York Journal,* "a complex citizen for you—this Jack Kriendler."

Each seemingly contradictory aspect of Jack observed by Sobol and all the other patrons of '21' did in fact coexist within the tall, handsome figure with a neat mustache who greeted them at the door or paused at their tables to inquire if everything was to their satisfaction. What astonished and amused them was that one day he could be dressed to the nines in one of dozens of suits specially tailored for him by the Spitz brothers in his apartment above the club, and the following day appear all decked out in a cowboy outfit of fringed shirt, chaps, boots with jingling spurs, holstered six-gun, and Stetson hat.

While emulating Uncle Sam Brenner's spiffy attire, Jack

had fallen in love with everything about the Old West. His wardrobe grew to a hundred custom-made getups, twenty-five each of four different styles. The collection quickly included 130 shirts, 160 pairs of pants, twenty-six pairs of boots, twenty-four belts, twenty complete rodeo outfits, and three dozen ten-gallon hats.

Jack had also become a collector, but not of books as Bob had. For Jack the attraction was to artifacts of the American West. In pursuing this hobby he added to the decor of '21' one of the finest private assemblages of Western art in the world, including numerous paintings and drawings by Frederic Remington.

A real prize of Jack's Westernalia was an item I bought for him at a bankruptcy auction in California. It was a fine Mission Saddle of hand-tooled Mexican leather studded with sterling silver conchos depicting Spanish missions. When Jack wasn't in it astride a horse, the saddle was displayed in '21' in a steel-and-glass case just off the lobby.

Jack's affinity for the West materialized in other ways in the club, including naming one of the upstairs dining rooms the Winchester Room. Displayed there were two pairs of Jack's boots with K's embossed in leather, and a pistol holster bearing silver miniatures of the iron gates.

Having been bitten by the Western bug, Jack naturally took vacations out West, where he delighted in taking part in local rodeos. A postcard from one of these events showed "Jack in the saddle again." The front pictured him in full cowboy gear on a handsome palomino horse. The reverse read: "Two-Trigger Jack Kriendler, Baron of Manhattan's noted '21' Club and one of the West's most colorful horsemen is shown with his famous California Mission Saddle, during his participation in a typically Western Rodeo recently held at the B-Bar-H Ranch, Palm Springs, California."

"Of course, he belonged no farther west than the Manhattan Transfer," remarked Bill Corum. "But he knew it and the nice part was that he could laugh with it, too."

Just as Jack's fascination with the wild and woolly West earned him the nickname "Two-Trigger Jack," his alternate attire—the sable-lined coat and elegantly tailored suits—garnered him the title "the Baron."

Although Charlie Berns was never as natty a clotheshorse and example of sartorial perfection as Jack, he was also well turned out in Spitz brothers tailoring. Jovial of manner and spirit, Charlie generally came across as reserved, unassuming, unpretentious, conservative, and substantial. Wearing glasses and a lot less hairy than the Charlie that Mark Hellinger described at the Red Head, he was seen by one customer as "a balance wheel."

This solid-image perception was not entirely right. Charlie could be as entertaining as Jack. He also nurtured a fondness for horses and riding. To outfit himself he turned to the man who made Jack's Western duds. A tailor from Philadelphia with the trade name Rodeo Ben (last name Lichtenstein), he'd met Jack at a Madison Square Garden rodeo and soon found himself creating both Jack's and Charlie's riding attire.

No matter how they dressed, together Jack and Charlie faced customers and the outside world, according to a caption above their photos in the 1936 edition of *The Iron Gate*, with an "extraordinary display of continuous amity, commercial harmony, and fructuous collaboration which would have warmed the hearts of the Cheeryble Brothers and their immortal creator, Charles Dickens."

In 1931 this colorful pair of restaurant owners, who'd been raised on Manhattan's Lower East Side surrounded by Dickensian scenes of poverty, went beyond dressing up like "dudes" and actually ventured into the countryside. They snapped up an opportunity to take over the lease of the financially strapped Westchester Embassy Club. Located north of New York City on Route 22 between Armonk and Bedford Village, it was a sumptuous resort hotel catering to "country squires," with a swimming pool, riding stable, eighteen-hole golf course, tennis courts, and dining and dancing under the stars. Much of the staff Jack and Charlie put together for it was imported from Cuba. Having just come back from a vacation in Havana, Jack gave the menu an international flavor by adding such Caribbean dishes as black bean soup.

The customers who paid two-hundred-dollar-a-year membership fees included Roosevelts, Farleys, and Whitneys, as well as a roster of judges, district attorneys, and attorney generals whose very presence assured there'd be no Prohibition agents rudely intruding on the fun of drinking Cuban rum. Blithely sipping, the top names in New York society and politics delighted in observing the new owners in white golfing knickers and cashmere sweaters, or riding pants and knee-high boots. Jack and Charlie also dared the minions of the law by introducing slot machines and roulette tables in defiance of state antigaming statutes.

Once again they had succeeded in turning the sow's ear of Prohibition into a silk purse. But when the nation came to its senses and repealed the Eighteenth Amendment, and '21' faced the financial crunch resulting from new competition by freshly opened and reopened spots, the Embassy was sacrificed to help keep '21' afloat. "Since Repeal had negated its noble purpose and it [Embassy] was a losing deal," Charlie noted, "we just didn't renew the lease."

A second attempt at putting money behind the opening of a new club fared better. When Bill Hardey came to Jack and Charlie with an idea for a spot in the brownstone house Jack and Charlie had bought on Fifty-fourth Street, they gave him seven thousand dollars for equipment and supplies. He named the place Bill's Gay Nineties. As a fond tribute to Uncle Sam Brenner, he decorated the entrance floor with four hundred silver dollars. Jack and Charlie eventually pulled out of the operation, opening the way for our brother-in-law Henry Tannenbaum to come in. He and Bill would be partners for a quarter century, after which Henry retired, leaving Bill Hardey the sole proprietor until he also retired in the 1960s.

But Jack didn't limit his excursion into the suburbs to the Embassy Club. He soon bought himself a country place near Hampton Bays on Long Island. Twenty acres on a bluff, it was promptly stocked with cattle, sheep, turkeys, and chickens, all of which were destined sooner or later for the '21' kitchen or the huge barbecue pit Jack constructed. In the basement of the house was installed a replica of the '21' back room. The bar was the one that had been taken from the Puncheon and kept in storage for the day Jack knew would come when he would build just such a "weekend getaway" in which to install it.

Incapable of enjoying his country retreat in solitude, Jack continued his role as genial host. Regulars at '21' were invited by the droves for "weekends" that started on Friday afternoon and ran to Tuesday. My favorite event of the fair-weather out-ings was the Saturday night dinner served on a huge patio in the glow of Japanese lanterns. Guests were offered unlimited supplies of a Bill Hardey–invented drink. Called Bill's Block

Buster, it was a double mint julep topped by cognac. The dinner menu usually had caviar as a starter, then Long Island oysters, Montauk lobsters, steaks or lamb, roasted potatoes, corn on the cob, and lettuce and vegetables straight from the garden. The Sunday brunch might include crisp Long Island duckling with a fine Burgundy and fresh strawberries.

To get to both the Long Island weekend place and the Embassy Club Jack drove a black Cadillac convertible. Just as he loved to ride spirited horses, he had a passion for lively cars, and the faster the better. One of his prized race cars was a 1908 Buick driven by famed race driver Louis Chevrolet. Jack's "No. 21" came in first in an "Old Car" race that was the curtain-raiser for the 1936 George Vanderbilt Cup at Roosevelt Raceway.

But a drive to Connecticut in the Cadillac one lovely summer day in 1935 ended with the Caddy wrecked and Jack's name splashed in headlines across the front pages of every newspaper in town. In the back of the car police found a big wicker hamper stuffed with champagne bottles, caviar, pâté, baguettes, Brie cheese, cold pheasant, pears, a complete silver service, and one red-and-white checkered '21' tablecloth. Bachelor Jack's partner for the romantic picnic in the country was to have been a beautiful woman. Unfortunately, before Jack could meet her for the tryst he misjudged a curve in the road and the Cadillac slammed into a tree. It fell onto the car and pretty much squashed the hood. But Jack got out in fairly good shape.

Unfortunately, the object of Jack's liaison in a rustic spot in the Nutmeg State happened to have a husband who wasn't exactly in the dark about what his spouse had been up to. The irate guy had, in fact, been keeping tabs on his missus for quite a while, including tapping their home telephone. Not only that, he'd had her romantic conversations with Jack transcribed.

The result was that in the suit for divorce brought by the husband, naming Jack as co-respondent, the word-for-word lovers' chats between Jack and the man's wife went public. In an era when gossip was a participatory sport engaged in by anyone choosing to follow the story in the press (I never met a soul who wasn't on tenterhooks waiting for the next sensation, especially the '21' guys and gals) got to read the sweet nothings Jack had whispered into the woman's dainty ear. Some of these utterances were not what you'd find in a dictionary. Jack tended to express his amorous feelings to her in barnyard vocalizations such as "Mooey! Mooey!" There was also lovers' gibberish and baby talk, including "Gooch, gooch." I found all this hilariously charming.

An affair which might have made Jack a laughingstock and hurt '21' had the opposite effect. "This touch of nature," said Stanley Walker, "made Jack Kriendler one of the most popular men in New York, and brought vast numbers of society folk to his restaurant."

Stanley expounded on the "scandal" and found in it evidence of how much the country's attitudes regarding such matters had changed during the years of Prohibition. "Certainly a lot of stuffiness and snobbery is gone," he wrote. "Everyone seems less inhibited, less afraid of making a mistake or being seen with the wrong people. The evolution of a new social set-up has produced some genuinely amusing characters, who should be appreciated as affording pleasant spectacles in a world which often appears unbearably drab and dispiriting. Off with the shackles. The telephone directory always was better reading matter than the Social Register."

More than a few of Stanley Walker's "genuinely amusing characters" could be found running other restaurants and clubs. In the block of West Fifty-second known as Swing Street you could come across Joe Helbock presiding at the Onyx, Eddie Davis and Leon Enken of Leon & Eddie's, John Popkin of Hickory House, and Jack White at Club 18, across the street from Jack and Charlie's.

Other personalities indelibly associated with their clubs were Sherman Billingsley, whose Stork Club at 3 *East* Fifty-second was Walter Winchell's favorite location for picking up gossip well into the 1960s before he and the Stork went out of business; Toots Shor, famous as host to a primarily sports-minded clientele; heavyweight champion Jack Dempsey holding forth in a spot near Madison Square Garden; John Perona, the founder of El Morocco; and guys at a number of joints who were "silent" partners or outright owners operating uptown in Harlem, including the Cotton Club, backed by Irish mobster Owney Madden.

Not all the "characters" you could run across in the saloons owned them. Many were customers. But of all the truly unique figures who ventured into '21' in the 1930s, none proved quite as fascinating as "His Imperial Highness, Prince Michael Alexandrovich Dmitri Obolenksy Romanoff." What was outstanding about him was that he was a fraud, impostor, and habitual check-bouncer. Yet virtually everyone (except persons engaged in law enforcement, or who had been duped by him) really liked the guy.

Standing five feet tall, with a debonair mustache, and dressed in fine Parisian-made or Savile Row suits, he swaggered around town swinging a walking stick, insisting that he really was Russian royalty—until one day in a conversation in '21' with Broadway columnist Louis Sobol.

"Old chap," he said to Louis, "my name truly is Michael Romanoff. However, I now confess to having been in error about the royal blood of the Russian Romanoffs coursing through my veins. I have discovered that I am a Romanoff with no connection with the Russian clan. However, I have my consolation. I have my own car, a valet, three months' rent paid in advance, and a checking account like any peasant."

Royal pedigree or not, in 1940 Mike managed to get John Hay Whitney, Joseph Schenck, and Bob Benchley to form a corporation to back him in the restaurant business. He set it up in Beverly Hills. Before long he turned Romanoff's, and himself, into the arbiter of status in Hollywood.

Despite the abundance of drinking and dining places in New York in the thirties, Jack and Charlie never faltered in the conviction that none of them amounted to serious competition for '21'. That Jack and Charlie created something unique is evidenced by the fact that '21' stands alone as a survivor from those years. A "current column" reprinted in the 1936 *The Iron Gate* but not otherwise identified as to its authorship, perfectly captured '21' in that decade:

> Jack and Charlie, one tall and one short, have long
> been known as the most successful club-restaurant opera-
> tors in the swank belt. During prohibition, they coined
> twin fortunes by serving the best liquor in town and excep-

tionally fine food. They lasted out every storm kicked up by the prohibitionists. Their place became a rendezvous for Hollywood stars, producers and society, and they were smart enough to emphasize the exclusiveness of their place by rigidly maintaining the scrutiny of those who rapped at the door and peered through the peephole-in-the-door. I imagine Jack and Charlie are worth $2,000,000 in cash. The experiment was noble in motive, if not downright generous to them.

Except for the two million in cash, this was all true.

Five

MR. PETE

With four guys named Kriendler usually on the '21' premises at the same time, when one of the staff said "Mr. Kriendler," he was likely to be answered by a quartet. The solution was for the "Mr." to be followed by a given name, which made me thereafter (and to the present day) "Mr. Pete."

Being in the restaurant business hadn't been my plan. After graduating from De Witt Clinton High School, I went to City College and then to Saint Lawrence University law school. I found studying law a cinch and passed the bar exam on my first try. I never practiced, but a classmate of mine did. Irving Lazar stuck with it and eventually used his mastery of law's ins and outs to become the most powerful agent (literary and talent) in Hollywood. He earned a reputation for closing lucrative deals for his clients in such a short time that he picked up the nickname "Swifty." Shortly after I completed law school in 1929 I sold my seat on the New York Curb Exchange, which Jack had bought me for twenty-six thousand dollars, and walked away with roughly ten times that amount.

Well-off financially at the tender age of twenty-five and not sure what I wanted to do with my life, I spent a lot of time at the Puncheon, much of it hanging out with Bob Benchley. The more time I spent there watching Jack's obvious talent for making the Puncheon and '21' more than ordinary speakeasies, the more I wanted to get involved. Switching from observer to participant was a short step, but not an easy one. My first job was handyman. I swept the floor, carted boxes of food, and worked behind the bar as a cashier and bartender. Jack put me to work.

Shortly after I began my apprenticeship, I met Jeannette Epstein. The attractive daughter of a very successful builder, she'd recently graduated from New York University. The first time I saw her she was arriving at '21' in a chauffeured Lincoln Town Car. What she found in me I don't know, but what I recognized in her was a beautiful, vivacious charmer. We got married in 1933 at the Waldorf-Astoria, honeymooned in Hawaii, and settled into the life of husband and wife which lasted almost sixty years.

As with all women of the Kriendler clan, Jeannette understood that the running of the family business was the province of the men. She was perfectly content to enjoy its fruits, and she did so with a zest that later prompted our nieces and nephews to liken her to the fabulous Auntie Mame in the play and film (based on the Patrick Dennis best-selling book).

When it came to enjoying the finer things of life, Jeannette certainly was never reticent. Neither was I. Nor should we have been. Thanks to '21' we could afford to have the best, and did. Jeannette's ideal vacation was an ocean crossing and a shopping tour of Europe. When I took off to indulge my passion for fishing, particularly for salmon, in Scotland,

Iceland, Spain, and Alaska, Jeannette stayed home. My sojourns were usually in the company of other dedicated anglers who frequented '21', among them Bing Crosby and Clark Gable. Both validated my opinion that it is not possible to find a fisherman who's not an all-around great guy.

For a time Bing became a fixture of the Christmas Lonely Hearts dinners, leading everyone in singing Christmas songs, frequently accompanied by a chorus of Salvation Army volunteers whom Jack took to inviting to the dinners.

To celebrate my birthday I organized the "Eighth of July or Thereabouts Club," to which only people who also had birthdays in July could belong. About fifteen of us would get together for a champagne lunch that began at noon and ran until two. A rule of the club required that no man could attend with his wife, and wives couldn't bring their husbands. Most of the members were women, so each year I picked one of them to rule the proceedings. A feature of these gatherings was telling raunchy jokes, and the rule was that if the joke included a dirty word, there could be no getting around it by spelling it or choosing a euphemism. Punishment for breaking the rule was banishment from the club. One charter member of the group who could be relied upon to regale us with a really off-color joke was Charlie Berns's wife, Molly.

When Jeannette and I moved into a spacious apartment across Fifth Avenue from the Metropolitan Museum of Art in 1947, she delighted in furnishing it with the things we both liked, along with my growing personal collection of fine art and good books. She also found enormous pleasure in entertaining, including parties for her dachshund, Mikimoto, who was adorned with a pearl collar. Through the years we had a number of dachshunds, each named Mikimoto, and all of them have been memorialized in sketches by the great illustrator Dong Kingman. Jeannette's fondness for the breed also resulted in a large collection of ceramic dachshunds. Another of her passions was collecting watches.

Like my brother Jack, I was interested in art and artists. As a result, the walls of our homes and the public and private rooms of the club soon resembled galleries. One of *New Yorker* cartoonist Peter Arno's works displayed in '21' is of a bartender peering over the bar to an unseen customer flat on the floor. The bartender is inquiring, "Will that be all, Sir?" Another famed cartoonist, Zito, took a sheet of '21' stationery and on the back drew a whimsical sketch of Charlie Berns. Another Charlie likeness, appearing in *Vogue* magazine, was put on display in the upstairs Puncheon Room. Zito also rendered a forlorn little mug of a dog sitting dejectedly outside the iron gate and looking at a sign that says, "No admittance without a pedigree."

The painter who became synonymous with '21' was Frederic Remington. Our collection eventually contained twenty-six paintings and drawings and five bronzes. A few of these came into our possession in strange ways. *An Ox Train in the Mountains* and *Mule Train Crossing the Sierras* were sold to us by the widow of a regular customer at the price her husband paid for them twenty-five years earlier. She said she wanted them to belong to someone who would not only appreciate them but would also make them available for others to enjoy. She dropped in from time to time to look at them. Another customer was so deeply in debt to us that he asked if we might be interested in tearing up his tab in exchange for a Remington he had under his bed. We gladly accepted the deal.

An artist who spent a lot of time in the club in the late 1930s was Ludwig Bemelmans. A refugee from Nazi Germany,

My parents, Carl and Sadie Kriendler, shortly after they settled on the Lower East Side of New York.

My mother's brother, Sam Brenner, provided the inspiration to Jack and our cousin Charlie Berns to open a speakeasy. Uncle Sam was regarded as the spiffiest-dressed saloon keeper on the Lower East.

That's me seated beside brother Bob. Behind us are Mac, Gussie, our mother, and Eunice. Where Jack and our sisters Beatrice and Anna were at the time this picture was taken I have no idea.

Left to right: Mac, me,
Jack, and Bob in
the 1920s (*left*) and
again in the 1940s at
Bob's wedding.

Jack (*right*) and Charlie in front of the Puncheon at 42 West Forty-ninth Street. When the building was torn down to make room for Rockefeller Center, Jack and Charlie bought a townhouse on West Fifty-second Street and created Jack and Charlie's '21' club.

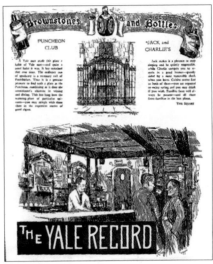

The earliest and most loyal patrons of the Puncheon were students from Yale University. Praise from the campus newspaper brought them down from New Haven in droves.

Sketch of 21 West Fifty-second Street in 1930 by the architect who designed the club, Frank Applegate Buchanan.

Yale men at a 1935 bachelor dinner held at '21' for George Vanderbilt ranged from newspaper magnate William Randolph Hearst Jr. to songwriter Hoagy Carmichael.

Another group of Yale men called themselves "the Comanches" and were treated to an annual dinner "on the house" at '21' for more than sixty years.

The iron gate that had been the entrance to the Puncheon Club on West Forty-ninth Street was installed at the front of Jack and Charlie's '21'. The tradition of decorating the front of the club with cast-iron jockey figures began with gifts of statues by stable owners Jock Whitney, Alfred Gwynne Vanderbilt, and Buckley Byers.

There are twenty-one jockey figures on the balcony.

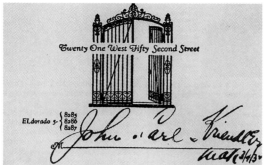

A sure way to be admitted to '21' was to be given a club business card marked with "OK" and signed by Jack. But if he wrote "34" on it, the headwaiter was being told, "Keep this bum out."

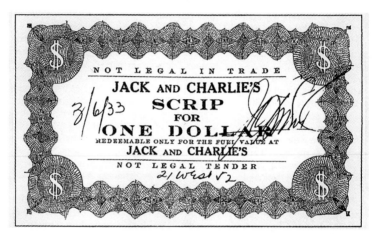

When many '21' regulars were hit hard financially during the depression, Jack and Charlie extended them credit in the form of scrip redeemable at the club for food and drink.

The '21' tradition of red-and-white checkered tablecloths was started in the Puncheon.

For his wedding party in 1936, the head of Warner Bros., Jack L. Warner (holding the drink), chose '21'. Among the guests were Ethel Merman (above Jack's shoulder) and, next to Ethel, heavyweight boxing champ Jack Dempsey. Thirty-some years later, Jack Warner offered to buy the club for $21 million. We turned him down.

Famed *New Yorker* cartoonist Zito found a cute way to poke fun at Jack and Charlie's policy of exclusivity. They achieved this primarily by charging very high prices.

Cartoonist Rube Goldberg, known for coming up with zany and complicated inventions, offered this device for gaining admission to the club.

The '21' bar through the years: above, 1930s; below, 1940s; at right, 1950s.

"A Mr. Peebles phoning from New York, Mr. President. He wants to know if you can push the button and open a place at 21 West 52nd Street?"

A *Life* magazine cartoon on June 12, 1931, emphasized the exclusivity of Jack and Charlie's '21' by showing an aide relaying a message to President Herbert Hoover from a man who wants to know if Hoover can get him into the club. During the 1932 presidential election campaign, columnist George Jean Nathan wrote that Jack and Charlie would make the best president and vice president because their club was the most efficiently run business in the country.

A customer of ours since the opening of the Puncheon, humorist Robert Benchley (*above*) introduced other wits of the famed Algonquin Round Table to the Puncheon and then to '21', including columnist Heywood Broun, who was notorious for dressing sloppily.

The original barroom of No. 21 West Fifty-second Street is now known as "the front room" and "the kitchen room" and is regarded as the most desirable seating area. A plaque on the wall behind table No. 3 at the far right indicates that it was the favorite of Robert Benchley. This table was also where Michael Douglas and Charlie Sheen filmed a scene in the movie *Wall Street*.

What was once 19 West Fifty-second Street is now the middle section of the barroom. Humphrey Bogart's regular spot, the table on the far right beneath the cartoon and a bust of Babe Ruth, is known as "Bogie's Table."

Located in the former 17 West Fifty-second Street, the "east room" was considered by some customers as the least desirable place to be seated. Consequently, it became known as "Siberia." Actually, the section provides a panoramic view of the whole barroom.

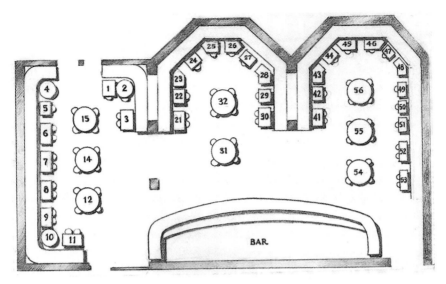

Favorite tables of some regular celebrity customers (past and present) and placement and numbering of tables (sketch by Kevin Gordon):

FRONT SECTION
1. Regis Philbin
   Molly Berns (Charlie's wife)
   Used by Walter Weiss when assigning tables
2. Larry King
   Ben Hecht
   Charles MacArthur
   Helen Hayes
3. Robert Benchley
   Alexander Woollcott
   Rex Stout
   John O'Hara
   Jimmy Carter
   Joan Rivers
   Otto Preminger
   Gordon Gekko (played by Michael Douglas in *Wall Street*)
4. Helen Gurley Brown
5. Laurence and Jonathan Tisch
6. Jean Kennedy Smith

   Heywood Broun
   Dorothy Parker
7. John Steinbeck
   Ernest Hemingway
   Richard Nixon
   Henry Kissinger
   Nancy Reagan
   George and Barbara Bush
   Fred de Cordova (when producing *The Tonight Show* in New York)
8. James Baker III
   John Connolly
9. Barbara Walters
   Donald Trump
10. Bob Considine's Corner
11. Gerald and Betty Ford
12. Marx Brothers
13. There is no No. 13
14. Frank Sinatra
    John DeLorean and family
15. Marvin Davis

MIDDLE SECTION
21. Maxwell (Mac) Kriendler
    Tom Brokaw
    Jackie Gleason

22. George Steinbrenner
    Joe Torre
23. Bo Jackson
25. Chris Evert
26. Arlene Dahl
30. Humphrey Bogart (Bogie's Corner)
    Lauren Bacall
    Robert Altman
31. Members of the Kennedy family

EAST SECTION
41. Luciano Pavarotti
42. Matt Dillon
43. Michael Nouri
44. Julia Roberts
46. Michelle Pfeiffer
49. Rod Stewart
50. Savion Glover
51. Bill Murray
52. Ivan Boesky
    Ed Koch
53. Alan King
    Andy Williams
    Frank Polk
    Pete Kriendler

The upstairs dining rooms, their walls decorated with the work of some of the world's greatest painters and illustrators, provided a more sedate atmosphere for dining than the sometimes raucous downstairs barroom. These spaces are now reserved for private parties and banquets.

For more than half a century, Walter Weiss has decided who sits where. The process is known in the restaurant business as "dressing a room."

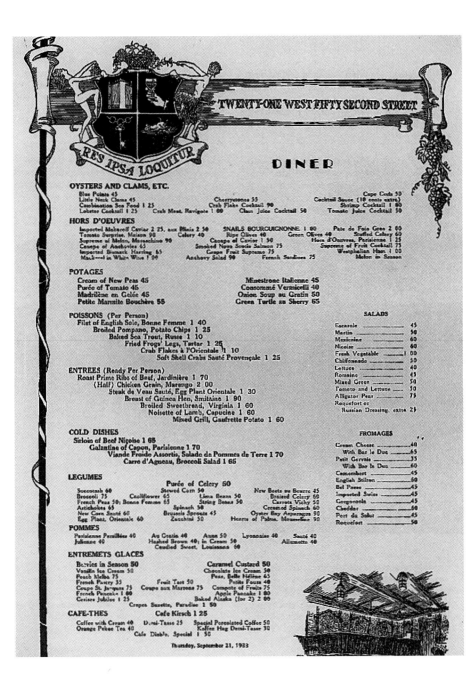

TWENTY-ONE WEST FIFTY SECOND STREET

RES IPSA LOQUITUR

DINER

OYSTERS AND CLAMS, ETC.

Blue Points 45
Little Neck Clams 45
Combination Sea Food 1 25
Lobster Cocktail 1 25   Crab Meat, Ravigote 1 00

Cherrystones 55
Crab Flake Cocktail 90
Clam Juice Cocktail 50

Cape Cods 50
Cocktail Sauce (10 cents extra)
Shrimp Cocktail 1 60
Tomato Juice Cocktail 50

HORS D'OEUVRES

Imported Malossol Caviar 2 25, aux Blinis 2 50
Tomato Surprise, Maison 90   Celery 40
Supreme of Melon, Maraschino 90
Canape of Anchovies 65
Imported Bismack Herring 65
Maakereel in White Wine 1 00   Anchovy Salad 90

SNAILS BOURGUIGNONNE 1 00
Ripe Olives 40   Green Olives 40
Canape of Caviar 1 50
Smoked Nova Scotia Salmon 75
Grape Fruit Supremo 75
French Sardines 75

Pate de Foie Gras 2 60
Stuffed Celery 60
Hors d'Oeuvres, Parisienne 1 25
Supreme of Fruit Cocktail 75
Westphalian Ham 1 00
Melon in Season

POTAGES

Cream of New Peas 45
Purée of Tomato 45
Madrilène en Gelée 45
Petite Marmite Bouchère 55

Minestrone Italienne 45
Consommé Vermicelli 40
Onion Soup au Gratin 50
Green Turtle au Sherry 65

POISSONS (Per Person)

Filet of English Sole, Bonne Femme 1 40
Broiled Pompano, Potato Chips 1 25
Baked Sea Trout, Russe 1 10
Fried Frogs' Legs, Tartar 1 25
Crab Flakes à l'Orientale 1 10
Soft Shell Crabs Sauté Provençale 1 25

ENTREES (Ready Per Person)

Roast Prime Ribs of Beef, Jardinière 1 70
(Half) Chicken Grain, Marengo 2 00
Steak de Veau Sauté, Egg Plant Orientale 1 30
Breast of Guinea Hen, Smitaine 1 90
Broiled Sweetbread, Virginia 1 60
Noisette of Lamb, Capucine 1 60
Mixed Grill, Gaufrette Potato 1 60

COLD DISHES

Sirloin of Beef Niçoise 1 65
Galantine of Capon, Parisienne 1 70
Viande Froide Assortis, Salade de Pommes de Terre 1 70
Carré d'Agneau, Broccoli Salad 1 65

LEGUMES

Purée of Celery 50

Succotash 60
Broccoli 75   Cauliflower 65
French Peas 50; Bonne Femme 65
Artichokes 65
New Corn Sauté 60
Egg Plant, Orientale 60

Stewed Corn 50
Lima Beans 50
String Beans 50
Spinach 50
Brussels Sprouts 45
Zucchini 50

New Beets au Beurre 45
Braised Celery 60
Carrots Vichy 50
Creamed Spinach 60
Oyster Bay Asparagus 90
Hearts of Palms, Mousseline 90

POMMES

Parisienne Persillées 40   Au Gratin 40   Anna 50   Lyonnaise 40   Sauté 40
Julienne 40   Hashed Brown 40; in Cream 50   Allumette 40
Candied Sweet, Louisanna 50

ENTREMETS GLACES

Berries in Season 50
Vanilla Ice Cream 50
Peach Melba 75
French Pastry 35   Fruit Tart 50
Coupe St. Jacques 75   Coupe aux Marrons 75
French Pancake 1 00
Cerises Jubilee 1 25   Crepes Suzette, Paradise 1 50

Caramel Custard 50
Chocolate Ice Cream 50
Pear, Belle Hélène 65
Petits Fours 40
Compote of Fruits 75
Apple Pancake 1 00
Baked Alaska (for 2) 2 00

CAFE-THES

Cafe Kirsch 1 25

Coffee with Cream 40   Demi-Tasse 25   Special Percolated Coffee 50
Orange Pekoe Tea 40   Kaffee Hag Demi-Tasse 30
Cafe Diablo, Special 1 50

SALADS

Escarole	45
Martin	50
Mexicaine	60
Nicoise	60
Fresh Vegetable	1 00
Chiffonnade	50
Lettuce	40
Romaine	45
Mixed Green	50
Tomato and Lettuce	50
Alligator Pear	75

Roquefort or
Russian Dressing, extra 25

FROMAGES

Cream Cheese	40
With Bar le Duc	65
Petit Gervais	35
With Bar le Duc	60
Camembert	45
English Stilton	60
Bel Paese	45
Imported Swiss	45
Gorgonzola	45
Cheddar	60
Port du Salut	45
Roquefort	50

Thursday, September 21, 1933

Prix Fixe Luncheon

Appetizers

Bouquet of Organic Greens with balsamic vinaigrette
Prosciutto with melon noodles and citrus-yogurt dressing
'21' Caesar Salad

Main Courses

Crisp Calamari Salad with lobster-port vinaigrette
Oak-Grilled Salmon Paillard with potato purée and oven-dried tomatoes
Hickory-Fired Sirloin Burger with pickled vegetables and potatoes

Desserts

Passion Fruit Sabayon Tart
Grand Marnier Chocolate Bomb
Classic Crème Brûlée

25.00
Beverage, Gratuity and Sales Tax not included

Menus: dinner, September 21, 1933 (*left*); prix fixe (*above*) and a la carte luncheon (*right*), October 1, 1998.

Luncheon

Appetizers

Grilled Japanese Yellowtail with eggplant, roasted tomato and aged balsamic 19.00
Maine Crab Cake with cucumber salad and curry-carrot sauce 18.00
House Smoked Salmon with red onions, capers and crème fraîche 17.00
Shrimp Cocktail with fresh horseradish sauce 17.00
Roasted Sweetbreads with mirepoix sauce 21.00
Fois Gras with red papaya, mango and vanilla bean 23.00
Bouquet of Baby Greens with cremini vinaigrette 12.00
Daily Market Selection of Atlantic & Pacific Oysters 15.00
Farmed Littleneck or Cherrystone Clams 15.00
Jellied Fisher Island Oysters with lobster and caviar 15.00

Beluga Caviar Service
75.00 per ounce

Main Courses

Wood-Fired Wild Bass with caramelized endive, broccoli rabe and a tomato-fennel sauce 38.00
Seared Peppered Tuna with a shrimp and avocado roll, soy-citrus sauce 39.00
Sautéed Shrimp, Scallops, and Clams with linguini, white wine-tomato sauce 37.00
Roast Monkfish with smoked bacon, fricassee of mushrooms and citrus zest 36.00
Steamed Red Snapper with basmati rice and organic vegetables, herb broth 38.00

Butternut Squash and Wild Mushroom Risotto 36.00
Roast Chicken with potato purée, shitake mushrooms, corn and natural jus 35.00
Sautéed Calf's Liver with purple potatoes, green beans, tomatoes and celery 34.00
Sirloin Steak with Anaheim peppers, Cognac and pan-fried potatoes 39.00
Grilled Filet Mignon with chive-mashed potatoes and crisp leeks 39.00
Spicy Marinated Lamb Chops with grilled vegetables and yogurt-mint rice salad 39.00

'21' Classics

Cold "Senegalese" Soup 11.00
Endive and Baby Arugula Salad 12.00
Crabmeat Cocktail 21.00
Mussels Marinara with Toasted Garlic 34.00
Fried Oysters with tartare sauce 37.00
Maine Lobster Salad with roasted potatoes, cucumbers and black olives 39.00
Chopped Cobb Salad with chicken, avocado and bacon 27.00
'21' Sunset Salad, Jack and Charlie's chopped barroom salad 27.00
Grilled or Sautéed Dover Sole with new potatoes and artichoke 59.00
Old Fashioned Chicken Hash 29.00
The '21' Burger with a choice of potatoes and green beans 24.00
"Speakeasy" Steak Tartare discreetly prepared tableside to your taste 33.00

Side Orders

Potato Soufflées • Creamed Spinach • Potato Purée • Sautéed Potatoes and Herbs
Creamed Corn • French Fries • Pan Roasted Brussel Sprouts
9.00

EXECUTIVE CHEF – ERIK BLAUBERG

There will be an additional 50% charge for appetizers, salads or
soup served as main courses or for main courses shared

SERVICE IS NOT INCLUDED

This photo of a quiet moment in the '21' kitchen was taken in mid-morning as cooks prepared for the lunch-time crowd. Since the club opened for business in 1930 the kitchen has been frequently updated and its space expanded.

Two legendary '21' chefs: Henri Geib (*sketch*) and Yves Louis Ploneis.

he was pretty hard up for money. Feeling sorry for him, I bought a few of his works for about two hundred dollars each.

Other works to adorn '21' walls included oils by Stephen Etnier and Georges Haquette, a honky-tonk piano player by Paul Sample, and various watercolors and cartoons by Russell Patterson, Bradshaw Crandall, Arthur William Brown, Dean Cornwell, and Charles Dana Gibson. Because our collection was so accessible to the public, art critic Maria Nayor wrote in *The Connoisseur* magazine, "The club is a setting far more suitable than the antiseptic galleries of a museum."

The strangest artist I got to know at '21' was surrealist painter Salvador Dali. Wild-eyed and sporting a bizarre mustache in the shape of the handlebars of a bicycle, he occasionally arrived with a pet ocelot on a leash. More often he came in with a pair of the most outlandishly dressed women I'd ever seen, then spent most of his time worrying about his wife showing up. On other occasions he was in the company of his male secretary, who astonished me one day by coming in alone and presenting me with the first of a couple of large Dali pastels and charcoal drawings that still claim places on walls in my apartment.

Dali claimed to have picked up so many commissions while dining at '21' that he exclaimed, "Is gold . . . is gold. I go at seven o'clock, and I come away with gold in my pocket."

Because '21' attracted many of the country's top writers, I frequently found my sleeve being tugged when I passed table 11 as John Steinbeck said in a gruff tone, "Pete, sit and talk to me." He'd be there alone for long periods with his head in his hands. I wasn't surprised when years later he published *Travels with Charley*, a book about a cross-country odyssey accompanied only by his dog of that name. John always seemed to be a very lonely guy.

"21"

With the exception of Bob Benchley, the author who most seemed to live in '21' was John O'Hara. Like Bob, he had followed Jack and Charlie in the move from the Puncheon. A native of Pennsylvania, he'd earned quite a respectable reputation writing short stories for the *New Yorker* and *Scribner's*, selling eleven of them to the *New Yorker* in one year (1932). One of them, "Early Afternoon," was so good that Dorothy Parker said to him that she'd bet if Hemingway read it "he'd want to cut his throat." This success meant that O'Hara was making a decent living. His problem was that he and his wife were living considerably beyond that income, partly because of O'Hara's desire to always go first class. Some of his friends said it was his envy of the wealthy that drove him to prove himself worthy of rubbing elbows with them. Whatever his motivation, he never shied away from the expense of drinking and dining at the Puncheon and then at 21 West Fifty-second Street.

What really launched O'Hara like a rocket was the critical acclaim for his first novel, *Appointment in Samara*, published in August 1934. Dorothy Parker hailed "this swift savage story, set down as sharp and deep as if the author had used steel for paper." The reviewer for the *Times* declared, "For contemporary truth I have seen little writing as searching as Mr. O'Hara's." Clifton Fadiman of the *New Yorker* said it was "the most sheerly readable novel within miles." Even Walter Winchell found it "grand" and worthy of "orchids." O'Hara was suddenly so renowned that an article in *Fortune* magazine on the subject of "status" in Manhattan expressed the opinion that the owners of '21' would rather have John O'Hara as a customer than any number of rich Texans or other persons with nothing but money to recommend them.

The trouble with O'Hara was that he was bad at handling

his liquor. Any remark to him taken the wrong way was greeted with either an insulting mouth or physical belligerency. An intended target of one O'Hara attempted punch was distinguished neurologist Dr. Howard Fabing. Only Jack's speedy intervention kept O'Hara from creating a violent scene.

A Yale man and regular '21' patron who found himself having to deal with an O'Hara outburst was tall, burly radio actor Paul Douglas, who would go on to stage stardom in *Born Yesterday* and convert that triumph into a Hollywood career in the film version and other 1950s movies, including *A Letter to Three Wives*, *Angels in the Outfield*, *The Solid Gold Cadillac*, and *The Mating Game*. Because NBC's Radio City studios were located in the RCA Building in the heart of Rockefeller Center, Paul was always popping in and out of the club before or after his broadcasts. On one of these visits he evidently said something that left O'Hara so miffed that he dashed after Paul, caught up with him just beyond the iron gate, and challenged him to a fistfight.

"Take it easy, John," Paul said, strolling away.

O'Hara raced after him, caught up a few doors along Fifty-second Street, and threw a punch at Paul's head. It missed. But Paul had had enough. He grabbed O'Hara's necktie, yanked it as tight as a hangman's noose, shoved O'Hara aside, and continued walking. O'Hara was damn lucky. One of Paul's punches could have landed him not only on his backside in the middle of Swing Street, but probably in Roosevelt Hospital.

On another occasion Jack listened to the complaint of a retired diplomat about tripping over O'Hara's feet as O'Hara lay sprawled in a chair in the lounge, drunk and mumbling.

A portrait of John O'Hara being drunk and belligerent in

the lounge off the '21' lobby was recorded by a legendary *New Yorker* writer. In his memoir *Here at the New Yorker*, Brendan Gill described a scene that unfolded at a time when he and O'Hara were estranged and O'Hara had boasted that the next time he ran into Gill he would knock his block off.

Not long after, Gill and his wife had been dining at '21' with friends. As they walked into the front hall to pick up their coats, Gill saw O'Hara standing there with a couple of friends. He had been drinking, but then O'Hara was always drinking in those days. Gill had been drinking, too, so he decided it was a fine time to challenge O'Hara to put up or shut up.

Gill went into the lounge and said, "Well, John, here I am. What are you going to do about it?"

O'Hara stared "dully, his lips working," wrote Gill about the incident. "At last there began to emerge from his lips a stream of vituperation. The words were conventionally scatological and were spoken with surprisingly little feeling, and when they began to peter out I said in a jeering tone, 'Is this the best you can do?'"

Gill waited for O'Hara to swing. But O'Hara went on muttering, as Gill put it, "in the way of the classic sullen barroom bully."

As Gill shrugged and started to leave, I said to him, "That was a close call."

"Not close enough," he replied.

James Thurber said of John O'Hara, "I guess a man cannot have an eye and ear as sensitive as O'Hara's without also having feelings that are hypersensitive. He brings into a room, or a life, a unique presence that is John O'Hara. If he sometime seems to exhibit the stormy emotions of a little boy, so do all great artists, for unless they can remember what it was like to be a little boy, they are only half complete as artist and as man. Who wants to go through life with only easy friends? Nothing could be duller."

I have no arguments with anything said about John O'Hara as a gifted, and subsequently mistakenly overlooked American author. But as a man I remember him as a pain in the ass.

It's a tribute to my brothers Jack, Mac, and Bob that they were able to be more tolerant and forgiving of O'Hara than I was. Certainly it became evident to me after Jack's death that O'Hara had a genuine fondness for Jack and for '21'. For the 1950 edition of *The Iron Gate* O'Hara wrote, "The overwhelmingly best thing about '21' is that it is the only investment where I put in a million dollars and get two million back."

O'Hara entitled his essay "'21' Is My Club."

How to handle drunks has always been a problem for anyone who runs a bar. But it's an especially delicate matter when the place has a reputation for being classy, and even more so when the inebriated individual is a valued regular customer. The policy in '21' was to deal strictly with someone "in his cups" by quietly ushering him out, taking away his keys if he had his own automobile, also taking his wallet, and then putting him into a taxi. The next day we would call him to tell him we had his keys and money. When he came in (almost always red-faced and terribly embarrassed) nothing more was said on the subject.

In some instances we resorted to other methods, including cutting the amount of liquor in a glass by half or refusing to serve a problem drinker beyond what the bartender believed was the limit. One such customer drank nothing but martinis and got drunk on the first one, so after he'd downed it, refills were water and lime juice with an olive.

No one was more astute at assessing a drinker's capacity to hold his liquor, and when to cut him off, than the guys who stood behind the '21' bar. But they were also talented in concocting new libations. Arguably the most famous drink credited as having been invented at the club is the Bloody Mary. Almost as famous is the combination of brandy and Benedictine known as a "B&B." Others with '21' birth certificates are the Ramos Gin Fizz and the Southside.

A policy at the '21' bar was that there are no stools. If you drank at "the long mahogany," you stood. Spaced along the brass foot rail were brass spittoons—unused, of course—as quaint reminders that '21' was and always would be a saloon.

When I came on board to start learning the saloon business, what set '21' apart from all other 1930s "watering holes" was not just a clientele celebrated in the worlds of literature, theater, journalism, and commerce, but also the staff Jack and Charlie had put together. My favorite description of our place comes from an essay contributed to the 1936 *Iron Gate* by writer John W. Rumsey. He wrote:

> As we enter we meet Jimmy. If you get past Jimmy you are 'in,' but if you don't then it is too bad. Walter and little Raymond help Jimmy boss the other boys in the front room, and after we get rid of our hats and coats we meet Headwaiter Phillip and his assistants Louie, Andrew and Mino, who have charge of the upstairs room. When we get inside the bar, or downstairs room, we find everybody on intimate terms with Gus the Steward who has done all the buying for the institution for many years. We are served by

Vincent, Raymond, Georgetti, and the others who know all the guests, and whether they prefer a white carnation or a red one. The bartenders, Harry, Bill, Mike, Nick, and Jack anticipate the orders of everyone as they come in. They start mixing your cocktail before you get through the door and they know if you want it sour or sweet, strong or weak. Incidentally, they also know just how many you should have.

The reference to carnations referred to a custom Jack established of presenting regulars with boutonnieres upon their arrival. This practice was duly noted in a poem by Ben Hecht, a stanza of which went:

Hark to the lads in their tete a tetes
Gossip and twitter and moldy pun,
Billboard amours and Broadway hates
Price tags for souls, and words by the ton.
Weep not, O Muses, be still. Art rates
A red carnation at 21.

While "art" rated respect at '21', being an artist did not provide exemption from club rules concerning attire. Men were required to wear coats and neckties. Should a patron appear at the door without one or the other (and sometimes both), a jacket and/or tie would be provided. One of the earliest customers to test the policy was Groucho Marx. Realizing there appeared to be no club rule on shirts, he showed up one day with a jacket over a T-shirt and a tie looped around his neck. He was admitted. A few decades later Sammy Davis Jr. came to the door wearing a turtleneck shirt under his coat.

He was given a club cravat and promptly tied it around his head.

A woman who'd heard that Katharine Hepburn had been let in wearing slacks decided to do the same. Informed she would not be admitted wearing trousers, she went to the ladies' room, removed them, and came out wearing only her blouse and panties. Her daring earned her a one-time exemption from the no-slacks rule.

Once inside the club, patrons were able to enjoy a number of amenities. Two of these involved telephones. First, there was a phone booth in the lobby connected to a switchboard operator who would not only place calls for customers, but would also serve as a message taker for regulars away on business trips or vacations. Rather than dial the phone company information operator for the number of a hotel, airline, theater, or a friend, regulars simply dialed the '21' switchboard. The second amenity was in being able to have a telephone brought to your table to either receive a call or to make one.

When Jack was trying to sweep actress Arline Judge Ruggles off her feet (or at least into his apartment and into bed) he took advantage of the '21' phone booth to further his campaign by way of a call to Hollywood so he could croon love songs to her.

When the editor of Sports Illustrated, Ed Fitzgerald, treated his daughter Eileen to a dinner at '21' to celebrate her high school graduation in the 1980s, she phoned her boyfriend from their table and giggled with delight as she said to him, "You'll never guess where I am!" Alas, in an age when it seems that everyone has a cellular phone in pocket or purse, that kind of thrill is pretty much a thing of the past.

To further cater to certain customers beyond serving them

food and filling their glasses, Jack had installed on the third floor a barbershop and a small gym, complete with steam cabinets, weights, and other equipment. When exercising was done, there was a masseur available.

Speaking of these amenities, the English character actor Sir Cedric Hardwicke once quipped, "A man can spend his entire life inside these walls enjoyably—except to leave now and then to eat." Sir Cedric did not have to leave if he wanted a fine cigar. A wide selection was for sale at a counter in the lobby, with an emphasis on Cuban cigars (even after the ban on their importation imposed by President Kennedy in the 1960s).

"They will fix you up with railroad tickets, tips on the races and free lights for your cigarettes," remarked journalist Thornton Delahanty. "You can get almost anything in the way of service at '21' except a drink on the house."

One thing you could not get was a table through bribery. The scene in many movies in which someone's palm was greased for a choice seat did not happen if the employee being offered a bribe wanted to keep his job. Of course, tipping for services rendered was okay. While some recipients of generous gratuities were able to pocket impressive amounts of cash to permit them to invest in such things as apartment houses and personal vacation homes, no one had to rely on tips for a decent living. Everyone on staff was paid enough to be unimpressed by someone waving cash around, or by anyone claiming to be rich in an effort to buy his way in.

Jimmie Coslove was proud of his ability to spot which person to allow in. "The day I'm unable to recognize a Brooks Brothers shirt," he said, "is the day I quit." Consequently, when a rather scruffy-looking person once attempted to enter and kept demanding to be admitted, the commotion at the door caught Jack's attention. Sent to the lobby to investigate, I asked Jimmie Coslove what was going on. He reported, "A guy at the door doesn't look right to me. He says his name is Lamont."

"I'll have a look at him," I said.

When I reached the door I immediately realized that the name of the man wasn't Lamont. It was *Du Pont*.

One evening in the late 1930s, Arline Judge Ruggles, looked around the dining room and jotted down on the table-cloth the names of other movie personalities having drinks or dinner. Later, she arranged the roster vertically with their first initials spelling out "Jack and Charlies Twenty One Club" as follows:

Joan Bennett	**T**allulah Bankhead
Arline Judge Ruggles	**W**esley Ruggles
Cary Grant	**E**dward G. Robinson
Katharine Hepburn	**N**orma Shearer
	Toby Wing
Ann Harding	**Y**vonne Dionne
Nancy Carroll	
Dolores Del Rio	**O**na Munson
	Nils Aster
	Edmund Gwenn
Charles Laughton	**C**lark Gable
Herbert Marshall	**L**upe Velez
Adrianne Ames	**U**na Merkel
Ramon Navarro	**B**etty Furness
Leslie Howard	
Irene Dunne	
Edmund Lowe	
Stewart Erwin	

At the age of thirty, as a novice in the food and drink business looking around the upstairs dining rooms and seeing so many celebrities, or rubbing elbows with Robert Benchley and many of the most famous people in the country as they crowded at the '21' bar, I could only think back to the gamble my brother Jack had taken in 1922 when he bought into a failed Greenwich Village tearoom, marvel at what he and Charlie Berns had accomplished, and wonder what the future held for all of us.

Six

JOCKEYS

The end of the 1930s was signaled in New York City by an extravaganza with the theme "Building the World of Tomorrow." When the New York World's Fair opened on April 20, 1939, Mayor Fiorello H. La Guardia said, "May I point to one exhibit that I hope all visitors will note, and that is the city of New York itself."

La Guardia had been mayor for almost six years, having taken over after winning a special election following the forced resignation of Jimmy Walker. A former congressman who'd opposed Prohibition, "the Little Flower" had come into office as a reformer vowing to rid the city of "tinhorns and chiselers" in government and to drive the gangsters out of town. Because doing so would require time, he counseled "patience and fortitude." By the opening of the World's Fair he'd made pretty good headway.

While the city La Guardia inherited from Jimmy Walker faced a lot of problems, it did so with a dramatic new skyline. During the 1930s Manhattan's profile was transformed by the two tallest structures in the world, the 102-story Empire State Building and the 77-floors-plus pyramid-shaped spiked tower of the Chrysler Building. In the heart of Rockefeller Center rose the elegant 70-story RCA Building. Also contributing to the city's splendors in October 1931 was the new Waldorf-Astoria Hotel on Park Avenue.

Visitors to the World's Fair who accepted La Guardia's invitation to also spend some time exploring the city itself had a vast array of places to eat. They ranged from street-corner hot dog stands, Horn and Hardart's automats (where how much you ate was a matter of how many nickels you slipped into the coin slots of help-yourself dispensers), several Schrafft's restaurants, and hotel dining rooms to what one guide glamorously termed "night clubs and supper places."

The choices available in 1940 to New Yorkers, out-of-towners doing business, and foreigners seemed limitless. There were the honky-tonks, jazz, and swing joints on Fifty-second Street, where they could eat, drink, and be merry (no one ever said "for tomorrow you may die," even though many young men came to town fearing that grim prospect of war might soon be a reality). Or they could party upscale in classy spots in hotels, rubbing elbows with celebrities at the Starlight Roof of the Waldorf, listening to the warbling of Hildegard at the Plaza, dancing to Guy Lombardo's "sweetest music this side of Heaven" at the Roosevelt, or jitterbugging with big bands at the Pennsylvania and New Yorker. They could drop a bundle at Sherman Billingsley's Stork Club, El Morocco, Au Cheval Pie, or La Vie Parisienne. And a guy or gal could soak up saloon atmosphere at Toots Shor's and at Bill Hardey's Gay Nineties.

But as one writer observed, "There is no place quite like the 'Club 21' and almost every notable visitor to New York has passed at least once through the iron gates. The patronage is select and many are those who visit the place merely to get a look at the celebrities ever present, either in the ground-floor room in front of the bar or upstairs. But the real reputation of the place has been made upon its cooking which is superlative."

Jack and Charlie's had come a long way from the ham and cheese sandwiches of the Red Head and the fare offered at the Fronton and the Forty-ninth Street spot. Among the dishes recommended in the 1940 guide were royal squab '21', made with wild rice, foie gras, and truffles and served with a Madeira sauce ($2.25); breast of guinea hen Smetana for four dollars; and for a buck and a half, English sole poached in white wine and served with creamed asparagus.

"There is no table d'hôte dinner," the writer continued, "and the dishes are not exorbitantly priced for what they are. There is a splendid wine list from which I would select a red Burgundy, *Nuits St. Georges* ($3.50) with the squab and Alsatian white wine, *Clos St. Odile 1937* ($3.50) with the filet of sole."

The phone number for reservations was ELdorado 5-6500, and the hours were 11:30 A.M. until 2:30 A.M., seven days a week.

The face that '21' presented to the "World's Fair City" had also changed. The expansion into the adjacent buildings had been accompanied by a blending of their facades with a second-floor front porch and outside stairway with New Orleans–style grille-work. Also added was a collection of cast-iron hitching posts in the form of jockeys in the colorful silks of some of the country's leading stables. It's a matter of dispute as to which titan of the horse-racing world contributed the first jockey. My memory is that it was a gift from Yale man John Hay "Jock" Whitney. But the distinction was also claimed on behalf of Alfred Gwynne Vanderbilt. A photo of the iron gate taken soon after the opening of the club proves that at the time the picture was snapped both stables were represented.

So many jockey figures were presented to the club that they became a symbol of '21' on menus and matchboxes and all sorts of advertising and souvenir items sold at the cigar counter. They eventually formed a line extending up the outside stairway and across the entire breadth of the porch. To avoid an appearance of favoritism, the placement of figures was periodically changed. Those on display also had to be limited in number to keep their combined weight from collapsing the porch.

But it wasn't only the proud owners of thoroughbreds who came up with ways of stamping their personal and/or commercial brand on '21'. Not long after the repeal of Prohibition, and at a time when travel by airplane was starting to catch on and airlines competed for recognition, an executive of Imperial Airways (later British Airways) walked into the barroom carrying a scale model of the "flying boat" used on its New York-to-England route. He asked Jack to hang the model from one of the ceiling beams. When Pan American Airways president Juan Trippe spotted the symbol of his chief competitor, up went a model of a Pan Am Clipper. This was followed by an American Airlines DC-3, contributed by American's boss, C. R. Smith. Next came Howard Hughes (never a man to be outdone) toting a model of one of the planes of his TWA.

Thereafter, the barroom ceiling turned into a display space not only for the captains of corporate America, but for the universes of sports, show business, politics, and virtually every other human endeavor. Among hundreds of items finding their way onto the ceiling were tennis rackets, football helmets, baseball caps, a Wagnerian headgear worn by opera star Lauritz Melchior, a souvenir bullet from Theodore Roosevelt's Rough Riders of the Spanish-American War, an elephant tusk, race cars, trucks, boats, and even a hangman's noose. Through the years, as in the case of the jockeys, so many items were contributed to adorn the ceiling that they had to be rotated. One writer, looking at all the airplanes, motorized vehicles, blimps, and other types of transportation in miniature, saw "a mechanized Mammoth Cave."

Authors Michael and Ariane Batterberry, in their book *On the Town in New York*, wrote that the bar looked like the storeroom of some sophisticated squirrel. "One had the feeling when speaking to a Kriendler or Berns not so much of life but of the deliberate magnification of it," they wrote. "Like Kosher salt and Christmas whiskey, it came to them in larger chunks and brighter packages than the regular kind. It was their talent to transmit the grandiose excitement to hand-chosen patrons that automatically led the twentieth-century New Yorker to associate expensive [dining] with the number '21'. [And it was] the great World's Fair of 1939, more than anything before, that attracted the eyes not only of the nation, but the world, to New York."

Unfortunately, that summer the city, nation, and world found themselves on the brink of world war.

A few months later, as the crisis in Europe centered on Nazi Germany's demands upon Poland to give up a territory known as the Danzig Corridor, I noticed a tall, military-looking gentleman in a dinner jacket sitting alone at a corner table. In the following three hours he had caviar and a pint of champagne, followed by a cup of green turtle soup; then roasted partridge, a salad of endives and chopped beets, and crêpes suzettes. The wine was Steinberger Kabinetwein Beerenauslese 1934. The brandy was Hine Triomphe. Cigars (two) were Belinda Fancy Tails. The check came to $57. Tips to the headwaiter, captain, two waiters, and the busboy brought the tally to $90.

After he'd departed, I asked Jack who he was.

"His name is Baron Frederick Von Oppenheim," Jack replied in an uncharacteristically melancholy tone. "This was a special occasion for him. Tomorrow he starts back to Germany. He told me it would probably be the last time for a long while that he'll have a meal like this—in peace—like a gentleman."

When Britain and France declared war after Hitler's attack on Poland in September 1939, I had no doubt that sooner or later the United States would have to join in the war. Being Jewish, I and all the other Kriendlers and Bernses were all for it. But not all Americans shared our views. Groups formed to oppose United States involvement in any way. Under the banner "America First," they called for American "isolation" from the affairs of Europe.

One of the leaders of the isolationists was New York Republican congressman Hamilton Fish Sr. When Jack saw Fish dining at '21' he personally handed him the check for the meal and said, "I don't like either you or your politics. I'd appreciate your not coming in here again."

Still welcome and likely to be encountered at the bar or in the dining rooms in the nervous months of 1940 were the leading lights of Broadway, radio, and films. Arguably the most fascinating movie star at that time was a Swedish-born actress who had shocked the entire world by quitting the screen at the pinnacle of her career. Leaving Hollywood behind, Greta

Garbo had settled into a reclusive life in New York, but her expressed desire to be left alone didn't extend to having meals alone at home. When she came to '21' she preferred an out-of-the-way table in a corner of the upstairs dining room.

It was there one night as she had a salad in the company of diet and physical fitness expert Gaylord Hauser (said to be her lover of the moment) that Garbo was spotted by Louis Sobol. Prodded by the idea that he could score a journalistic coup by getting an interview with "the Aloof One" (as Louis described her), he approached her table. Perhaps if Miss Garbo had been alone Louis might have succeeded. But Mr. Hauser was manning the barricades and stopped Louis cold with a look Louis described as "one of the dietician's spinach-juice stares."

Undaunted, Louis begged my brother Bob to intervene. When he did so, Hauser said, "What? Can't you see Miss Garbo is in a highly nervous state? Talking to a newspaperman would spoil Miss Garbo's evening completely. No, no, no."

Louis did not get the interview, but he left '21' that evening with a story for his column that was almost as good, even if it did reinforce the Garbo "I want to be alone" legend, which is probably what Garbo had hoped for.

The literary world at '21' in the 1940s was still represented in the persons of Steinbeck, Hemingway, Sinclair Lewis, Somerset Maugham, Robert Sherwood, John O'Hara, and the ubiquitous Mr. Benchley. After Benchley left the club early one morning in his customary state of giddy intoxication, he barged back inside after a minute or so, waving his arms and exclaiming, "Elephants in the street!" Bemused pals assumed Bob was pulling a prank. But when he insisted his claim was not a joke or the result of imbibing, we followed him outside and gaped with amazement at a line of Barnum & Bailey's circus pachyderms plodding along Fifty-second toward Eighth Avenue and Madison Square Garden.

No number of elephants in front could have been as startling to regulars and employees of '21' as the announcement by "Two-Trigger" Jack in 1940 that he was getting married. His bride-to-be, who at the moment was married to a Belgian count, was the beautiful Baroness Luisa Dumont de Chassart. Soon after she obtained a divorce in Florida, Luisa became Mrs. John Carl Kriendler in a ceremony in Miami. The happy couple set up housekeeping in Jack's apartment above '21'. Now, in addition to the nicknames "Two-Trigger" and "the Baron," Jack was addressed as "Count."

At the time of Jack's wedding—when much of Europe was under the jackboot heels of Hitler's armies, Great Britain was standing alone, and much of Asia was either conquered or under attack by the Japanese—Bob Kriendler was wearing the uniform of the Marine Corps, and Mac Kriendler had his heart set on pursuing an interest in flying by going into the Air Force. Of course, while all of us prayed that somehow the United States could stay out of the war, we were prepared for what seemed to be inevitable American involvement.

Just how seriously the U.S. government took that possibility was driven home to us by the arrival at '21' of a pair of FBI agents. They showed up in 1941 with a request that we cooperate in their surveillance of one of our customers. A German diplomat, he always insisted on being seated with his girlfriend at the same table in the upstairs dining room. What the G-men wanted was our cooperation in their plan to conceal a microphone in the wall behind the table. The mike would be wired to a transmitter in the basement which would relay the German's conversations to an FBI listening post in an apartment across Fifty-second Street. Whether the agents heard anything more than the German's whispering of sweet nothings in his mistress's ear, I never found out. He was booted out of the country when Germany declared war on the U.S. following the Japanese sneak attack on Pearl Harbor.

Another customer in the prewar years was none other than the head of the FBI. Although J. Edgar Hoover was best known for palling around with Walter Winchell at the nearby Stork Club, he always found time during weekend excursions to have a cozy Sunday lunch with his deputy, Clyde Tolson, safe from the prying eyes of a gossipy press. Some folks in '21', including me, speculated even then that more was going on between J. Edgar and Clyde than catching criminals and keeping tabs on the diplomats of potential enemies.

A problem for my three brothers and me arose during the professional football season. We were all fans of the New York Giants, as were quite a number of longtime patrons. When the Giants were playing at home we treated those regulars to tickets that we'd gotten gratis from the team's owner. We hired a bus to take them to the Polo Grounds. The catch was that one of us had to be on duty in the club. Who stayed was determined by drawing lots.

One time during the 1941 season, when the Giants took on the other local eleven, the Brooklyn Dodgers football team, I got the short straw. This meant that if I were to follow the game I'd have to stop supervising the dining room and duck into the kitchen to listen to the radio.

As it happened, Hoover and Tolson were having a late lunch upstairs. Satisfied they'd been well served, and with the game under way, I went down to the kitchen for the play-by-play on station WOR. As I came in, the Dodgers held a 7–0 lead after a touchdown by Ace Parker. Describing the Dodgers' kickoff, the announcer was saying, "Merle Condon comes up. He boots it. It's a long one, down to around the three-yard line. Ward Cuff takes it, coming to his left, he's over the ten—nice block there by Leeman—Cuff still going. He's up to the twenty-five, and now he's hit, and hit hard, about the twenty-seven-yard line. Bruiser Kinnard made the tack—"

Then, another voice: "We interrupt this broadcast to bring you this important bulletin from the United Press. Flash. Washington. The White House announces Japanese attack on Pearl Harbor. Stay tuned to WOR for further developments."

In the next instant cooks, waiters, busboys, and others, including a cluster of drinkers at the bar, witnessed something unseen in '21' since the last alarm of a Prohibition raid (and never repeated)—a Kriendler racing through the barroom and up the steps to the second floor.

Catching my breath, I reported the radio bulletin to the director of the FBI and asked, "Is there anything we here at '21' can do for you, Mr. Hoover? A telephone? May I get you a taxi?"

With a shake of his head and dabbing a napkin to his lips, he managed a slight smile and replied, "Thank you, I have my car waiting in front. But I'm afraid you will have to tell our waiter to cancel our order for coffee and dessert."

With Mac and Bob gone off to war (Mac to England with the Eighth Air Force and Bob to the Pacific with the Marines), Jack and I, along with Charlie and Jerry Berns and the rest of our extended '21' family, did our best to contribute to "the war effort on the home front," to use the phrase of the day.

Soon after we got into the war, Jack came up with the idea for a radio show to boost civilian morale and offer a bit of hospitality to soldiers, sailors, and airmen passing through New York on their way to overseas posts. Jack offered the '21' second-floor dining room as the studio. Produced in association with the Music Corporation of America and sponsored by Mennen, makers of men's aftershave lotion and other products, it was hosted on CBS by Broadway columnist Ed Sullivan. The weekly broadcasts featured an all-star roster of guests. Among them were Jack Benny, Ethel Merman, Greer Garson, Marlene Dietrich, Jeanette MacDonald, Jean Arthur, Myrna Loy, Raymond Massey, George Raft, Fredric March, Jack Haley, and Humphrey Bogart.

The show also brought on a number of GIs. One of the first was Marine Corps sergeant John Basilone. A hero of the battle for Guadalcanal in 1942, he was the war's first enlisted man to be awarded the Congressional Medal of Honor. He'd been brought home for a tour to help sell war bonds.

When Basilone came through the iron gate and into the lobby he looked around with a huge smile and said, "So this is '21'! I heard about it but never dreamed I'd ever see the inside of such a classy place." He'd barely reached the stairway when he found himself looking at the stars on the shoulders of Air Force General Francis Brady. Spotting the pale blue Medal of Honor ribbon on Sergeant Basilone's chest, Brady gave him the salute demanded of any rank when in the presence of a Medal of Honor recipient.

"Nobody ever enjoyed New York as much as Sgt. Basilone," Sullivan recalled. Writing in the 1950 edition of *The Iron Gate*, Ed noted that Basilone had said, "This life is sensational but I belong back with my outfit."

Return to his unit he did, only to be killed in the first wave of Marines fighting ashore at Iwo Jima.

Another Marine recipient of the Medal of Honor who appeared on Ed's broadcast from '21' was Captain Kenneth Walsh. He'd shown the valor required to receive the medal by flying combat missions at Bougainville. Appearing on the show with Walsh that week was Pat O'Brien, who repeated his dramatic "win one for the Gipper" locker-room speech from *Knute Rockne All-American*.

The distinguished actor Raymond Massey performed as Cyrano de Bergerac with similarly big-nosed comedian Jimmy Durante. "You mean to tell me the bum had a bigger schnozz than me?" Jimmy exclaimed. "Everybody wants to get into the act."

Just back from entertaining troops in overseas camps close to the front was Jack Benny. Irving Berlin came on the show to tell about how he'd written "God Bless America" and to sing it in a raspy, nasal style. Ann Sothern let radio listeners in on how she had created the role of Maizie (one of the era's most popular characters on radio and in movies).

Because the program went on the air live in the East, it had to be repeated three hours later for listeners on the West Coast. This delay provided a real test of willpower for Humphrey Bogart. Renowned for his drinking, Bogart promised Sullivan, "I won't take a drink until after the repeat." He kept his word, but as soon as the show was off the air, Bogie wasted no time getting down to the bar. (More about Bogart's zest for liquor and life, as well as his two wives, later.)

What amazed Ed Sullivan about the show was that the person who'd come up with the idea didn't try to run it, or even make an appearance on the air. "I'm a saloon keeper and restaurant man," Jack had said, "not a performer."

Another way we did our bit for the war effort was inviting a group of socialites to set up a table in the lobby to sell dollar raffle tickets to benefit camp shows being put on around the country by the USO. One evening when an army private came in and handed the woman at the desk a hundred-dollar bill, she gave him back ninety-nine. The private told her to keep the C-note. As she chided the twenty-dollar-a-month GI not to be foolish, I came up behind him and said, "Your table is ready, Mr. Rockefeller."

Around the same time, our ambassador to England, Joseph P. Kennedy, whose sons Joe Jr. and Jack were serving in the war, was joined at the bar by Lillian Hellman, William Powell, polo player Winston Guest, and Errol Flynn, a New Zealander who served his adopted country by making patriotic war movies. Guest turned to Flynn and said, "I would like to serve under you, Errol. You always seem to come out of every battle so well, and even if they bump you off you're still around the next day."

It was during the war that '21' introduced "ladies' lunch," at which women were allowed for the first time to lunch in the barroom and in the upstairs dining rooms without a male escort. One day Lieutenant Putnam Humphreys and Paul Douglas stood at the bar as an attractive woman came in alone. "May I join you for one drink for old times' sake?" she asked. Her name was Gerry Higgins. She'd been married to both of them.

Elsa Maxwell did her part to bolster the morale of the '21' patrons who had gone off to war. She sent them copies of current menus and notes filled with gossip so the men wouldn't feel they were missing something.

Gone-to-war customers who had been on leave would go back to duty carrying scotch and leaving orders for 21 Brands caviar and booze to be shipped to camps, overseas addresses, and even ships at sea. Bob was delighted to share a steady supply of '21' goodies with Marine buddies as they island-hopped across the Pacific.

In 1942 Captain Robert Kriendler was serving with the Third Marine Division as adjutant, Twenty-first Regiment. The delicious irony of the number was not lost on Bob. But that was only the first coincidence involving the number 21 while Bob was in the Pacific. Assigned to his unit was Major Malcom K. Beyer of Delaware. His wife's birthday was October 21. And they participated in landings on Guam and Iwo Jima on the twenty-first of the month.

Since the bad/good old days of Prohibition, a fact of life for my family, the Bernses, and everyone else involved in Jack and Charlie's enterprises was reading about the clubs in newspapers. Items ranged from stories about raids successful or hilariously embarrassing for the raiders, Jack's unfortunate collision with a tree while on his way to a country tryst with another man's wife, to the tidbits in columns by Louis Sobol, Ed Sullivan, and Lucius Beebe. But on October 22, 1943, the club and a pair of our regulars became minor players in a sensational news story that none of us liked being dragged into.

The chain of events began as the result of famed novelist W. Somerset Maugham's dread of being alone. The Englishman who had scored tremendous literary successes with *Of Human Bondage*, *The Moon and Sixpence*, and *Cakes and Ale* never dined at '21' by himself. He was usually accompanied by his secretary, Gerald Haxton, who also had the job of arranging bridge partners for Maugham in Maugham's suite at the Carlyle Hotel. A frequent member of the foursome was Lucius Beebe, who often found himself partnered with another '21' patron, a young Royal Canadian Air Force cadet.

What qualified Wayne Lonergan for admittance to the Maugham-Beebe circle was his marriage to stunningly beautiful twenty-two-year-old Patricia Burton, the daughter of a renowned portrait painter (recently deceased William O. Burton) and granddaughter of Stella Bernheimer Housman, heiress to a brewery fortune and wife of stockbroker Frederick Housman.

After Lucius discovered that Lonergan not only shared his passion for the Broadway theater, but also that the young man was an assistant to a drama critic (and often wrote the man's reviews), Lucius and Lonergan either dined at '21' before going to a show, or came in for after-theater supper. Neither Lucius nor anyone else seemed to notice that Wayne and Patricia rarely went out together.

Some people did notice that Patricia was developing a taste for the nightlife without her husband. Headwaiters regarded her as an attractive, personable, and photogenic asset in what we in the restaurant business call "dressing" a room. From time to time Patricia even contributed a bit of luster to '21'.

No wonder, then, that on Monday, October 25, 1943, we were all shocked to read in the *Times* that Patricia Lonergan had been found bludgeoned to death in the locked bedroom of her three-floor apartment on East Fifty-first Street in the swanky confines of Beekman Hill. A couple of days later came the announcement by the police that they'd charged Wayne Lonergan with her murder.

In reconstructing Patricia's activities on October 22, the night she'd been killed, detectives determined she'd been at '21' without Wayne. On November 15, when Wayne appeared in court for his arraignment, a reporter asked him how he was faring in jail. Wayne replied with a shrug and a backhanded compliment: "Of course the food is not as good as what a fellow could get at '21'."

Covering the case, along with the biggest horde of reporters since the Lindbergh kidnapping, was another '21' patron, Dorothy Kilgallen. A bright star in the journalistic firmament of William Randolph Hearst, she wrote a column, "The Voice of Broadway," and came up with an angle to the story that really set so-called café society on its ear. Following through on a pledge to "unfold the whole unsavory story" of Patricia's father, Kilgallen reported a homosexual relationship between William O. Burton and Wayne. Another gossip columnist, Thyra Samter Winslow of the *New York Mirror*, reported that Patricia had once explained to a friend why she was marrying Wayne by saying, "If he was good enough for my father, he's good enough for me."

Describing Lonergan during the trial, Kilgallen wrote, "He looks as little like a murderer as anyone in the courtroom." Nevertheless, Wayne was convicted of killing Patricia. He spent twenty years at Clinton State Prison in Dannemora, New York. Paroled in 1964, he was deported to his native Canada.

Married to Broadway producer (and '21' regular) Dick Kollmar in 1940, Dorothy Kilgallen had celebrated her engagement with a huge party at '21'. The couple teamed on radio in 1945 with a daily morning show, *Breakfast with Dorothy and Dick*. But press coverage of sensational murder trials notwithstanding, Dorothy would not become immediately identifiable until the 1950s when she became a permanent panelist on the hit TV program *What's My Line?*

When she died in 1964 in what many people saw as mysterious circumstances—just after she had said she was about to expose the truth behind the assassination of President Kennedy—many people believed she had been murdered to silence her. I didn't buy any of it.

Probably the weirdest individual to come into '21' during the war first appeared right after Pearl Harbor. He arrived in an army uniform and with the rank of private first class. A couple of months later he showed up as a sergeant. Not long after that he arrived with a first lieutenant's bars on his collar. Then we did not see him for a few months. He next appeared sporting the full regalia of a major general. A day or two after this amazing apparition, a detective of the New York City police department came in with a photo of the man who had meteorically risen from private to general. I told the detective that the man came in often. "Well, the next time he does," said the cop, "please give me a call. He's an escapee from a mental hospital."

When the guy appeared the following evening with yet another star on his uniform, I informed the detective of his presence and asked him to do '21' the favor of not taking the man into custody in the club. "No problem, Mr. Kriendler," he said. "We'll grab him very quietly on the street when he leaves."

Another customer who really enjoyed coming into the club in a uniform was comedian George Jessel, but the outfit he sported was strictly an honor bestowed on him for his work on behalf of the USO. His talent as a master of ceremonies at gala banquets earned him the title "Toastmaster General." Outliving many of his showbiz buddies (he died in 1981 at the age of eighty-three), he seemed to have a new career as a deliverer of eulogies.

Georgie is best remembered at '21' for a wisecrack that was turned into a joke on him. He had quipped to a columnist, "You can get a pretty good meal at '21' for about twenty-one grand." The next day after he finished lunch at the club he was handed a bill for $21,000. Fortunately, Georgie's luncheon companion was Harpo Marx. True to his image as the nonspeaking and zaniest Marx brother, Harpo grabbed the bill, popped it into his mouth, rolled his eyes, chewed slowly, and swallowed.

Harpo's oldest brother, Groucho, had also turned the issue of stiff prices on the '21' menu into a joke by ordering one bean. When it was brought to him on a plate, he protested that it was undercooked and demanded the waiter take it back to the kitchen.

Millionaire show-business impresario Billy Rose, who'd owned his own pricey nightclub, once shrugged off a fifty-dollar tab for lunch for himself and stripper Gypsy Rose Lee. "What the hell," he said. "It's only half a point on the one hundred shares of AT&T I bought this morning."

Some regular customers couldn't be bothered with bills and arranged to have the tab mailed to them. The truly classy actress Anne Baxter made such a request before she brought her parents to dinner because she wanted to avoid having a tussle with her father, whom she knew would insist on paying.

Critic George Jean Nathan was fond of saying that he once eavesdropped on a meeting of the Kriendler brothers at which we roared with glee as we made up outlandish menu prices. Jack's explanation for the expense of a meal at '21' was blunt: "We don't charge high prices to rob people, but to keep out riffraff, bums, and heels."

When Mac and Bob returned to the club after the war, John Steinbeck quipped, "They served the country well. They did not lead the charge up San Juan Hill but this does not mean there will be no charge."

During the war years I hadn't seen much of my friend Bob Benchley because he was in Hollywood. But Bob's son Nathaniel was all grown up and a regular customer. With the outbreak of the war he'd joined the navy. In January 1943 he was a public relations officer of the Third Naval District. Based in New York City, he often came to '21', and once did so after attending a concert at Carnegie Hall. What transpired next, according to Nat, was "by far the silliest" thing to happen to him in the entire war.

Standing at the bar, he struck up a conversation with another naval officer, Lieutenant Commander Frederick Wolsieffer, executive officer of a destroyer that was in port. The two men drank far into the night and then parted ways.

When Nat dressed for duty the next morning he found Wolsieffer's card in his jacket pocket. Written on the back was the name and location of Wolsieffer's destroyer. At that moment Nat recalled with horror that he'd agreed to join Wolsieffer on some kind of secret mission to some unnamed port.

What was worse, Wolsieffer remembered the promise and expected Nat to keep his word. In short order, Nat was formally detached from his PR job and given "temporary duty under instruction," whatever that meant.

The secret mission turned out to be a convoy to Casablanca. "As we nosed out of New York harbor, one black and freezing midnight," Nat recalled, "I wished to God that I had been an habitue of Leon & Eddie's or Toots Shor's. Only in

'21', I whimpered to myself, could a man get himself into a predicament like this."

After arriving in Casablanca, Nat and his companion learned that they were to be assigned to duty on a French destroyer by the name of *Fantasque*. As Nat recalled, "The captain was still fighting the First War, the officers were fighting the captain, and the cook was fighting a losing battle against beriberi."

To the amazement of Nat and Wolsieffer, the destination of the French ship was New York City. The trip took two weeks, and Wolsieffer and Nat kept up their courage by planning what they would do their first night home. Standing on the bridge, with wet Frenchmen zinging back and forth around them, they would go into detailed anticipation of their first hours ashore.

"We'll go straight to Twenty-One," Wolsieffer said on one of these occasions. "And we'll get a shave, shower, and manicure."

"And a drink," Nat added.

Wolsieffer nodded. "Double bourbon sour, with lime juice." A faraway look came into his eyes. "Then," he said slowly, "then we'll have—let me see. Prosciutto or smoked salmon—which do you think?"

"Both," Nat said.

"All right. Both. Then maybe a steak, or venison, with fried eggplant and a mixed green salad—"

"How about a fish course first?" Nat asked. "Maybe they have some Dungeness crabs now."

"Oh, sure. Crabs first, with mustard sauce."

Every day they planned a '21' menu. And every day it became more elaborate. Finally, they noticed that the

Frenchmen were looking at them queerly, so they became even more rapturous, and at last one of the French officers took Nat aside.

"Qu'est-ce que c'est, ce Twenty-One?" he asked guardedly.

"C'est un restaurant," Nat replied.

The Frenchman nodded silently and walked away.

It was fifteen degrees below zero the night Nat and Wolsieffer landed again in New York. Hurrying off the *Fantasque*, they made a beeline to 21 West Fifty-second Street. Shave, shower, and manicure were forgotten in favor of drinks at the bar. After a few had been downed, Nat turned from the bar to look for familiar faces. At a corner table sat five officers of the *Fantasque*, sipping pony glasses of brandy.

While Nat Benchley was wearing navy blue-and-gold in 1945, his dad was in Hollywood making one of his short subjects. Entitled *I'm a Civilian Here Myself*, and made on behalf of the U.S. Navy, it was an instructional film in which Bob portrayed a discharged sailor encountering fantasy versions of problems that an ex-sailor might confront upon returning home. He also made a version involving a returning soldier.

After completing the project, Bob returned to New York and '21'. Unhappily, I found him changed. The carefree guy from the Puncheon and so many evenings at '21' appeared to me to be tired and embittered. He believed he'd wasted his talents by going Hollywood. The move had also cost him his job as the *New Yorker* drama critic. Harold Ross had replaced him with Woolcott Gibbs.

Soon after arriving in New York, Bob was at lunch at '21' with Ross, James Roosevelt, music critic Deems Taylor, and

Mrs. Donald Ogden Stewart. Suddenly turning to Ross, Bob said, "I'm tired of being a mime, Harold. Can I have my old job back?"

Ross snapped, "Certainly not. Woolcott Gibbs is doing a better job than you ever did, or ever could."

As Bob sat silent and seemed to age before the eyes of the others at the table, Deems Taylor said indignantly, "You know what, Harold? You're a son of a bitch."

James Roosevelt gave a sharp nod of his head and said, "I second the motion."

Ross stormed out.

Not long after this ugly scene, the distinguished actor John Carradine was leaving '21' just as Benchley was coming in. John asked him, "How are you?"

"I'm tired," Bob replied. "I'm tired."

On the weekend of November 17, 1945, he was rushed to Regent Hospital with a nosebleed that wouldn't stop. It was the result of a cerebral hemorrhage. In one of those amazing co-incidences of life, or perhaps a bit of Benchley whimsy, he died on November 21.

A bicoastal memorial service was arranged. Bob's New York circle were to gather at '21' at six o'clock, with playwright and former Round Tabler Marc Connelly in charge. The Hollywood group would assemble simultaneously under the auspices of Dorothy Parker. With the New Yorkers fortified with scotch and gathered around Bob's usual place at the bar precisely at six, Connelly placed a call and announced to Parker, "We're here. Now, Dottie, if you all will raise your glasses. . . ."

Parker replied, "Raise our glasses? Marc, you silly son of a bitch, I told you to have the service at six o'clock *West Coast time*. You're three hours early!"

In cherished memory of Bob a plaque was put up at his customary spot in the barroom:

ROBERT BENCHLEY—HIS CORNER.

It's still there.

Seven

THE SWEET SMELL OF SUCCESS

On July 19, 1947, the *New York Journal* depicted '21' as an "estaminet" famed from coast to coast and ocean to ocean, lording it like a solitary lily over a fretting quagmire of Manhattan between Fifth and Sixth Avenues on Fifty-second Street.

I appreciated what was meant by "a fretting quagmire." In the changed social atmosphere following the war a number of the surviving clubs from the prewar era had shifted their entertainment offerings from jazz groups to women who danced while taking off clothing. Swing Street had become Strip Street. And worse. The distinguished jazz critic Leonard Feather pointed out that the street's reputation "has been blackened by reports of dope raids and arrests."

Time magazine would also note the transformation. "Even the customers had changed," the magazine observed. "There were fewer crewcuts, pipes and sports jackets; more bald spots, cigars and paunches."

When I read the *New York Journal* article I had to be sure '21' wasn't being insultingly lumped together with such tawdry places, so I looked up "estaminet" in my dictionary. It's French for bistro. That was okay, but it fell far short of saying what '21' was and would remain even though the neighborhood was turning a bit shabby. As Louis Sobol pointed out at that time, "Here assembled for lunch or cocktails or dinner, the elite of the country. If you linger around this place long enough, you'll meet everyone in Who's Who worth knowing."

One of those individuals was Walter Bedell Smith. During the war, "Beetle" had been General Dwight Eisenhower's chief of staff and had presided over the ceremony at which Germany surrendered (Ike had refused to see or speak to any German officer). In 1946 when President Truman appointed General Smith as our ambassador to Moscow, we at '21' immediately recognized a possible advantage of having one of our regular customers in a position to clear up a problem that had plagued us during the war: caviar.

Made from the roe (eggs) of four species of Caspian Sea sturgeon (beluga, sterlet, osetra, sevruga), the delicacy had always been part of the '21' menu. Because we had been unable to import it from the Soviet Union during the war, we'd switched to Iranian, which was fine, although Iranian caviar somehow never enjoyed the cachet of the Russian. Now, with Bedell Smith going off to Moscow, we asked him to see what he might be able to do (unofficially, of course) to assure us a supply of Russian caviar for the club and for our Irongate Products. He came through for us, as he did for Ike and everyone else in the war, with flying colors. Although we didn't see him much during his ambassadorship, he again showed up at the club on a fairly regular basis between 1950 and 1953 as he traveled up to

New York City from Washington as director of the Central Intelligence Agency.

In addition to Russian and Iranian caviar we offered postwar gourmets the delights of other exotic foods. For six months of the year Bob's wartime pal—now General Breyer, retired, USMC—searched the world for delicacies. In August it was grouse hunting in Scotland (an expedition which I was always glad to join). Whatever we succeeded in bagging in a day was immediately packed in ice and shipped to New York via Pan American Airways for the next day's menu. At Grimsby, England, the general picked up Dover sole. In Holland it was green herring; rare rose jelly and trout in Denmark; prawns in Dublin; hazel hens and snow geese in Sweden; smoked reindeer tongue in Finland; eel and salmon in Poland; pâté de foie gras in France; truffles in Yugoslavia; and deer and boar in Australia.

While Bob maintained a link with his wartime experiences in the person of Malcolm Beyer, and by serving in the Marine Corps reserves, Mac came back from service with the Eighth Air Force as a lieutenant colonel wearing the Legion of Merit, the Air Force Commendation Medal, and the Exceptional Service Award. Finding a lot of customers who'd also served in the air force, he promptly organized the Iron Gate Chapter of Air Alumni. One of the members added a model of an SBD bomber to the ceiling. Gatherings of the Air Alumni usually included Mac leading the group in a loud rendition of the air force song. Somehow, with all the airplanes dangling from the barroom ceiling, it seemed perfectly appropriate to be serenaded with "Off We Go into the Wild Blue Yonder."

Judging by what was happening in New York City in the two years immediately after World War II, there would be no limits on how far you could go in that wild blue yonder, figuratively and in fact. Along with a general economic boom fueled by public optimism, air travel was taking off and everyone appeared to want to come to New York. This would provoke writer E. B. White to gripe, "The city has never been so uncomfortable, so crowded, so tense. Money has been plentiful and New York has responded. Restaurants are hard to get into."

Of course, this was always the case at '21', and not because of a limitation on tables and standing room at the bar. Guardians of the gate were expected to be as discerning as they'd always been as to whom they let in and whom they didn't. However, with New York chosen as headquarters of the newly formed United Nations, a rather more international tone was noticeable as regular patrons introduced diplomats to the club in much the same manner as a few pals had done for David Niven in the early 1930s.

In a postwar "gustatory guide" to New York in a book entitled *New York Confidential*, journalist Lee Mortimer and coauthor Jack Lait listed '21' as a place where you could dine "without orchestral din," adding the caveat, "if you can get in."

Mortimer and Lait expounded as follows:

> In defiance of police regulations, two lines of sleek and fancy limousines are parked nightly outside Jack and Charlie's famed 21 Club on 52nd Street.
>
> One reason why the cops close their eyes while pounding that beat is that the cars, with liveried chauffeurs, are owned by the rich and prominent townsfolk. Another is that many of the machines carry burnished seals, signifying they belong to, or at least are assigned to, high city, state and national officials. West of Fifth Avenue, 52nd Street

was long a street of wealth. Today, the 21 Club is wealth's
last outpost.

Also returning from military service during the war was our
nephew Sheldon Jay Tannen, son of Anna and Henry. While
enrolled at New York University, he came into the family business possessing a fair amount of experience gained while working for Henry and Bill Hardey at the Gay Nineties. After
assessing Sheldon's performance as a waiter, Jack decided
Sheldon didn't present the proper posture. He thought he
didn't hold himself erect enough. His shoulders slouched. The
remedy for this, Jack decreed, was to have Sheldon wear a cor-
rective brace.

On the subject of Jack's image as a Napoleon in the restaurant business, longtime '21' veteran Steve Hanagan would
write, "Jack was a disciplinarian—of others as well as himself.
He was the master sergeant, ever looking after his pursuits.
When Mac came into the store only his size kept him from
quailing under the injunctions of his older brother. Bob, more
sensitive and just out of Rutgers, got a grounding in drink and
decorum that made a jest out of boot training in a Marine
camp. Jerry—cousin Charlie Berns's brother, coming into the
store from a reporter's plight on the *Cincinnati Enquirer*—found
the first year, under Jack, his toughest assignment. Only Pete
seemed to escape the lash of training, because, perhaps, he
entered later in life and elsewhere had acquired self-discipline.
I could notice all these things, in detail, because I was around
at odd hours, often between meals, and what I didn't see I heard
in frail rancor from the younger set. I have a shoulder padded
with a crying towel. It wasn't that the boys rebelled at Jack.
They respected his authority, his experience, his success. They

just didn't know whether they were made of the stuff that Jack demanded for '21' service."

Most of Steve Hanagan's observations were accurate, except what he said about my having been spared Jack's "lash." I'd felt its snap as often as my brothers, cousins, and nephews. And like them, I understood Jack's intent. When Sheldon was asked why he'd complied with Jack's demand that he wear a shoulder brace, he smiled and replied, "We know how to separate family love from business."

That truth asserted, there wasn't one of us who didn't feel a twinge of anxiety and apprehension when Jack signaled his desire to have a few words with us. I certainly did one Friday evening, August 13, 1947, when Jack gestured to me to come to his table. He usually sat at table 1. Next to the kitchen door, it provided him a view of both the barroom and the entrance to the club. He'd been chatting with a pal, Air Force general Andy Anderson.

As I approached them, I thought Jack looked as if he were upset about something, so I braced myself for a possible bawling out. Instead, he said, "Pete, I'd like you to keep Andy company while I go up to my apartment for a couple of minutes."

Assuming he'd remembered some business he had to take care of using his private phone line, I settled down in anticipation of a brief but lively conversation with the general. He could usually be relied on to relate amusing war stories or the latest Washington gossip.

When Jack didn't return after a few minutes, I was at first curious, then concerned. Excusing myself on the pretext of having to check something in the front of the club, I went to the fourth floor. Opening the door to Jack's apartment, I heard a groaning from the bedroom. Rushing in, I found Jack on the bed, his hand pressed to his chest, sweating heavily, gasping, and writhing in obviously deep agony. Despite the heroic efforts of our family physician, Dr. Herman Brush, Jack died in his bed of a massive heart attack. He was only forty-eight years old.

My first concern was notifying my brothers. But Mac was in Bermuda running after a girl, and Bob and his wife were in Canada. Jewish law required burial the following day, unless it fell on the sabbath, so arrangements were made for the service to be held on Sunday. I feared Mac and Bob might not be able to get back to New York City in time, but they did, joining our four sisters and their families, the Bernses, Jeannette and me, scores of Jack's shocked friends, and hundreds of stunned '21' regulars. Tributes in the form of more than two thousand telegrams came from around the nation and world. Wreaths were sent by New York mayor William O'Dwyer, Postmaster General James Farley, and many '21' regulars.

A *Herald Tribune* editorial said, "It took imagination and a kind of genius for perfection to evolve what shortly became a national institution, and these qualities Jack Kriendler possessed in determined abundance."

For the *New York Sun* Ward Morehouse wrote, "The passing of John Carl Kriendler removes a dramatic and colorful figure in the life of New York. He had friends in all parts of the world and in all walks of life. His genius for organization contributed greatly to the success of Twenty One, the Fifty-second Street meeting place, that is recognized as one of the finest restaurants of our time."

Dean of New York's sportswriters Bill Corum: "For me there will never be another host in a public place like my friend, Jack Kriendler. Not only because I liked him and know the feeling was mutual, which is true. But also because he had the knack somehow of making me feel that a party was afoot. That we were conniving a little together toward the goal of a good time."

I couldn't imagine then, and can't conceive now, of a nicer eulogy for my big brother Jack—or for anyone.

Unfortunately, among these glowing and heartfelt tributes to Jack there was a glaringly offensive column from Walter Winchell, quoted here with all his infamous venom and vitriol:

Novelette at '21': People who belonged to the inner circle at the renowned Manhattan restaurant gave the creeps to intimates with this alleged lowdown on what killed Jack Kriendler.

The story tellers rarely note that Mr. K. had suffered numerous heart attacks. They prefer this legend: Two weeks before he succumbed, Kriendler had a scene with a man in his place. The man had no police record but was influential in both the upper and underworlds. Kriendler signal'd a captain to seat this man and his lady on the third floor in the rear so he wouldn't be seen. The man was incensed. He sent for Mr. K. and told him off. 'Why did you do this to me?' he thundered, 'I will kill you, do you hear? I will kill you!'

Kriendler, pals insist, tossed every night in bed for two weeks worrying about the threat—killing himself.

Nonsense.

The idea that a man who twice defied Legs Diamond, gave the bum's rush to other hoods, and once bounced a boss of the underworld, Frank Costello, would worry himself to death over a threat was—and remains—a ludicrous notion.

Reading Winchell's words then, and having reread them in the process of writing this book, I found my outrage tempered by a sad realization that Winchell supposed he could get a modicum of revenge for having been banned from '21' by taking a swipe at a dead man.

The truth is that Winchell never understood what was at the heart of Jack and '21'. But Ben Hecht did, as he proved in this poem, "To Jack," written in 1950 for *The Iron Gate*.

Nobody gives a good God damn
For Fame or Glory in Twenty One—
Milit'ry Brass and Movie Ham,
Money Bag and Political Gun,
Poet and Poohbah are lost in the jam.
This dizzy tavern is overrun
With muttering Fascists and camouflaged Reds,
All tying on an identical bun.
And Genius and Wizard are so many heads
Of Gothamite cattle at Twenty One.
You can corner the market or write King Lear
Or sail to the moon in a scientist's pram.
It'll get you exactly bubkes here
For nobody gives a good God damn
Who's Who or What in this house of fun—
For the shade of Jack still makes salaam
To only a friend in Twenty One.

With Charlie Berns remaining in charge of 21 Brands and Bob and me continuing in roles Jack had never fully delineated, Mac became president of '21'. Service in the air force had given him a managerial experience that enhanced all he'd learned from Jack about running a successful restaurant. Tall and broad-shouldered, he was cheerful, cordial, and cultured.

Gifted with an operatic-quality voice, he had no misgivings about demonstrating it. As Jack had relished amusing customers by donning one of his cowboy outfits, Mac enjoyed regaling patrons with songs, especially arias.

Our nephew Kermit Axel noted that Mac reserved his grand opera arias for top-drawer personalities and that lesser lights received a blast of something like "Old Man River." Customers quickly learned that the sound of an aria signaled the presence of somebody worth getting a look at. But on one notable occasion, as Mac burst into something from *The Barber of Seville* and customers abandoned the bar and tables to ogle the beneficiary of Mac's performance, it became immediately obvious to everyone but Mac that a mistake had been made. The perplexed object of Mac's singing was a burly, bearded fellow whom Mac had mistaken for Ernest Hemingway.

Should it become known that it was a customer's birthday, Mac would corral a group he named "the Chuck Wagon Glee Club" and lead them in singing "Happy Birthday to You" with all the verve of the chorus of the Metropolitan Opera. George Jean Nathan hailed their performance as a "Must!" What Jean meant was, "As soon as they start singing you must blow the joint."

Chuck Wagon member Frank Conniff contended there was a subterfuge in the singing of "Happy Birthday." He alleged that as the glee club was in full throat "captains and waiters tenderly deposit a cake brightened by a single candle on a guest's table," but as the chorus "reaches a crescendo under Herr Kriendler's baton, a busboy snatches the cake and whisks it back to the scullery. It is always the same cake and candle. The Kriendlers, you see, like to have their cake and keep it, too."

Women whom Mac serenaded with a solo were invariably charmed and flattered, which was what Mac intended. He had always been a ladies' man, constantly declaring he'd fallen in love. One day he called me to his office to announce he'd met a young woman from California and intended to marry her immediately. He wanted to know if the wedding could be held in my apartment. Naturally, I agreed. Arrangements for the ceremony were expertly supervised by Jeannette and were splendid.

The marriage lasted two weeks.

On another occasion Mac's friend Anthony Paget Jr., who was living in Madrid, was surprised by Mac calling him on the phone and saying, "Hey, Tony, I'm in town. Meet me in the hotel bar and bring along a couple of gorgeous Spanish gals."

"But Mac," replied the mystified Tony, "aren't you just married and on your honeymoon? Where's your bride?"

"Oh Lord, I forgot," Mac laughed. "She's upstairs."

Mac would eventually be married four times and father four outstanding children.

With the deaths of Jack and Bob Benchley less than two years apart and the welcoming home of Mac, Bob, and others from the war, I felt bittersweet as the 1940s came to a close, but I also shared with the city and country a guarded optimism about the dawning decade.

A glimpse of '21' at the start of the 1950s has been immortalized in the movie *All About Eve*. This is the classic film in which Broadway star Margo Channing (Bette Davis) warns the guests at a party held in her apartment, "Fasten your seat belts, it's going to be a bumpy night." While Bette certainly was capable of providing fireworks both in movies and in real life, whenever she came to New York she couldn't leave town without at least one *non*-bumpy visit to '21.' But the scene in *All About Eve* did not involve her.

It was Celeste Holm, playing a playwright's wife, who drew up in front in a taxi, proceeded through the iron gate, and went down the steps and into the lobby. Against the background of the reception desk, cigar counter, check room, art-bedecked walls, stairway to the second-floor dining room, and customers going in and out, she encountered the cunning theater critic portrayed by ever-suave George Sanders. Accompanying him on his way to the door was the unscrupulously ambitious actress of the title, Eve Harrington, played by Anne Baxter, the sweet lady who had once arranged to have her dinner bill sent to her home to prevent her father from grabbing it and insisting on paying.

What Celeste Holm, as the playwright's wife, learned in the lobby of '21' provided a dramatic turning point in the plot. The movie afforded not only a tantalizing peek into '21' for moviegoers in places far from New York City who probably would never have the opportunity to dine at the club, but also an opportunity for people in future generations to see how the club looked at the inception of a decade that would be marked by historic changes in the American way of life.

"To say that '21' is an institution of our times and to a great extent a mirror of our manners is to state a banality which everybody knows and nearly everybody accepts," wrote Louis Bromfield in 1950. "I can go to '21' and know that I am going to see quite a lot of friends from New York, from Dallas, from

Kansas City or Cleveland or Hollywood or where you will. And
I also know that I am going to encounter some actors, some
brokers, some advertising men, some pretty and entertaining
women, some Hollywood people, some ranchers, some oil men,
in short pretty nearly everything."

Shortly after *All About Eve* put '21' on the nation's movie
screens the front door was redesigned. This by no means sig-
naled a change in policy regarding who passed through it.
Among the keen-eyed watchmen whose orders were to careful-
ly screen who came in were Chuck Anderson, Michael Bemer,
Tom Ray, and Monte Sideman, who was married to my sister
Bea. And still on the job after more than twenty years was
Jimmie Coslove.

In the description of one customer, Jimmie was "an ani-
mated supply of hospitality, blessed with an eye which has the
inordinate quality of segregating a patron from a poltroon."
One of Jimmie's tried-and-true methods to keep out someone
who'd made a reservation but really wasn't welcome was to
express shock and declare, "We thought you made your reservation for tomorrow. I'm sorry, we're full tonight."

As Jerry Berns put it, "Legally, '21' is a public restaurant,
and we're glad to welcome any strangers, so long as there is
available space." What constituted "available space" depended
upon who hoped to occupy it.

Still snobbish? Sure. Being choosy was one of the reasons
for the club's continued success. Those who were admitted took
pride in claiming that the men's room attendant could make
fifty thousand dollars a year in tips. One regular customer said,
"I can eat in just about any other restaurant in town for what it
costs me in the men's room at '21'."

A new entrance was not the only dramatic architectural change in the block of West Fifty-second between Fifth and Sixth. Many of the graceful old townhouses that had become speakeasies and then legitimate clubs and restaurants were being taken over and torn down to make room for skyscrapers and other bastions of American business.

On the floodtide of this construction a new type of customer began passing through the iron gate, entering the new portal, and being met by Jimmie's discerning eye. We'd entered the brave new world of the expense account.

One longtime customer, lyricist Howard Dietz, whose collaboration with composer Arthur Schwartz in 1948 (*Inside USA*) starred Bea Lillie, observed the phenomenon and joked, "The elite are the guys who can deduct the tabs from their income taxes, the new expense account society. The government may pull a raid one of these days, not like the old raids to find bottles of liquor, but in order to round up tax-evaders. I understand Mac is considering a device whereby, in case the Internal Revenue Department barges in, all the checks can be destroyed in three minutes. A section of the bar slides out and the checks go down a chute."

What the new breed of customers found in '21' was exactly what their predecessors had embraced. The mood was best described by financier Michel Apostol: "It's a clubby house. I go to certain bars where there are a lot of people I know and I feel very much at home in them, but they are not hospitable in the sense that '21' seems to be. You go through this lounge and suddenly you're protected."

On the other hand, there was the busty platinum blonde who walked in on the arm of a businessman with an expense account, looked around, and exclaimed to her escort, "You call this place something special?"

Since the end of the war, the person who had the job of arranging seating was Walter Weiss. Fresh out of the Marine Corps in 1945, Walter first went to work at Toots Shor's, which was best known as a watering hole for the celebrities and near-celebrities of the sports world. (The place of athletes in the story of '21' will be related in my next chapter.) Walter stayed at Shor's less than a week.

When it came to "dressing a room," no one proved better than Walter. Reporting to work at ten in the morning, he parked himself at table 1, next to the kitchen door, and for the next two hours booked lunch reservations. The task was like putting together a jigsaw puzzle with 150 parts (the number of tables upstairs and in the three sections of the barroom). The barroom space appeared to be a single one, but the ground-floor dining area was divided by the structural supports of the three houses (17, 19, and 21).

Where a customer would be placed was entirely up to Walter. The challenge was in striking a balance between tradition, the prominence/ego of customers, and the '21' reputation for style and class. Tradition played a role in the sense that regulars expected to be seated at the table where they'd always been placed; this was frequently so cherished a spot that some patrons felt they had a right to bequeath their '21' tables as part of their estates. Rich and famous customers with egos to match demanded to be located where they'd be noticed. And there were the people whose placements were deemed beneficial to the club, because, as the Bible says, a candle belongs where it radiates most light.

The architecturally dictated divisions came to be identified variously. Some customers spoke in geographical terms.
The area encompassed by No. 17 was "east" and "Siberia."
No. 21 was often called "the kitchen room." The middle area
(No. 19), which consisted primarily of banquettes facing the
long bar and afforded a commanding view of all the sections,
tended to be favored by guests with roving eyes.

A few customers didn't give a damn where Walter Weiss
sat them. Journalist Robert Ruark said, "I have heard that there
is a tyranny of customer location. I have heard that when some
customers do not come in often enough to eat all they can for
a hundred bucks, then the management becomes testy and ban-
ishes these people to the boondocks. Of these inner politics I
know nothing. My practice is merely to walk in the joint and
flop into a seat. I sit where there's room to sit."

What happened if a customer had booked a favored table
and was due to come in and claim it at the appointed time, but
found it still occupied by the previous patron? While such a
dilemma was generally avoided by carefully timed bookings, a
first occupant might still be seated when the second customer
was due at the door. This situation required a good deal of tact.
Alas, in the case of showman Billy Rose's slowness in departing
so that George Jean Nathan wouldn't be told that his usual
table wasn't ready, Billy was bluntly ordered to hurry up and finish his meal. Only the fact that Billy had been in the restaurant
business and clearly understood the situation saved the day.
When Mr. Nathan arrived Billy was gone, though only a few
paces to the bar.

A middle-section table in close proximity to the bar was
the preference of Humphrey Bogart. When he first became a
customer he was married to a tempestuous actress, Mayo

Methot. The story of their legendary fights has been told elsewhere, as have tales of Bogart's penchant for getting into public rows that as often as not involved a lot of drinking and
ended in fisticuffs. Indeed, there were many evenings when
Jack or Mac, by virtue of their robust physiques, advised him of
the wisdom of his leaving the premises sooner rather than later.
But after he made the movie *To Have and Have Not* he divorced
Mayo Methot. The catalyst for the split was his costar, Lauren
Bacall, who had made her film debut in the story based loosely
on a Hemingway yarn. I'm proud to note that they became
engaged at '21' and that Bogart's combative disposition
changed dramatically. A bronze plaque behind table 30 now
identifies the spot as "Bogie's Corner."

Similar stratification regarding seating also pertained
upstairs. There were two rooms. The main formal dining space
was called the Front Room, and the one in the rear was the
Tapestry Room, off of which was a private-party apartment
known as the French Room.

The second-floor pecking order was described in a 1952
Holiday feature by Lucius Beebe:

> There is a certain contingent of 21 patrons, mostly
> older persons in the upper social brackets, who advance
> determinedly to the staircase leading to the upstairs restau-
> rant and proceed directly to their table, squired by Floyd
> Flom, who announces them to Philip or Pierre at the land-
> ing. The cream of Jack and Charlie regulars, old-timers and
> social and professional personages to whom appearances
> are a necessity are given the super-deluxe treatment in
> the Front Room. Every table and banquette in this
> gracious apartment is advantageous from the equally

urgent standpoints of seeing and being seen. An entry or exit through its doorway with its accompanying courtesies from the service staff cannot possibly go undetected. No new hair-do, beau, or date, no Valentina evening gown or Cartier necklace can go without notice.

Lunch or dinner, it matters not the time of day, is ritual in the Front Room, a ceremonial elegance presided over by masters of the grand manner and awash with rolling tables of Westphalian ham, flaming desserts, cut flowers, silver wine buckets, foil-topped bottles and the most perfect service of any restaurant in the world. Pierre Pastre, the headwaiter, and Philip Caselli, the maitre d'hotel, are the two men who make the pageant of the Front Room click with a soothing and cheerful precision.

The diplomacy of a Metternich and the courage of a lion tamer are the requisites for administering the Front Room. A preponderance of the regulars demand the same table whenever they put in an appearance, a contingency not always announced in advance and one which presents obvious problems of displacement of bodies. [Cosmetics queen] Elizabeth Arden, who is so regular as to present no problem at all, must have her accustomed place at the west wall banquette. [Broadway producers] John Golden and Lee Shubert must be shown to table 150 on boiled-beef-with-horseradish day, which is usually Wednesday. George Vanderbilt, Lawrence Tibbett, Helen Hayes, David Sarnoff, Moss Hart, Cole Porter, Greta Garbo, Leland Heyward and John Steinbeck each has a whim about seating and each is a whim of iron.

Nor would it be judicious to forget that Mrs. Ogden Reid likes to be seated with the windows to her back,

facing the entrance, that Mary Martin must be near the
door to make her curtain hours in the show of the moment,
and that such notables as John Jacob Astor, Joshua Logan,
Gen. Jimmy Doolittle and George S. Kaufman don't want
to be behind any big hats.

Among customers of the 1950s who expected special
treatment were stars of the blossoming new medium of entertainment, television. On TV's roster of new "names" who
became steady patrons were CBS-TV newsman Edward R.
Murrow, actresses Betty Furness and Faye Emerson (married to
FDR's son Elliot Roosevelt and later to bandleader Skitch
Henderson, Emerson was famous for her gowns with plunging
necklines), comics Steve Allen and Sid Caesar, Arthur
Godfrey, Jackie Gleason, and numerous writers, producers, and
directors who went on to careers in Hollywood.

Nearly every day the founder of CBS, William S. Paley,
came over from the network's headquarters at 485 Madison
Avenue at the corner of East Fifty-second Street for lunch or
dinner. Seated in the Front Room, he exhibited an amazing
capacity for attracting the attention of beautiful women,
including those who at the moment happened to be in the
company of their husbands.

While couples had always been part of the '21' mix, no
pair made quite the impression in the 1950s as Tex McCrary
and Jinx Falkenburg, popularly known through their newspaper
column and radio and TV shows as "Tex and Jinx." In a contribution to the 1950 edition of *The Iron Gate* they asserted,
"What lures New York's most fascinating people to '21'? More
than anything else it's other fascinating people." Tex and Jinx
then listed those they had recently encountered in the club:

Mike and Fleur Cowles, founders of *Look*, *Quick*, and *Flair* magazines; department store magnate Bernard Gimbel; Herbert Bayard Swope; William "Hopalong Cassidy" Boyd; Dorothy Shaver, president of Lord & Taylor; Kent Cooper, boss of the Associated Press; Mrs. Edna Woolman Chase, head of *Vogue* magazine; Jimmy Durante; Anita Loos, author of *Gentlemen Prefer Blondes*; Roy Howard, chief of the Scripps-Howard news syndicate; Paulette Goddard; jockey Eddie Arcaro; Laraine Day Durocher, movie actress and wife of baseball manager Leo (first for the Brooklyn Dodgers and then the New York Giants); Sid Caesar; and Mae West.

In addition to his teaming with Jinx Falkenburg, Tex McCrary ranked as one of the top theatrical impresarios. He was also an ardent Republican. Combining these interests in the early 1950s, he played an important role in the efforts by some GOP leaders in persuading General Eisenhower to run for president of the United States, and in producing major "We Like Ike" campaign rallies.

Although the Kriendler brothers had a policy of never mixing '21' in politics, we all had our allegiances. Jack and Mac were Republicans, Bob and I Democrats. I'd been especially fond of Harry Truman since I first met him when he came to '21' as a senator. My admiration for him grew when he was vice president, and it soared after the death of FDR thrust him into the White House.

When Truman ran to become president in his own right in 1948 Jeannette was working for NBC News in its coverage of the nominating convention of the Republicans in Philadelphia. She was in charge of makeup for everybody who appeared on the podium.

Being a Democrat, I was delighted that Truman got the

nod at the Democratic convention, also held in Philly, and I was even happier when he confounded the pollsters and the pundits by beating our old nemesis from Prohibition days, Thomas E. Dewey, who had reluctantly advised raiders that the mere odor of liquor was insufficient evidence to make a case against Jack and Charlie.

The next time I greeted Truman at '21' was after he'd left office in 1953. It started with a phone call from Judge Samuel Rosenman, whom I knew well because he usually sat next to me in services at Temple Emanu-El. "Pete, I need a favor from you," he said. "I know this is very short notice, but I'm bringing some special people to dinner at '21'. We'll be there at six o'clock. Please tell me there'll be no problem about getting a table."

This was short notice indeed, but Sam was an old friend, and what are friends for, I thought as I asked warily, "How many?"

"My wife and me, President and Mrs. Truman, and Margaret."

Luckily, Walter Weiss's reservation plan for the Front Room on that evening contained the names of no regulars who would object to being displaced even if the move were to make room for a president of the United States. Looking over the layout of the room with Walter, I chose table 120. Thereafter known as "the Presidential Table," it subsequently accommodated Eisenhower, John Kennedy, Richard Nixon, Gerald Ford, Jimmy Carter, Ronald Reagan, George Bush, and Bill Clinton.

As for Truman's unexpected visit that evening, I'm pleased to record that it went very well, although I confess that I felt so excited at meeting a man who was my political hero that all I could say was, "Good evening, Mr. Truman. I'm Pete Kriendler, the boss of this place. It's been a while since we've had the honor of seeing you at '21'."

"Well, you know, young fella," he said with a chuckle and a twinkle in his eyes, "I've been kind of busy down in Washington these past few years."

While I found politicians fascinating as individuals and as customers, I had no interest in getting personally involved in politics. It was Bob who had that passion. He was so attuned to politics that I could easily envision him running for and winning a seat in the U.S. Senate. A keystone of Bob's philosophy was the belief that the United States could not escape the role of leader of the free world.

Among '21' customers who shared Bob's "internationalism" in the years immediately before the war and following it were Aleck Woollcott, Robert Sherwood, and Rex Stout. All became active in the formation of a group called the Fight For Freedom Committee, forerunner of Freedom House. Its purpose was the promotion of the principles of freedom and the dissemination of freedom's concepts. Bob became a member of the board, and '21' became the site of many of the board's dinner meetings.

Naturally, in the 1952 presidential campaign that pitted Eisenhower against the Democratic governor of Illinois, Adlai E. Stevenson, I was for Adlai—until I met him. When I shook his hand and found it as limp as a dead fish, I said to myself, "How the hell can I vote for this guy when he doesn't even give you a proper handshake?" It was the first time I voted for a Republican.

Eisenhower had come to '21' after he'd become president of Columbia University in 1948. He was usually accompanied by men from the worlds of business and sports. Then he was recalled to duty in 1950 by President Truman to take command of NATO. After he was elected president in 1952 I thought he was the right man for the time. Even though his critics labeled him a "do-nothing" president and "chairman of the bored," I found him to be exactly what the country needed. Steady. Cool. Tough with the Russians.

But I do think Ike fumbled the ball in dealing with Senator Joseph R. McCarthy and his chief henchman, Roy Cohn. I'd known Cohn's father, a prominent State Supreme Court judge in the Bronx, and his mother was a charmer whom I saw frequently at the opera. How such fine people could produce so evil an offspring as Roy Cohn mystified me.

I also knew the father of one of Roy Cohn's buddies, who became the controversial main character in Joe McCarthy's war with the U.S. Army for allegedly protecting "communists." In an embarrassing debacle carried on television as "the Army-McCarthy hearings," we learned that Roy Cohn had tried to muscle the army into giving preferential treatment to his pal David Schine. (Some people whispered that Roy was in love with David.) I'd known Schine's father, Meyer, a glove manufacturer who'd parlayed his fortune into a string of movie theaters in New York state.

It was with more than a little satisfaction that I watched the downfall of McCarthy, which was initiated in large measure by a customer of '21', Edward R. Murrow. In one of the most dramatic broadcasts in the early history of television, Murrow exposed McCarthy as the demagogue he was, while at the same time revealing the power of TV to affect politics. I also felt a twinge of pleasure that Joe McCarthy's demise as a malevolent political force rubbed off on his persistent champion in the press, Walter Winchell.

Except for gossip columnists of the Winchell ilk, '21' had always been attractive to journalists, and never more so than in the 1950s. One of them was show-business columnist Earl Wilson. He liked to joke that he could get anything he wanted at '21' except a glass of water. "They do have it," he wrote, "but the battery of captains, waiters and busboys that surround you naturally assume you're a man of the world, and expect you'll be drinking wine." Earl said that one day he left a five-cent newspaper at the checkroom and it took a quarter tip to the attendant to get it back.

Other luminaries of 1950s journalism who beat a path to '21' were Arthur Krock, Bob Considine, Robert Ruark, Bill Corum, Adela Rogers St. John, Lucius Beebe, Frank Conniff, John Crosby, and even Hollywood's queen of harmless screen gossip, Louella Parsons.

And there was the perennial Ben Hecht, who worked for the only New York newspaper with initials for a name, *P.M.* In his autobiography, *A Child of the Century*, Ben related an attempt in 1955 to end a twenty-year estrangement with Sherwood Anderson. Ben decided the place to do it was '21'.

"I sat down with him as if not two decades but two weeks had passed since our last sight of each other," he wrote, adding that he found Sherwood's laugh intact and that the "intimate purr, the glowing eyes, the delicately trembling features" were the same, although he'd grown "paunchy, gray-haired, and a sort of pelican pouch had been added to his neck." Sherwood informed Ben he was off in the morning to South America, where he planned to live the rest of his life.

"We drank wine again together, laughed loudly over a few long-ago names," Ben wrote. "The magic I had felt in him in his youth seemed unchanged."

The next day Ben handed in to his editor a story of his reunion with Sherwood that described Anderson as a man leaving not a country but life, and that Anderson was "like a wearied animal going off to an unfamiliar place to die."

The day the column appeared in *P.M.* Ben found that a small news item had been inserted at the top announcing that Anderson had died the night before aboard a ship bound for Brazil. He'd accidentally swallowed a toothpick and punctured a vital organ.

As melancholy as Ben's memory of his last meeting with an old friend was, it illustrates the bond so many customers felt concerning '21'. That emotional connection was also experienced by author Louis Bromfield. He wrote, "The place is full of memories for me of good food and wines and excellent company, of dinner parties which have been the gayest in the world, even of at least one long-after-hours session ending up at daylight. It was a purely accidental gathering that lasted until the grey morning light came in the windows. It is a great place— Twenty One—and I'm old enough, thank God, to have known it through many phases and at least three periods of great economic growth and sociological interest, not to mention the good company, the good food and the pleasure of seeing old friends."

Given the affinity for '21' of journalists such as Louis Bromfield and Ben Hecht, I was not surprised that the producers of a movie about a newspaper columnist wanted to shoot a scene in '21'. It was great fun to have the gang there for a couple of days while we closed down the club. And when the picture came out, we were all invited to a movie house in the neighborhood where many of the '21' employees and the movie's stars lived. The film, released in 1957, was entitled *The Sweet Smell of Success*.

In the '21' scene Tony Curtis as Sidney Falco, an ambitious and unscrupulous publicity agent with a "hot" item, has tracked down a powerful newspaper gossip columnist in the middle section of the barroom. Played by Burt Lancaster, J. J. Hunsecker is a fictional composite of Ed Sullivan and Walter Winchell. The movie was written by Clifford Odets and Ernest Lehman and produced by the partnership of Lancaster and Harold Hecht. For the privilege of shooting the barroom scene the company promised '21' a fee of ten thousand dollars. (Just for the record, we never got the check.)

As the scene between Curtis and Lancaster continues in front of '21', the changing character of West Fifty-second between Fifth and Sixth is visible in the background. There are empty spaces. The parallel rows of brownstone houses that had become speakeasies in the 1930s and then legitimate clubs through the forties were one by one being torn down to make room for towers for the 1960s—all but one.

Ten years after the *New York Journal* saw "a fretting quagmire," our neighborhood was at the beginning of a renaissance in which, I felt confident, '21' could not only survive, but could attain an even more fabulous success.

Eight

I ALWAYS WANTED TO JOIN THIS CLUB

"To say that the fame of Jack and Charlie's 21 Restaurant is national is a triumph of understatement," wrote Lucius Beebe in the 1950s, "for its fame abroad is almost as well established as that of Maxim's, Claridge's, or the Tour d'Argent. It possesses the added distinction of being the hardest restaurant in the world to gain admission to."

When Tex McCrary was asked to define the essence of '21' he called it "the catalyst on the hot tin roof" of New York. John Steinbeck quipped, "If you build a better mouse trap mice will come from all over to enjoy it."

But the fact is that '21' was not *created*. There was no such thing as a master design. Jack and Charlie never sat down to draw up a business plan. If they had, it might have been along the lines of how another customer summed up the '21' experience: "Everyone who comes in the door is treated like a person who has not yet had his morning coffee."

Working in a place with that reputation, even though I was a member of the ownership and management, was both an honor and a daunting responsibility. With Charlie devoting almost all his time to running 21 Brands, the overall boss in the club was Mac—a dynamo of energy, apparently carefree, always ready to sing. Under him were Bob, a lot like Jack—clear-thinking, sober-minded, nattily decked out; Jerry Berns, a detail man; Sheldon Tannen, in training for some future date when he would inherit administrative duties; and me.

Looking over this team and coming up with a few thumbnail sketches, John Steinbeck saw romance-minded Mac as a guy with "a jolly eye for a well-turned ankle and an appreciation of a well rounded heel." Marine Corps Reserve officer Bob was "Grandson of Battle." Jerry was "a gentleman of the old school who says he is not a Communist, which proves he is." Sheldon Tannen somehow managed to avoid a tarring with the Steinbeck brush.

I was "Peter, also known as Lucky Luciano."

Our *maestro extraordinaire de cuisine* at this time was Yves Louis Ploneis. He'd succeeded Henri Geib and was in the process of training Anthony Pedretti, who would follow him in 1966.

In devising menus Louis was guided by the seasons. Despite improvements in technologies for preserving food for long periods by freezing them, the '21' policy was never to yield to the urge to store a large repertory of out-of-season items. Discussing the policy in an interview, Bob said, "We're old fashioned enough to believe that salmon and green peas belong on the seventeenth of June and that California figs should appear only on the menu when they are naturally ripe and intended by God for consumption."

The time for grouse, for instance, was after the twelfth of August when the hunting season began in England. We did not save some in a freezer to spice up the menu on the Fourth of July. At the appropriate times customers knew they would find Dungeness crabs, Lynnhaven oysters, Guayamas shrimp, hardboiled pheasant eggs, grilled black bear chops, saddle of antelope, Norwegian ptarmigan, Mexican quail, Delaware terrapin, and mallard and canvasback duck.

When sitting down for a meal of game a customer knew that it was very likely to have been bagged by no less a big-game hunter than Frank Buck, or perhaps by journalism's most famous sojourner into the wilds of Africa with gun in hand, Robert Ruark. Trophies of their marksmanship could be perused on the walls of the upstairs Hunt Room.

Some of these delicacies were served with great fanfare, but not always flawlessly. When Winston Churchill was guest of honor at a private party it was Walter Weiss's privilege to present the wartime British prime minister with pheasants Souvaroff. This was an elaborate dish of four birds in a large copper casserole with a truffle sauce and foie gras in a pastry crust. Walter's job was to dramatically unveil it before Churchill. But the cover was so hot that Walter dropped everything at the great man's feet. For a breathless moment no one in the room dared move. Then Churchill let out a roar of a laugh and helped Walter scoop the birds from the floor. Fortunately, or perhaps presciently, Henri Geib had a backup quartet of pheasants standing by in the kitchen.

Yet a fancy array of rarities never matched in customers' fervor one specialty of the club's menu, especially on Monday night during the opera season. Served at midnight, it was chicken hash and scrambled eggs. The dish also appeared on the menu as chicken hash '21', served with wild rice; chicken hash St. Germaine, with a puree of peas and grilled cheese topping; and chicken hash Beyers, with both wild rice and pureed peas. It was favored by William Paley's daughter, Mrs. Hilary Beyers, hence the name. In one style or another, chicken hash became a '21' staple.

As anyone who saw the movie *Wall Street* starring Michael Douglas and Charlie Sheen knows, another favorite is traditional (raw) steak tartare. Made with a pound of freshly ground top round, two large egg yolks, chopped hard-boiled egg whites, finely diced raw red Bermuda onion, diced shallots and anchovy, Dijon mustard, Worcestershire and Tabasco sauce, chopped capers, parsley, and olive oil, it was invariably the choice of the popular singer Dinah Shore. As chef Michael Lomonaco warns in *The '21' Cookbook*, "While an entree-size portion would cost you a week's allowance of cholesterol, an appetizer-size Steak Tartare shouldn't do you in for more than a day."

Michael noted in his book that the longest-steady-diet award would have gone to perennial patron Hubie Boscowitz, who enjoyed a nightcap of steak tartare topped with two raw egg yolks after the theater nearly every night. He remained cheerfully unrepentant until the day he died at age ninety-four.

Except for steaks, far and away the most frequently ordered meat on the menu has been the '21' hamburger. Although details of the recipe have varied throughout the years, the '21' burger has always been served with brown sauce and no bun. So renowned was the '21' hamburger that it was Jimmy Carter's choice when he came in for lunch during the 1976 Democratic Party Convention that nominated him for president. Carter was accustomed to having a hamburger for seventy-five cents at a restaurant owned by Mr. and Mrs. David West a few miles from his hometown of Plains, Georgia. After the election some of the reporters who'd covered the campaign treated Mrs. West to lunch at '21', where her hamburger cost twelve dollars. She attributed the difference in cost to "high rent" in New York and to the '21' atmosphere.

Other items continually on '21' lunch and/or dinner menus included crab cake, caviar in a pastry cup, smoked salmon, foie gras with sweet and sour cabbage, prosciutto, Cuban black bean soup, Manhattan clam chowder, Senegalese soup, Sunset and Hunter salads, all sorts of seafoods, steak Dianne, poussin with red wine sauce, Long Island duckling, venison, hash brown potatoes, pommes soufflées, creamed spinach, and a variety of pastas.

Then there are the desserts. As best anyone can recall, the first to appear on the menu was rice pudding, followed closely by apple pancakes. Both are still served and are highly popular. Others much in demand are profiteroles (puffs) with vanilla ice cream, chocolate torte, port-laced chocolate mocha terrine, strawberry shortcake, poached pears in flaky phyllo overcoat with Madeira Zabaglione, chocolate-coconut truffles, chocolate pecan brownies, soufflé, sorbets, and apple pie.

For many years menus were handwritten in a combination of French and English in red and blue on both lunch (*déjeuner*) and dinner (*dîner*) menus. They are now printed (and dated).

As to the wine cellars, in the opinion of Andrew Simon, head of the British Wine and Food Society and one of the greatest wine experts of the day, '21' had the finest collections of claret and Burgundy in the United States and some of the most remarkable champagnes and spirits. For example, there was a Madeira 1804 that had been imported to the United States in 1810 and a couple of bottles of Margaux 1870.

"21"

A wine lover once got trapped in the cellar when an electric lock malfunctioned, and he was invited to help himself to anything in the bins while he waited to be rescued. He was so overwhelmed by the choices that nearly an hour later when the door was opened he was still trying to decide.

Occupying the hidden room that once confounded Prohibition agents, the cellar developed into a veritable museum of wine, as well as of vintage whiskey bottles kept as souvenirs of the foolish dry spell. The wine bins generally held more than six hundred varieties (reds, whites, and champagnes) ranging in size from ordinary bottles to magnums and gigantic Nebuchadnezzars. At any one time our temperature-controlled rooms contained over two thousand cases. Some bins also held bottles laid down for regular patrons. Over the years these private stashes were allotted to patrons ranging from presidents of the United States to corporate executives, film stars and directors, sports celebrities, and writers.

Among the reserves to be found in the cellar in 1998 were vintages set aside by the late John Huston, Richard Nixon (La Tache, a gift from Frank Sinatra), and actor Burgess Meredith, as well as bottles for Chelsea Clinton (champagne earmarked by her parents for her twenty-first birthday), David and Julie Nixon Eisenhower, Elizabeth Taylor, cosmetics tycoon Ronald Lauder, Gerald Ford, financier Ivan Boesky, and others whose names are meaningful in their social and business circles but not to the general public.

Drinks at the bar have always been a measure of the reigning taste in liquors, ranging from the "three-martini lunch" of the 1970s to the "I'll just have a glass of white wine" and Perrier fads of the fitness-conscious 1980s and the cognac and single-malt scotch fervor of the 1990s. One constant in all this has been the ability of the fellow behind the bar to produce whatever was being ordered—and to sense when the time had come to quit refilling someone's glass.

Certainly there was no one better at tending the bar than Henry Zbikiewicz, who came to work at '21' in 1946 and served until his retirement in 1987. The way to get Henry's attention (or that of any of the bartenders) was to ring a Siamese temple bell suspended at one end of the bar. Its clang meant that all the glasses on the bar or in someone's hand were to be topped off.

It was also a clarion call to storytelling. According to columnist Frank Farrell, when he came up short on ideas all he had to do was tug the bell and characters converged to spin yarns, some of which might have been true.

The bell was Mac's idea and gave rise to the formation of the aforementioned serenading Chuck Wagon Bunch, which Frank Conniff called "a boys' choir of lofty ambitions but rather restricted talent."

One version of how the "Bunch" got together was related by humorist Peter Donald, chief joke-teller on *Can You Top This?*, one of radio's most popular programs. He explained, "Somehow this gang formed around one corner of the bar like moss building up on the north side of a barn. It was kind of a luncheon club that met every day and just never got around to lunch. Only eight or ten boys for the nucleus—no two in the same racket and therefore no two equipped to bore one another with shop talk. A symphony conductor, a lawyer, a jeweler, a carpet tycoon, a steel magnate (I'm not going to gag around with that one), a comedian, an ad man, sundry newshawks, devalued millionaires and generally speaking the best damn bunch of drinking, laughing gents you'd ever want to drink or laugh with. We congregated every day to compare doctors' warnings and comfort each other's maladies and scare off intruders—snug in our own little Hangover Heaven. Then it all began to really jell. One day Mac politely asked us to join the busboys in serenading a birthday guest. That's what pulled these raggle-taggle gypsies together in a common bond of brotherhood and musical mayhem. Tonsils that hadn't been lubricated since choirboy days, lungs that couldn't wheeze through two mornings of the Camel cigarettes' 30-Day Test, harmonies that might have been achieved by rubbing two whooping cranes together—all these were unleashed."

Another group that congregated at the bar called itself the East Enders. Movie moguls, Madison Avenue ad men, and real-estate executives, they milled around the east end of the bar.

The third congregation of regulars at the bar called itself the Skeeters. Organized by sports broadcaster Ted Husing, it was made up of "admirers of the breed" who ventured to racetracks in the wilds of New Jersey, a state notorious for vast swarms of bloodsucking mosquitoes ("skeeters"—get it?). One of its charter members was sportscaster Clem McCarthy, whose gravelly voice was heard describing some of the greatest moments in horse racing, including the Kentucky Derby wins of Whirlaway (1941) and Citation (1948), and Native Dancer's victory in the 1953 Wood Memorial. In those days, if Clem McCarthy wasn't at the microphone to growl "Rrrrrr-ace-ing fans" and "They're OFF," it couldn't have been much of a contest.

That jockey hitching posts became symbolic of '21' was because so many leading figures in the world of thoroughbred racing were patrons of the bar and dining rooms. Among them was Warren Wright, owner of Citation and the stable Calumet Farms, named for the baking powder company. To celebrate

Citation's Kentucky Derby win he flew all the owners to '21' for a banquet and, of course, made sure the club got a jockey figure in Calumet's red silks.

While the '21' association with horse racing was well known, thanks to the jockey figures in front, not many people beyond the club's iron gate were aware of our close association with the New York Yankees. It began in 1945 when Larry MacPhail, formerly of the Brooklyn Dodgers, signed a deal to buy the New York Yankees for $2.8 million. The problem was, Larry didn't have the money, so he struck up a conversation with an old friend by the name of Dan Topping, who was fresh out of his military service in the Pacific. What Larry had in mind was making Topping a partner. Figuring that they were still short of the mark financially, they phoned Bing Crosby. Because Bing owned a racetrack (Del Mar) and could never be approved as a club owner by baseball commissioner Judge Kennesaw Mountain Landis, Bing put Larry and Dan in touch with multimillionaire Del Webb. The bargain was struck on the phone, and Larry walked out of '21' to close the deal.

Three years later, on October 12, 1948, '21' was chosen as the place to announce that the Yankees would have a new manager by the name of Casey Stengel. Speaking for the Yankees, Red Patterson explained why '21' was chosen for the press conference. "We were the Yankees. We went first class."

Casey, famed for his tangled syntax and meandering way of thinking out loud, got Topping's first name wrong; then, when asked how he felt about managing Joe DiMaggio (sitting right there), said, "I can't tell you much about that, being as since I have not been in the American League so I ain't seen the gentleman play, except once in a very great while." On his way out

Casey looked around '21' and said, "Ya know, I always wanted to join this club."

That remark was almost equaled when boxing champion Rocky Graziano came to the club as guest of honor at a luncheon. "Can you imagine them letting me into '21'?" he asked. "I'm lucky I can count that high."

For me, a personally rewarding result of Larry MacPhail's being a regular was the blossoming of a friendship between us. Being a lifelong baseball fan, I'd admired him since his debut in 1938 as the manager of the Brooklyn Dodgers. When he took the helm at age forty-eight he was a fabulous character. With red hair and a brash demeanor, he could be noisy and quarrelsome one minute and a real charmer the next.

What surprised me was his love of classical music. This was revealed to me one afternoon when I took a break from work to go to the gym for a massage and found Larry and Dan Topping getting rubdowns and listening to Mozart on radio station WQXR. They were not just listening. They commented on Mozart's genius as though they were music critics rather than partners in the Yankees.

My own appreciation of great music had started in my youth and included towering admiration for conductor Arturo Toscanini, maestro of the NBC Symphony, whose concert broadcasts originated only two blocks from '21' in Radio City's Studio 8H. Knowing he was so close, I hoped that one day he might drop in for dinner so I could meet him. But another NBC "man of music" came in often. He was Dr. Frank Black, head of the network's music department and conductor of the symphony when Toscanini was not wielding the baton. Marshaling the nerve to ask Dr. Black if it were possible for me to attend a

Toscanini rehearsal, I was thrilled to be told there'd be no problem, but there had to be a quid pro quo.

"It's quite a coincidence that you brought up the subject of Maestro Toscanini," Dr. Black explained, "because he's asked me to make arrangements for him to bring his wife and another couple to '21' for lunch. I know you give all of your customers class A treatment, but I hope you'll give the maestro class A-plus."

"For Arturo Toscanini," I exclaimed, "I'll personally assure that his welcome and our service will be triple-A-plus."

Indeed they were. I seated the party at a table in the Front Room where he could be easily seen and admired but not disturbed. To wait and serve only that table I assigned Walter Weiss, and Louis Ploneis prepared the food. The wines were our cellar's choicest. The desserts were as heavenly.

As promised by Dr. Black, the quid for my quo was tickets for me and Jeannette for a Toscanini rehearsal. But that wasn't the end of it. As an expression of my gratitude and admiration, I sent Toscanini several bottles of Italian cordials accompanied by an admiring note. He graciously reciprocated with an autographed photo which to this day holds a place of honor on a shelf in my living room.

Adjacent to my valued souvenir of Toscanini is a prized memento of a man I probably could not have come to know, and an experience I wouldn't have had, were it not for my association with '21'. It's a foot-tall bronze bust of Dr. Albert Schweitzer. This amazing relationship began on an afternoon when I was passing a small movie theater, the Guild, on Fiftieth Street. It specialized in "art" films. A billboard announced that the feature of the day was a documentary on the world-famous humanitarian and his work as a medical missionary in Gabon in equatorial Africa. With time to kill before I was expected at the club, I decided to see it. I came out deeply moved and wishing that somehow I might meet the good doctor and see what made him tick. I certainly did not expect to look up one day and see him dining in '21', so if I were to make his acquaintance I'd have to go to Africa. By the time I got to '21' I'd made up my mind to look into it.

I began by tracking down the photographer of the film and asking her how I might go about arranging a trip to Schweitzer's hospital on the island of Lambarene on the Ogooué River. If she could help me, I said, I'd put her in touch with my friends in the film industry to see about arranging wider distribution for her film. To my delight, she took me up on the proposition. I kept my end of the deal and she made inquiries about my going to visit Dr. Schweitzer.

A few weeks later she phoned to tell me that my visit had been approved and how to go about getting there. Thrilled by the prospect, I consulted with two '21' customers who knew their way around Africa, Frank Hunter and Robert Ruark. I then contacted British Overseas Airways and booked a flight to London and onward to Libreville in the Congo. This was not exactly the kind of journey that appealed to Jeannette, so the plan was that while I plunged into African jungles she would bide her time in Europe.

Accompanying me was a noted surgeon specializing in facial reconstruction who went to Lambarene once a year to treat victims of leprosy. To reach Schweitzer's hospital camp required a trip worthy of a Tarzan movie. At the end of a wild dugout canoe ride up the crocodile-infested Ogooué was the Nobel Prize winner, physician/surgeon, philosopher, proponent of the theory of "reverence for life," classical organist, and authority on the music of Bach—the most celebrated European in Africa since newspaper reporter Henry Stanley tracked down a supposedly "lost" missionary in 1871 and greeted him by saying, "Dr. Livingstone, I presume?"

Tall, thin, straight as a ramrod, with a bushy mustache and wearing white pants and shirt, black bow tie, and pith helmet, Dr. Schweitzer greeted me in German. Although I didn't know the language, I'd grown up speaking Yiddish, so we had no trouble understanding one another. We got along very well.

Having brought a few bottles of scotch, I also hit it off nicely with a group of Schweitzer's young medical assistants. They gave me excellent advice on how to get along in the camp. I was told to never leave any possessions out in the open because to do so would be interpreted by the natives as an indication that I did not want them anymore. I was also advised not to assume that a thick canopy of foliage would protect me from the sun; I should always wear a hat.

My most vivid memory of Schweitzer was not of him tending to patients, but of him shaving in the morning. Perched on his shoulder was a brilliantly feathered jungle bird. The doctor always greeted me with a smile and "Good morning, Herr Kriendler."

The most difficult memory of that journey is a visit to a leper camp operated by a young Japanese doctor and his wife.

When the time came to leave I asked Schweitzer what I might do immediately to help him in his work. His reply caught me off guard. He said, "Send sneakers for the patients and staff. Not shoes. Sneakers are best for getting around."

This was a truth I wished I'd known before I left for the Congo. The boots I'd bought at Abercrombie and Fitch proved to be very stylish and would have been fine for wearing while fishing for salmon in Scotland, but they were utterly wrong for tramping around in a jungle.

Upon my return to the United States, I phoned the chairman of U.S. Rubber Company and told him of Schweitzer's request. He quickly arranged to ship several hundred pairs of sneakers. When I returned to Lambarene the next year, I was pleased and proud to see them on the feet of hundreds of Schweitzer's patients.

Another need expressed by Schweitzer that I was able to be of assistance in satisfying was a particularly hard-to-get medicine for the treatment of leprosy.

I was also glad that a result of my visits (I made a total of three trips) was a burst of publicity on television for Schweitzer's work by NBC-TV's late-night talk show host Jack Paar, who was a frequent customer in '21'. After listening to me tell stories of my visits with Schweitzer, Jack decided to go and see for himself and to take along a camera crew. Jack's reports on his visits became a staple of his *Tonight Show* and provided national publicity for Dr. Schweitzer's work, which resulted in an outpouring of financial assistance from viewers.

I liked Jack Paar, but I thought he made a terrible mistake when he retired as host of *The Tonight Show* and told him so.

While '21' was a popular spot for celebrities of TV, movies, and the stage, and for owners and managers of sports teams, it never became a hangout for athletes. They liked Toots Shor's or Jack Dempsey's, primarily because they never had to pay for drinks and meals. From time to time we did see DiMaggio, who generally came in alone and sat by himself. Babe Ruth made rare appearances, always with an open collar so that he had to be handed a necktie, usually one of Jack's Western-style leather bolos.

The absence of players was offset by a plethora of sportswriters, starting with Heywood Broun and Damon Runyon, followed by Bill Corum, Bob Considine, and others.

A sports star who did frequent the club was the tennis pro Big Bill Tilden, friend and doubles partner of Frank Hunter. Big Bill's biographer and renowned sportswriter Frank Deford found the two men a real odd couple. He wrote, "A man's man in every way, Hunter has shot big game and chased good-looking women all over the world. But if he was completely different from Tilden in many respects, he was just as strong-willed, and he could dominate Big Bill on or off the courts."

Of his first visit to '21' in 1934, Tilden himself wrote, "Seeking congenial companionship and feeling that I should have with me one whose gastronomic abilities and activities were worthy of the best food in the world I naturally invited my friend and doubles partner Francis T. (Smarty) Hunter. I was slightly embarrassed to discover that he was an old standby at '21,' a habit instituted by friendship with Jack and Charlie but developed and intensified by natural gluttonous instincts that led him toward good food."

After a couple of drinks, Big Bill continued, the pair journeyed above "for a snack." Having been warned to expect steep prices, he had brought two hundred dollars to pay for "a modest bite of melon, steak, potatoes, peas, rolls, coffee with some ice or chocolate soufflees for dessert," but Hunter "added asparagus, salad, a soup and other minor details."

After taking a few minutes from his meal to table-hop among friends who included Helen Hayes, Charles MacArthur, Bea Lillie, Robert Montgomery, and Noel Coward, Big Bill finally made his way to his table, only to find that Frank was not there.

"Where is Mr. Hunter?" he asked a waiter.

"Mr. Hunter was called away unexpectedly on business," said the waiter as he handed Tilden the check.

Realizing Frank had taken him for a good-natured ride, Big Bill pulled the two hundred-dollar notes from his pocket and handed them to the waiter without looking at the sum on the check, which was considerably less than that. As the waiter tried to point this out, Bill grumbled, "The change is your tip, *if there is any change.*"

A few customers went beyond merely being sports observers and fans. Ted Husing, Gilbert Kahn, and William Randolph Hearst Jr. formed a '21' bowling team and were often seen leaving the club in white ties and tails heading off to an alley. There was also a baseball team whose roster included Hearst, Topping, Ben Hecht, drama critic John McClain, and jockey Eddie Arcaro. While not exactly a sports team, there was also a group of regulars who in winter challenged the customers and staff of Club 18, across the street, to snowball fights. An occasional participant was Ernest Hemingway. For the athletically oriented who didn't care for team activities, there was the upstairs gym.

One of those who wasn't given to physical exertion was the cartoonist Ham Fisher, creator of *Joe Palooka*, a popular comic strip about a boxer. Claiming to have found inspiration for "the American ideal" in Mac, Ham explained, "His manly grace, his handsome face appealed to me so that I knew this was to be the prototype of my heroic creation." He also said he based Joe's fight manager on doorman Jimmie Coslove, and that a moneybags character named Humphrey Pennyworth was based on Charlie Berns. But Ham warned, "If any of these bums expect any royalties, they're crazy."

Any 1950s cartoonist looking for inspiring characters need have looked no farther than '21'. As one writer noted, a customer in the club at this time would have rubbed elbows with Edward R. Murrow, Marlene Dietrich, Rex Harrison and his wife Lilli Palmer, Henry Fonda, Mary Martin, the Gabor sisters, Alfred Hitchcock having an ice cream dessert first and then a steak, Prince Rainier of Monaco, and the reigning beauty of Hollywood and one of Hitchcock's stars, Grace Kelly.

There was also to be observed a tradition (mercifully short-lived) of giving hot feet. This quaint prank appears to have been started by Monty Woolley (famous for playing Aleck Woollcott-inspired Sheridan Whiteside in *The Man Who Came to Dinner*). Monty was known to slip several matches under a victim's shoe, light them, and retreat to the bar to await the result.

If the festivities in the barroom weren't stimulating enough, there frequently were private parties which might be crashed a la Hemingway. One such bash in 1953 that attracted a good deal of attention in newspapers was held to mark the publication of *A House is Not a Home*, the memoirs of the Prohibition era's most famous madam, Polly Adler. When Jerry Berns was asked why we'd allowed a notorious brothel operator to throw a party at '21', Jerry asked, "Why not? Where else would Polly go?"

Actually, '21' and Polly had enjoyed an informal business relationship during the dry spell. She bought her whiskey from us, and if one of our patrons was seeking temporary companionship we gave him Polly's phone number.

A party receiving almost as much press attention was a spur-of-the-moment affair. To celebrate delivery of his new Constellation airplane Howard Hughes loaded the sleek four-engine craft with twenty-five starlets of his movie studio and flew them and a large number of friends to New York and took over the whole club for the night.

When Frank Loesser, Jo Swerling, and Abe Burrows celebrated opening night of their smash-hit musical *Guys and Dolls*, based on Damon Runyon characters, they decided the logical place for their party was Runyon's old hangout, '21'. As Abe Burrows reported in his autobiography, *Honest Abe*, after I made my way through the jubilant barroom crowd to extend my congratulations I gave him a pat on his bald pate and said, "Abe, with a show like this you can now afford to eat here."

Because of mounting demands for banquet services in the years after Polly's and Abe's parties, '21' developed an informal department to handle them. More than forty years after Polly and Abe celebrated within the walls behind the iron gate and the jockeys, the club was handling hundreds of private parties, from cozy dinners for two in the same (but greatly spruced-up) cellar room where Jimmy Walker hid away, to banquets in the sixty-foot-long main dining room. These affairs have ranged from wedding receptions to an extravaganza of two thousand for winners of the music industry Grammy Awards, held in the nearby Museum of Modern Art.

While '21' has never been a "take-out" place, there have been instances when meals were delivered to customers' homes. But none has matched in desperation and urgency the frantic call we got one evening from the wife of Broadway showman Joshua Logan.

The occasion was their twenty-fifth wedding anniversary, and Nedda had planned a dinner for 150 in their elegant apartment in The River House. She'd engaged a chef from the South to prepare one of native Louisianan Josh's favorite dishes—gumbo. But something went wrong. With the arrival of guests imminent, the chef announced that the gumbo had turned out to be inedible.

Frantically, Nedda asked Josh if he could think of a restaurant that might be able to rescue the evening. She answered her own question. "I know. Twenty-One."

I took her desperate call.

"Have you got anything prepared that you can send over?"

I told her we had some nice lobster Newburg.

"Fine," she said, sighing with relief.

"And chicken hash."

"That's good, too."

"And creamed chipped beef."

"That's fine."

"How many orders would you like? Six? Ten?"

"A hundred and fifty," she said, laughing a little. "Send everything you've got, as fast as you can get it here."

I'm proud to record that the food arrived well ahead of the 150 guests. And that Mr. Logan's check in payment was delivered the next morning.

Collecting on tabs was not always so effortless, and not every check presented by a customer could be assumed to be good, no matter how well-heeled the person who made it out and signed it. Unfortunately, a man whose checks always bounced was William Randolph Hearst Jr., one of four sons of the legendary newspaper and magazine tycoon. Evidently Bill

Jr. simply could not keep track of his bank balance. Faced with a string of rubber checks, we finally made an arrangement with the Hearst headquarters in which a phone call from us resulted in a messenger arriving in short order with cash.

One "paying the check" episode involved another customer for whom the problem wasn't being short of money, but the opposite. The customer was ensconced cozily at a corner table with a young woman. They'd been there for hours, closing time had come, and he showed no inclination to call for the check so we could all go home. When he continued to linger, I had the house lights brought to full brightness. Still no movement. At last, I came right out and told him we were closing and presented a bill for about one hundred dollars.

"All right, if that's your attitude," he said in a huff as he drew out his wallet. "Take your money out of this."

He handed me a one-thousand-dollar note.

Deciding two could play at that game, I signaled two waiters to accompany me upstairs to the office. Opening the vault, I directed them to gather all the bags of coins and bundles of small bills until we'd assembled on a waiter's trolley the change the man was owed.

As the mountain of money was rolled to the man's table, I said, "Your change, sir. Would you care to count it?"

Flushed with embarrassment, he pulled out his wallet again, took out a hundred-dollar bill and a twenty, shoved them in my hand and said, "Okay, you win. Give me back my G-note."

The next evening he was back. "I had a little too much to drink and got out of line last night," he said apologetically. "Can we forget the incident ever happened?"

With a smile I asked, "Last night? What incident?"

A contributor to the 1950 edition of *The Iron Gate*, Erich Brandeis, captured the essence of '21' in that decade in which the nation, New York, and '21' savored the sweet smell of success. He wrote:

> "21" is a significant number.
>
> At "21" the young man reaches his majority. He becomes a citizen. He is entitled to vote. His father no longer has to support him. He is on his own.
>
> At "21" the young woman has reached the age of consent, although in some states it's earlier. Whatever she does, she is responsible for it. She can no longer be called a "juvenile." She is a "woman of the world."
>
> But "21" has another significance. It is the name of a place where people reach their social majority. To be an habitue of "21" means to be in the swim, to be recognized as a connoisseur.
>
> New York has many fine places to eat and drink. At "21" one does not eat. One dines.
>
> At "21" one does not drink. Drinking at "21" becomes sheer delight because here the liquids served are members of the nobility.
>
> At "21" one enjoys himself but one does it with good manners and in good company.

Nine

CAMELOT NIGHTS

Someone once said (it could have been Bob Benchley or Aleck Woollcott) that January in New York City is a time for either sober resolution or a good time to think about flying south. For those who elected to stay or had no choice but to tough out the short, bleak, cold days and long nights the town offered plenty of diversions: white sales in the department stores, hockey and basketball at Madison Square Garden, boat and antiques shows, museums, concerts, opera, movies, and the Broadway theater.

Or you could go out to eat.

In January of 1960 there were about 15,000 restaurants ready to serve you. In the block of Fifty-sixth Street between Fifth and Sixth Avenues alone there were twenty-three. Between the same avenues on Forty-ninth you'd find thirty. If you could afford to eat in a different restaurant for every meal of every day you'd still be at it after fifteen years. But in that time a couple of thousand more would have opened and many would have gone out of business before you got around to trying them.

Should celebrity-watching have been a desired part of your dining-out experience in 1960 you could have gone to Danny's Hideaway (the showbiz crowd), the Oak Room of the Plaza (politicians), Sardi's (Broadway headliners), the Russian Tea Room (musicians), Toots Shor's (the sports world), or '21'.

If your bank account permitted you to partake of what food and restaurant reviewers called haute cuisine you could have cut your list to Cafe Chauveron, Forum of the Twelve Caesars, La Caravelle, La Cote Basque, La Grenouille, Le Pavillon, Lutece, Quo Vadis, Voison, and '21'.

Selections on the '21' menu on Saturday, January 9, 1960, included:

Fruits de mer:
  Bluepoint oysters ($1.60), cherrystone clams ($1.50), steamed clams ($3.50), combination sea food cocktail ($2.50), shrimps à la Russe ($2.25), and lobster cocktail ($3.50).
Hors d'oeuvres:
  Beluga caviar (price unlisted; if you had to ask . . .), French boneless sardines ($1.50), Morecombe Bay potted shrimp ($2.50), Bismarck herring ($1.50).
Potages:
  Philadelphia pepper pot ($1.00), clam broth ($1.15), consommé alphabet ($1.00), onion soup gratiné ($1.25), green turtle soup ($1.50), borscht ($1.00).
Poissons:
  English sole poché Condorcet ($5.00), Long Island Bay scallops fines herbes ($4.75), brook trout sauté Nantaise ($4.75), frogs' legs Provençale ($4.75), sea food Newburg, rice ($4.75).

Entrees:

Half chicken sauté chasseur ($5.00), escalopines of veal Gismonda ($5.25), roast quarters of lamb Judic ($5.50), sweetbreads under bell Tosca ($5.00), half Long Island duckling aux cerises ($5.75), braised sirloin steak Flamande ($5.50).

From the grill you might order royal squab en crapaudine ($5.50) or suprême of capon Virginie ($5.50).

Specialités de la Maison (prices unlisted): Scotch grouse (flown to '21'), baby pheasant, chuckar partridge, rock Cornish game hen, honey bear, wild boar, terrapin Maryland, baby turkey, chicken casserole '21' (for two).

Prices for vegetables (a la carte) ranged from a dollar to a dollar and a half. They included braised celery, boiled zucchini, spinach, imported French peas, heart of palm mousseline, cauliflower hollandaise, brussels sprouts, string beans, eggplant orientale, and carrots Vichy.

Potatoes (*Pommes*) a la carte: Parisienne persillés ($1.00), au gratin ($1.25), Lyonnaise ($1.25), baked Idaho ($1.25), hash brown ($1.25), and several other varieties.

Choices in desserts included a frozen soufflé with strawberry sauce for two ($4.50), Napoleon slice ($1.25), baba au rum ($1.75), crêpes suzettes ($2.75), compote de fruits ($1.25), pêche melba ($1.50), apple pancake ($2.25), rice pudding ($1.00), seasonal berries with Devonshire cream ($1.75), melon ($1.25), and macédoine de fruit maraschino ($2.50). Or you could have ice cream in the popular flavors ($1.00), an ice (lemon, lime, raspberry, pineapple, or orange) for a buck, or baked Alaska for two at four dollars.

Café diablé and café kirsch cost $1.75, espresso seventy-five cents, and regular coffee or orange pekoe tea half a buck.

And there would be a one-dollar-per-person cover charge.

Among those having dinner in the Front Room a year later (January 19, 1961) was the man who the next day would be sworn in as president of the United States, John Fitzgerald Kennedy. His father, Joseph P. Kennedy Sr., had been a customer at '21' for years. Of course, on that night when the president-elect and his wife, Jacqueline, dined with us no one expected that the offspring of a man who'd made a fortune in liquor after the end of Prohibition and would then become a movie mogul and have a torrid affair with Gloria Swanson would be the closest America would ever come to having a royal family. Nor that John F. Kennedy's abbreviated term in the White House would be seen as romantic and noble as the "brief shining moment" of a mythical kingdom then being re-created by Richard Burton and Julie Andrews on the stage of the Majestic Theater in Lerner and Loewe's *Camelot*.

I'd voted for Kennedy. Except for backing Eisenhower over Adlai Stevenson I'd been a Democrat since I'd gotten my feet wet politically as a ten-year-old kid sitting at tables in Uncle Sam Brenner's saloon and showing immigrants how to vote the way the neighborhood Democratic bosses wanted them to. But brother Jack had laid down rules for us concerning politics in the club:

Never let a customer know what party you vote for. There's no difference between Democrats and Republicans when it comes to the color of their money.

If a politician books a private room for a function make sure you get the dough up front.

Following this credo one day in July of 1976 nearly put me in a very embarrassing situation. It began with a phone call from a guy claiming to be a member of the Democratic National Committee. He introduced himself and said, "We want to take over your restaurant on Sunday for a fund-raising event."

Remembering Jack's admonition, I said, "Look, I don't know you, and unless I can talk to someone I do know, I'm not going to commit to closing '21' without a guarantee as to who's going to pay for it and when."

He paused a moment, then said, "Someone will be in touch with you, Mr. Kriendler."

The someone turned out to be the party chairman and an old friend, Robert Straus. He said, "Pete, that fellow you spoke to the other day was my man. Don't worry about getting paid. I'll guarantee it."

"No problem, Bob," I said. "I'll be away on a fishing trip, but I'll make certain before I leave that everything's set."

An hour or so later I got a call from New York governor Hugh Carey, another old friend. "Pete, what's this I heard about you not going to be there on Sunday?"

"That's right. I'm going fishing."

"The hell you are. You're staying put. You're the only guy I know who I can count on to make this thing go right."

"So what's the big deal? What big shot is this bash for?"

"Be there," Carey said, "and you'll see."

Come Sunday morning, in walked Jimmy Carter, wife Rosalynn, his mother, sister, and brother Billy. They were followed by five hundred of the Democratic Party's deepest pockets.

One of the leading figures in motivating contributions at the event was U.S. Senator Daniel Patrick Moynihan. Tall and dignified, he worked the room with drink in hand and radiated a combination of the beguiling charm and wit of the Irish and the erudite intellectuality of a Harvard don. And not a Democrat in the place appeared to hold it against him for having held a job in the Nixon administration.

Another frequent political presence beginning in the 1950s was the other U.S. senator from New York. As brainy and shrewd as Moynihan, Republican Jacob K. Javits had built his reputation in the realm of foreign policy and was the author of the War Powers Act, which placed limits on presidential authority to commit U.S. troops to combat without prior congressional approval. It was his custom when campaigning to not eat before he delivered a speech, but to come to '21' afterward for a hearty meal. Accompanying him was his beautiful and glamorous wife, Marian, whom I knew well because of our mutual interest in art and in spotting the up-and-coming young painters.

Although Richard Nixon did not come to '21' while he was in the White House, he frequently had lunch or dinner in the club in the years between his terms as vice president and his election to the presidency in 1968, and again in the post-Watergate debacle when he became a semi-recluse in New Jersey.

For most of his visits he was in the company of either or both of his business friends, Bebe Rebozo and Robert Aplanalp, who'd made his fortune from his invention of the nozzle which made possible the aerosol can. Rebozo was a Florida real estate developer and banker. He was best known to the public as Nixon's host at Key Biscayne, Florida, during Nixon's vacations. He and Nixon were fond of chopped steak, medium rare.

Of the two Nixon cronies, I was better acquainted with Bob Aplanalp. Puzzled as to why he was a steadfast friend of Nixon even after the disastrous Watergate scandal, I found the chutzpah to ask him. He shrugged and replied, "Pete, I just am."

I liked Aplanalp, but he had one peculiarity about which I could not bring myself to inquire. Despite being a very wealthy individual, he always wore the same pants and shirt. Sartorial criticism and his devotion to Nixon aside, I found Bob to be a warm, wonderful guy.

When he and Bebe joined Nixon at '21' they would arrive first, but the moment Nixon appeared their attention was riveted on him. Observing him from my vantage point at table 53 in Siberia, I was amazed and amused by Nixon's keen awareness that he was being watched, and that he clearly relished it.

President Ronald Reagan dined at '21' only after he'd left office, while Nancy Reagan came in several times, usually in the company of fashionable New York women friends. Yale man George Bush and wife Barbara showed up once in 1993 on short notice. And Gerald Ford lunched with us in 1994 on chicken salad from the $19.94 prix fixe menu. New York restaurants cooperate in a city-sponsored effort to encourage dining out by offering meals priced according to the year. A 1997 lunch, for example, was $19.97. It was a gimmick, but '21' had never been too snooty to go along with a clever marketing idea that was potentially good for the city—and for '21'.

Among city politicians who would prove to be not as willing as presidents and ex–chief executives to come to '21' were mayors Edward Koch and Rudolph Giuliani. Perhaps this was because they feared that a lot of voters might resent their presence in a high-class and expensive restaurant. Or maybe they simply didn't like the menu. Perhaps they were afraid they'd be seated in Siberia.

Not all patrons looked aghast at being seated there. Comedian Alan King preferred it. He told me, "I want everybody who sees me sitting here to know I'm enjoying *real* security."

One of the delights that first attracted Alan to '21' in the "Kennedy Camelot" years was our enormous supply of Cuban cigars, even after JFK struck back at Fidel Castro and his communist regime in Havana by imposing a ban on importing them.

In a brilliant move made in anticipation that Castro's takeover of Cuba might cut off our stock of Cuban cigars, Mac and Sheldon Tannen flew down there in 1959 with a quarter of a million dollars in cash in their luggage and went on a buying spree. When they came back with a deal for over a million cigars, a special humidor warehouse was constructed for storing them at sixty percent humidity. So when JFK slapped the embargo on imports of Cuban cigars in 1961, '21' aficionados were assured of long-term post-prandial lighting up of Cohibas and other prized Havana brands.

Not knowing how long the embargo would last (it was still in effect after thirty-seven years), we began acquiring cigars elsewhere, including Florida, the Dominican Republic, Honduras, the Canary Islands, and Nicaragua. Some of these bore our own '21' brand. Like everything sold in the club, the cigars were not inexpensive. When George Jessel bought three, he paid with a check he'd gotten for six months of royalties for one of his songs. After calculating the cost of the cigars and noting the amount of the check, the cigar counter clerk announced, "I'm sorry, Mr. Jessel, but you still owe forty-two cents."

The sales of cigars, cigarettes, and smoking accessories bearing the iron gate and '21' symbols, marketed as "'21' Selected Items," totaled almost a million dollars a year. They were sold at a counter in the lobby opposite the check room where we still offered copies of the latest books by our author-patrons.

One of those whose works we were proud to offer was Edna Ferber. Unfortunately for another regular, Moss Hart, a Ferber book was the cause of a confrontation between them that was fraught with suspense for Moss.

Edna had given him a copy of her latest book to read. While lunching with Irving Lazar, Moss saw her across the room and said to Swifty, "I haven't read her book yet. Hell, I haven't even had a look at it. How do I get out of here without her seeing me?"

Swifty said, "Let's try to sit here until she leaves."

They'd almost finished their meal, Moss had to get to another appointment, and Edna had barely started her lunch, so the only recourse Moss could think of was to try to conceal himself behind Swifty and depart as quickly as possible in the hope of not being spotted.

Almost clear of the room, he heard Edna's distinctive voice. "Moss, I'd like to see you a moment."

Trapped, Moss went to her table, all smiles, and lied, "I read your book, Edna. I just loved it."

"What did you think about the part of the priest? Do you think I was right to leave it in?"

With the sheepish look of a guy figuring he'd been caught, Moss confessed, "You got me, Edna. I haven't read it."

With the satisfied smile of a person whose suspicion has been justified, she crowed, "I thought not."

Evidence of the changes taking place in the 1960s could be found in the celebrities who came to the club. They were increasingly less likely to be authors and more apt to be recognized for their work in films and television.

From almost the first day that Jack and Charlie opened the iron gate at 21 West Fifty-second the front sidewalk became a popular location for celebrity-watching fans hoping to get an autograph, or perhaps a photo snapped with a star coming or going from the club. Earl Wilson made note of the phenomenon in one of his "Midnight Earl" columns. "A dozen autograph kids hang around outside waiting to see Paulette Goddard, Dorothy Lamour, Lana Turner or other stars who may be in town," he wrote. "It's Humphrey Bogart's favorite spot."

Those who were being gaped at called the crowd of onlookers "spotters." So fascinated by them was the playwright and former Algonquin Round Table member Marc Connelly that he wrote about the breed in the form of a fictional letter from a spotter named Roy. Part of it read:

> Two of the most interesting stellar material I have ever
> dealt with in front of the club are Bogey and Lauren, or
> "Betty" as Bogey calls her in private life. I never lose an
> occasion to greet them as they arrive and depart from the
> club. Sometimes Bogey turns a little when too many of us
> cover his arrival and jab their autograph books at him and
> the Missus. Like one time Bogey and Betty were making for
> a show or something and he found himself up against quite
> an eruption of spotters. There was a new spotter there
> named Hermy that we called Wormy Hermy on account of
> him having a rash. He was also older than the rest of us

being about maybe 18 and I am frank to admit a guy not very used to contacting big people like Bogey and Betty. "Right here, Bogey," he said. "Sign it to Hermy from his pal Bogey."

"Look, buster," Bogey said, "Why don't you commit insecticide?"

"You're a jerk!" Hermy called after him. Everybody laughed, but it was agreed that Bogey had come off best in the duel. And so it goes. Every day there is always something doing around the old '21' Club.

One customer who could walk past the spotters without being bothered happened to possess a fabulous collection of celebrity autographs. He was Irving Lazar, my law school classmate and the country's top talent agent. The signatures were on contracts he'd negotiated for some of the biggest names in show business, which included Bogart.

Although based in Hollywood, Swifty often came to New York and to '21', usually with someone he was representing or hoped to sign up as a client. A superstar who Swifty did not have in his stable was Frank Sinatra, although he could have signed Frank years before Frank hit it big in the early 1940s as the "crooner" who made girls in bobby socks squeal and then swoon in the aisles of the Paramount Theater.

Irving had heard about a skinny youngster singing in a club in New Jersey. When he went to hear him he liked what he heard and reported on Sinatra's talent to Harry James. The big-band leader gave Frank a listen himself and hired him. Frank was so grateful that he offered to give Irving the usual agent's fee of ten percent of his salary of seventy bucks a week. "It seemed silly to take a seven-dollar-a-week commission,"

Swifty told me (and later recorded in his autobiography). "So I suggested the kid wait till he was making real money."

Not long after that Frank was the singing sensation of the era. He went on to become so huge a success that twenty years after Swifty had passed up the chance to represent Sinatra they were neighbors in Beverly Hills. They were also close friends.

But it could be a stormy relationship. One night in the 1960s Frank was dining at '21' with his pal Jilly, owner of Frank's favorite New York hangout, Jilly's, on West Fifty-second on the other side of Sixth Avenue, which had a menu of Chinese food and a special chair that was brought out only for Frank to sit in. Turning to Jilly as Swifty came over to their table, Frank asked, "Is this the week I like Swifty, or the week I don't?"

Content to be the man behind the success of so many stars and to be able to slip past the gawkers with autograph books in their hands in front of '21', Swifty suddenly found himself in the flash of news photographers' cameras on January 9, 1966. The night before, he'd come to '21' with his wife, Mary, to join Truman Capote and socialite Slim Keith for dinner. They were given a choice table in the Front Room next to the table occupied by movie director Otto Preminger, his wife, Hope, and Louis Sobol and his wife.

They chatted for a little while as Swifty sipped from a glass of scotch. Always aware that he had a column to write, Louis asked Swifty, "Any news?"

"We just got into town," Swifty replied.

In the thick accent that had made him chillingly villainous as a Nazi in the movie *Stalag 17*, Preminger interjected, "Why don't you print that Frank Sinatra is going to punch Mr. Lazar in the nose and beat him up?"

darity numbers of people ...

WET SPOT GOES DRY AS RAIDERS ARRIVE

Agents Armed With a Warrant Get a Cordial Welcome at Speakeasy, but No Liquor.

TRICK SHELVES REVEAL WHY

Push-Button Had Dumped Bottles Into Chute and Only Odor Remained, Federal Men Complain.

Prohibition agents of the staff of Administrator Andrew McCampbell went to the Federal Building yesterday to complain about the way they had been treated Friday night at an establishment in West Fifty-second Street which the agents said was a speakeasy, but this allegation they were unable to prove.

The fact that liquid proof was lacking was the burden of their complaint. However, they were informed by Thomas E. Dewey, Acting United States Attorney, and David Marcus, his assistant, that they could do nothing about it.

When Montrose Rice, an agent, visited the establishment on June 20 and 22, he swore in an affidavit, he had been able to buy liquor on both occasions. Francis A. O'Neill, United States Commissioner, was sufficiently satisfied with his story to issue a search warrant.

Armed with this document, Agents Benjamin Lippi and Benjamin La Rosa called at the place on Friday night. Lippi pressed the doorbell and waited. In a minute an outer door opened and a door tender came out. An inner metal door closed behind him. He asked the agents what they wanted.

"You sell liquor here," said Lippi. "It's against the law."

"Yes," La Rosa seconded. "We are going to search the place. We have a warrant."

Another attendant, who had been listening to the conversation through a peephole in the inner door, opened the portal. He was cordial to the agents and greeted them, they said, as if they were long-lost friends.

After columnist Walter Winchell was banned from gathering gossip about '21' customers he ran an item pointing out that the club had never been raided by Prohibition agents. They did so a few days later and found liquor out in the open. This resulted in the building of secret liquor closets and a wine cellar with a special "invisible" door. The next time the raiders descended they found, as the *New York Times* reported, a cordial welcome but no liquor. (Photo courtesy New York Public Library)

This is the trick door made
of brick that concealed a
secret storage room holding
thousands of bottles of
wines and spirits. As
demonstrated here by Bruce
Snyder, it could be entered
only by pushing a metal
bar into a tiny hole, which
triggered an unlocking
mechanism. During one
raid that lasted more than
twelve hours, the feds never
discovered the camouflaged
door and the treasure
behind it. The room still
serves as the club's wine
cellar. And the door still
works.

Stored in the wine cellar behind the secret door are bottles of whiskeys and cognacs that date back to the Prohibition era. Bins also contain bottles held in reserve for regular customers. Three of these still bear the name of President Richard Nixon and were gifts to him from Frank Sinatra.

The success of Jack and Charlie's '21' created an acute shortage of space, so they decided to expand into the adjoining building at No. 19 and in 1935 sent a Christmas card to patrons announcing a "breaking thru" in 1936. The building at No. 17 was taken over later, forming the facade shown in this 1950s drawing.

New Yorker magazine cartoonist Zito's works have been displayed in the '21' barroom for more than half a century.

"Will that be all, Sir?"

This cartoon by Tom Laughlin, a founder of the group of loyal patrons from Yale University known as "Ben Quinn's Kitchen," depicts "Ladies going to the Third Floor," which for many years was the location of the club's only women's rest room.

NEW YORK WORLD-TELEGRAM, MARCH 18, 1936.

Jolly 21 Club Is Crowded
by a St. Patrick Day Party

Helen Hayes, Looking Like Victoria Regina in Person, Is Center of Brilliant Gathering.

By HELEN WORDEN

HELEN HAYES changes type when she changes plays. Yesterday at Jack and Charlie's 21 Club the star of "Victoria Regina" looked like a beautiful young Queen Victoria with her straight light-brown hair parted in the middle and slicked down over her ears. A little black taffeta hat that might have been a Victorian bonnet was worn far back on her head.

St. Patrick's Day was very gay at 21 W. 52nd St. Every table was taken. Among the familiar faces about us were Erskine Gwynne, the cousin of the Vanderbilts who has just returned from California; Dudley Field Malone, the divorce attorney; Myra Kingsley and her husband, Howard Taylor; Lois Long Arno, Helen Meany, the diving champ, Lady Montagu, John Rumsey, Charlie MacArthur. Helen Hayes' husband —and giving his party, Mervin Le-Roy, Quentin Reynolds, Eddie McIlvaine, George Atwell, Jr., Mrs. Morton Downey, Marjorie Franklin. George Monnet, Francis T. Hunter, Willard McKay, John (Shipwreck) Kelly and Norman Todd.

A birthday/St. Patrick's Day party for Helen Hayes in 1936, given by her husband Charles MacArthur, garnered this attention in the press. Helen was the only woman to be honored by having a '21' sandwich named for her.

Cartoonist Feg Murray paid tribute to five women movie stars and a champion swimmer who were regulars at '21' in the 1930s and '40s.

Because '21' was always regarded as a men's club, popular illustrators added to that perception by contributing work such as these to the club's walls. Dean Cornwell's drawing of the woman in the chair was captioned, "But I don't want to see your etchings! I want to go to '21'." Arthur William Brown titled his picture, "Censored for '21'."

With four Kriendler brothers on the premises most of the time, any employee who said "Mr. Kriendler" was likely to be answered by a quartet. Consequently, when we were addressed, the "Mr." was followed by a given name. Shown here in the 1940s (*left to right*) are Mr. Pete, Mr. Bob, Mr. Jack (also known as "Two-Gun Jack" and "the Baron"), and Mr. Mac.

Bob (*center*) and I mingle with President John F. Kennedy at the Football Hall of Fame dinner in 1961.

JOHN CARL KRIENDLER

When Jack died in 1947 at age forty-eight, newspapers hailed him as a colorful figure in the life of New York and a restaurateur with a genius for perfection. He is remembered in the club with an oil portrait above the lounge fireplace and a bronze plaque in the entrance vestibule.

With the untimely death of Jack, the running of the club fell to Mac (*above*), while Charlie Berns devoted most of his efforts to a club offshoot, 21 Brands, importers of fine liquors and wines.

HERE'S TO THE FANS
UNDER TWENTY-ONE WHO
HANG OUTSIDE OF TWENTY-ONE!

Betty Betz

Because so many celebrities were '21' customers, the entrance was frequently thronged by autograph seekers, as humorously drawn by Betty Betz in the 1950s. It was said (but not confirmed) that Humphrey Bogart brushed off a pimpled, pesky stargazer by telling him to go away and commit "insecticide."

Prince Valiant takes the long count at "21"

HAL FOSTER

©K.F.S.

A Royal Entrance
By
O. SOGLOW

O. SOGLOW

The '21' reputation for being expensive was reflected in these cartoons included in the 1955 edition of a commemorative book, *The Iron Gate*, marking the club's twenty-fifth anniversary.

"I TOLD YOU NEVER NEVER TO PRESENT THE CHECK TO A PATRON FACE UP!"

SWAN

QUICK, CINDERELLA! GET YOUR FAIRY GODMOTHER!

WALT DISNEY

SUNDAY NEWS, JANUARY 9, 1966

Otto Presses 50-Stitch Charge

By LEE SILVER and PATRICK DOYLE

Writers' agent Irving Lazar was arrested at his Park Ave. hotel suite late yesterday on a felonious assault charge pressed by movie producer-director Otto Preminger. A drinking glass had been crunched against Preminger's forehead at the 21 Club late Friday. Fifty stitches were required to close the wounds.

The fracas was said to have been over the film rights to the new book sensation, Truman Capote's "In Cold Blood."

Lazar, 58, was arrested at the Ritz Towers, 465 Park Ave. He said:

"We had an altercation. I didn't think it was this serious. It's too bad it happened."

Fingerprinted and Released

Taken to Police Headquarters, the highly successful literary agent was photographed, fingerprinted and released at 6:35 P.M.

His attorney, Sidney Cohen, said Lazar had been paroled in his own recognizance by Supreme Court Justice Gerald Culkin for appearance in Criminal Court tomorrow morning.

What actually happened in the usually sedate confines of the posh club? The accounts given by Lazar and Preminger to NEWS reporters vary widely.

"Tried to Hit Wife"

"He (Preminger) tried to hit my wife, Mary," Lazar insisted at headquarters. "He called me names, such as crook, thief; he embarrassed me and my wife in front of people; he was insulting and he leaned over, as if to try to hit her."

Explained Lazar about the crucial moment of injury:

"I tried to stop him from hitting my wife. A glass was in my right hand and it had broken."

Lazar said Preminger threatened him, but before he could elaborate, his wife and Cohen rushed up and put an end to talking. All drove off from police headquarters in a Rolls-Royce.

The 58-year-old Austrian-born Preminger expressed "shock and surprise" over the suddenness of the incident, which left him with a gash over the left eye and a cut lip.

The Argument Flares

Preminger said he was sitting with his wife, Hope, when the Lazars came into the club. The producer chided Lazar for selling the screen rights to Richard Brooks for $500,000 and 33% of net gains without first informing him and Frank Sinatra.

Lazar had offered Preminger a bid on the book two years ago as a vehicle for Sinatra, the producer said.

Lazar replied he hadn't made a firm promise and Preminger teased him about not fulfilling his promises.

"Lazar said, 'Don't call me a liar.' He got very angry and before I knew it he picked up a water glass and broke it on my head," the producer said.

"Lazar started to leave," said Preminger. "I got up to go after him, but his wife blocked me and they left.

"People from the restaurant stopped me from following, and I am glad now they did. I am a very large man and he is small (Preminger is 6 feet, Lazar 5-feet-3) and I am glad I did not have to hit him."

Bleeding From Face

Blood streaming from his face, Preminger was taken to a rest room and an attempt was made to stop the bleeding. He was removed to New York Hospital, stitched up, X-rayed and given a sedative.

He then returned to his home at 129 E. 64th St.

"I did not lose a fight; there was no fight," said Preminger. "I'm just shocked over how it happened. I was never angry. I was, in a sense, maybe teasing."

One thing both men agreed upon: Preminger did lose screen rights to "In Cold Blood," a saga of murder in Kansas.

Otto Preminger Gets bopped on head

(NEWS foto by Bill Quinn)
Detective Eugene Casey (right) escorts Irving Lazar from Police Headquarters.

This is the kind of newspaper attention a restaurant can do without. The occasion was an argument in the '21' barroom on January 9, 1966, between Hollywood super-agent Swifty Lazar and movie director Otto Preminger in which Swifty clobbered Otto with a scotch glass. This account appeared in the *New York Daily News*.

The New York Times
Maxwell A. Kriendler

M. A. KRIENDLER OF '21' CLUB DIES

President, 1947-'55, Served Liquor Affiliate 18 Years

Maxwell Arnold Kreindler, who was president of the famous "21" Club from 1947 to 1955, died yesterday at Mount Sinai Hospital. He was 65 years old and lived at 1016 Fifth Avenue.

Mr. Kriendler, who was known widely as "Mac," had been ill for some time. He had been hospitalized for cancer, but a spokesman for the restaurant, at 21 West 52d Street, said the immediate cause was pneumonia.

At his death Mr. Kriendler was a consultant for 21 Brands, Inc., a liquor distributor with headquarters next door, at 23 West 52d Street.

He had joined Twenty-One Brands, Inc., as president and treasurer in 1955 and in 1963 was elected chairman of the board of directors.

When Onassis Is Hungry, Onassis Eats

NEW YORK, Nov. 23 (NYT). —Sheldon Tannen and Bob Kriendler waited on Aristotle Onassis at the "21" club yesterday. Mr. Kriendler recommended the knockwurst and Mr. Tannen fetched the order.

Mr. Kriendler and Mr. Tannen were there because they are two of the owners of "21" and it has been struck by cooks, waiters and bartenders. Mr. Onassis was at the club because he was hungry.

Not since President Franklin Roosevelt and First Lady Eleanor hosted the king and queen of England at Hyde Park, New York, in 1939 and served them hot dogs for lunch had the lowly wiener gotten so much attention in the press as the day in 1972 when Greek shipping tycoon Aristotle Onassis settled for knockwurst and beer during a citywide strike by cooks, waiters, and bartenders.

GUIDING MENTORS
OF
 "21"

JERRY

Drafted from a drama desk in Cincinnati, a worthy replacement for his big brother Charlie . . . a man for detail as myriad and varied as the parts of a multiple stained glass . . . a shoulder sought after for advice and sympathy . . . whose devotion to his associates is matched by their fraternal love . . . whose nature takes knowing . . . whose spare hours are spent on a bridle path or puttering with camera film . . . whose hair is unruly and whose appearance is unstudied carefreeness . . . that's Jerry Berns of "21."

PETE

Making friends is his joy . . . fishing is his hobby . . . giving service to guests his watchword . . . from the trading of the exchange he joined his brothers to assist during trying times and remained as a mainstay . . . a bundle of nerves and energy exploding in constructive directions . . . sought after by people of all walks and climes . . . the giver of sound advice . . . always with the sparkle of joviality in his eye . . . that's Pete Kriendler of "21."

BOB

As much like his late brother Jack as Jack himself! . . . adds to his own stature by his intelligent approach to difficult situations . . . a clear thinker yet one modestly looking for advice of others . . . his mark made in many years with Marines in the Pacific is raised as a standard around which his division of the corps rallies . . . his indefatigable work for Rutgers has brought him Alma Mater's honors . . . his sartorial assortments are envied . . . his friendship is deep and sought after . . . that's Bob Kriendler of "21."

SHELDON

In training for administrative duties the younger generation moves in to give continuity to an institution and a tradition . . . from army duty in France this Kriendler nephew has moved to a multitudinous assortment of duties covering the entire premises of "21" . . . whose broad shoulders are the relief for chores necessary and important to the smoothness of a well oiled machine . . . whose youthful refreshness is remarked upon with universal acceptance by the patrons . . . whose future prospects are bright in his chosen field . . . that's Sheldon Tannen of "21."

Upon the deaths of Mac and Charlie Berns, responsibility for the operation of the club fell to Jerry Berns (Charlie's brother), Bob, me, and our nephew Sheldon Tannen.

Left to right: Jerry, Sheldon, Bob, and me.

When Bob's death in 1974 left me as "the last of the Kriendler boys," I seemed to be everywhere at once and became known by the club's employees as "the Electric Jackrabbit." But when I greeted a customer at the door, such as Michigan governor and Republican presidential candidate George Romney, I usually introduced myself with, "Welcome to '21'. I'm your saloon keeper."

Jeannette and me.

This signed photo of Arturo Toscanini was given to me by the legendary conductor of the NBC Symphony Orchestra. Because my wife Jeannette loved dachshunds, we had a succession of them through the years (each one named Mikimoto). These portraits of six Mikimotos were painted by famed watercolorist Dong Kingman.

This portrait of me by Gordon Wetmore hangs in my apartment and was commissioned by a customer who insisted on remaining anonymous.

"Mr. Pete" the fisherman, St. Lawrence River, circa 1960.

Had I not been associated with '21', it's quite unlikely that I would have found myself in Rome in 1958 on the chariot-race set of *Ben-Hur* with Ed Sullivan and Charlton Heston.

The guy on my left with the stogie helping me celebrate my seventy-fifth birthday is broadcaster Curt Gowdy. Coming in the door and looking more surprised than I was is Jeannette, followed by Jerry Berns.

My longtime secretary Judith Channell is regarded as much a part of the '21' tradition as the red-and-white checkered tablecloths and toys hanging from the ceiling.

According to Swifty, Preminger wanted to stir up a little trouble because Swifty had sold the movie rights to Capote's best-seller *In Cold Blood* to producer Richard Brooks instead of to Preminger. The remark about Sinatra looking to beat up Swifty referred to a story going around that Sinatra had wanted to star in the film based on the Capote book about a pair of wandering misfits who massacred a Kansas farm family. The juicy role went to Robert Blake instead.

"Louis, please don't print this," Swifty said, putting down his drink. "Otto thinks I'd promised him Truman's book. I never did. As for Sinatra being mad that he won't get to star in the movie, that's rubbish. I've seen him several times since the book was sold with no fisticuffs."

Louis asked if he could print simply that Frank Sinatra and Otto Preminger wanted to buy the book but Swifty Lazar had sold it to someone else.

"Okay with me," said Swifty. "How about you, Otto?"

Preminger answered, "Swifty sold it for five hundred thousand. I wouldn't have paid that much. It's not going to be that good a movie."

Exasperated, Swifty pleaded, "Otto, it's academic. Let's just drop it."

Turning red from his shirt collar to the top of his bald head, Preminger growled in his *Stalag 17* tone, "You, Lazar, are a liar, a cheat, and a crook."

"Otto, please," Swifty begged. "You've got to stop this or we can't be friends. It's one thing to insult me—I can take it. But this is offensive to Mary."

Preminger leaned close to Sobol. "I tell you right now, Sinatra is going to beat Lazar up when he sees him. And to prove it, I'm going to call him."

As Preminger signaled a waiter to bring a telephone to the table, Swifty said to Mary, "Otto has been getting roles as a Nazi in the movies, and now he's trying to be one."

"Not at all," said Preminger as the phone was placed before him. "Sinatra is going to tell me how he's going to beat Lazar up, and Mr. Sobol is going to print it."

"You're making it impossible for us to remain here, Otto," Swifty said in dismay, gesturing to the waiter to bring his bill.

As Mary Lazar got up from the table, Preminger said to her, "You pitiable creature. I feel sorry for any woman who has to go home and go to bed with that crook."

"You're a dirty old man," Mary replied as she underscored her outrage with a slap across Preminger's face.

When Preminger leapt to his feet and lunged at Mary, Swifty grabbed up his scotch glass and brought it crashing down on top of Preminger's bald pate. This was quite a feat. Preminger was over six feet in height, while Swifty seemed barely taller than five. The force of Swifty's blow shattered the scotch glass.

Blood streaming down his forehead and cheeks, Preminger was rushed to a hospital. His head needed fifty stitches. Once that was done, he told police he wanted to press charges. The next day Swifty was arrested at his hotel for felonious assault, bailed out, and taken back to his hotel by his lawyer in a Rolls-Royce.

A newspaper account of the incident noted, "This is not the first time Swifty Lazar has drawn blood from a producer. He does it every time he negotiates. This is merely the first time he used a deadly weapon."

In the forty years in which the Kriendler family had been in the business of selling drinks, and in the thirty-six-year history of '21', that was the first time (and the last) that a drink at '21' was described as potentially lethal.

"Still the snappiest restaurant in New York," declared *Spy* magazine in 1960. "Bar for lunch, upstairs for dinner. Lunch for two can easily cost $35 and the prices for the drinks are really outrageous. A caste system operates in this plush spot separating the big from the small and the biggest from them all."

The theme of exclusivity was also made in a long article on the club in *Cosmopolitan* magazine. Writers Richard Harrity and Aileen St. John Brenon reported, "Through an iron gate on West Fifty-second Street in New York City there passes daily from noon to past midnight a procession of wits and worldlings, artists and writers, some of the world's most beautiful women, titans of big business and potentates from the five continents. They are the 'in' people of the world—the rich, resplendent and renowned. It is a favorite of the Duke and Duchess of Windsor, the Shah of Iran, the Prince and Princess of Monaco. The Astors, Vanderbilts, Rockefellers and Roosevelts maintain active charge accounts there. Nobel Prize winners Ralph Bunche and John Steinbeck are frequent patrons. Joan Crawford, David Niven and Rex Harrison are in almost daily attendance while in Manhattan."

In this period we were open every day but Sunday, serving about a thousand customers daily, and taking in around three million dollars a year. Out of that sum we were paying the salaries of a staff of 287. We employed 120 in the dining rooms as captains, waiters, and wine stewards. Then there were barmen, greeters at the door, check room and cigar counter folks, the telephone switchboard operators, powder room and men's room attendants, and housekeeping staff.

Between the 1968 and 1969 professional football seasons one of our employees was the New York Giants' placekicker Pete Gogolak, who thought he might go into the restaurant business himself after his football career was over. It lasted another ten years, but Pete instead became an executive with R.R. Donnelly Company of Chicago, the largest printing firm in the country.

While Pete was apprenticing, Louis Ploneis and assistant Anthony Pedretti supervised a kitchen staff of a hundred as they prepared, among other '21' menu specialties, filet mignon Sorti Rossini at fourteen dollars (for two), a brace of partridges for fifteen dollars, and breast of capon aux amandes at eleven dollars (also for two).

Often the kitchen was called on to satisfy customers who'd traveled a long distance just to dine at '21'. One such gourmet was an oilman who telephoned from Oklahoma to make a reservation for the next evening. He would be dining alone, he said, and proceeded to dictate to me the following order:

Course	Wine
Golden caviar	
Green turtle soup	Victoria sherry
English sole bonne femme	Batard Montrachet 1959
Scotch grouse roti	Grands Echezeau Domaine de la Romanee-Conti 1955
Braised celery	
Wild rice	
Chocolate soufflé	Dom Perignon 1955
Demitasse	
Havana cigar	Hine Triomphe cognac

The tab for this indulgence was eighty-seven dollars. The tip was another twenty-five.

Another patron phoned to carefully order dinner for himself and a woman companion. He told me he wanted caviar, a consommé Bellevue, Chinese pheasant, endive and beet salad, and for their dessert a soufflé Grand Marnier. I informed him, regretfully, that the Chinese pheasant wasn't available, but that we had very nice hazel hen.

"But I must have two Chinese pheasants," he said, almost shouting. "Don't you know that everything I have ordered is an aphrodisiac and that Chinese pheasant is the most potent of all?"

"I didn't know," I said, "but now that you've told me, it doesn't alter the fact that we have no Chinese pheasant. Might I suggest Scotch grouse?"

Obviously figuring he had no choice but to put his trust in the combined power of the rest of the menu and hope for the best, he grudgingly accepted the grouse. When I told Mac and Bob about the alleged benefit of Chinese pheasant Mac laughingly suggested that when we put it on the menu the next time we ought to give serious consideration to hiking its price.

In five decades in the food and drink business we'd gotten used to eccentricity on the part of some of our regulars. There was, for instance, a gentleman who came in daily for a lunch that lasted a minimum of five hours. He began with a couple of cocktails and an assortment of hors d'oeuvres, followed by a catnap at the table. Then came the entree, a bottle of wine and another brief snooze. The meal continued with cheese and dessert, coffee and cognac, topped off with another rest. When he awoke he asked for another helping of the entree. You might suppose that if he knew he was going to have seconds of whatever entree struck his fancy he would order a double portion in the first place, yet he never did.

Other regulars who took advantage of New York's nightlife and slept throughout the day arrived at midafternoon for a Bloody Mary or another pick-me-up and then sat down for "breakfast." One of these night owls invariably ordered cold roast duck. Another's routine began with four whiskey sours, half a dozen Lynnhaven oysters on the half shell (in season), a Napoleon, and coffee.

The leading man of swashbuckling movies, Errol Flynn, also dined early. He'd come in around four in the afternoon and start with a Jack Rose cocktail (Apple Jack, Rose's lime juice, splash of grenadine). The entree was whatever game was on the menu. The wine was Bordeaux. By 5:30 he was gone.

Greek shipping tycoon Aristotle Onassis expected to find on his table the makings of a Bloody Mary, which he mixed himself, and a dish of garlic pickles. Businessman Jack Hausman knew that waiting for him when he came in for a lunch was a single-pretzel appetizer.

Customers also knew they could order "off the menu." Some of these requests could be pretty bizarre. Charles W. Lubin, founder of the Sara Lee cake company, wanted a particular kind of triple-whipped thin pancake, the recipe for which he brought with him. Another liked scrambled ground beef laced with a potent sauce. A third always ordered chipped beef in cream sauce with grapes. As long as what was requested could be made with ingredients we had on hand, we did our best to deliver it—and charged accordingly.

Upon the retirement of Louis Ploneis in 1966 the kitchen became the domain of Anthony Pedretti. Although he'd been born in the United States, as a child he'd been taken back to

Italy by his parents and had been forced to join the Italian army during the war. When he returned to America in 1946 he worked as a fry cook at the Barclay Hotel, then worked in the kitchens of the McAlpin and other hotels. He'd come to '21' in 1959. His specialty was hollandaise, made in two-gallon batches twice a day.

The sauce was a favorite of the boss of a firm that became a neighbor of ours in its new headquarters at 51 West Fifty-second on the northwest corner of Sixth Avenue (renamed Avenue of the Americas during the war, but never called that by old-time New Yorkers). Presiding over CBS in a grand black marble tower, which was promptly dubbed Black Rock, William S. Paley had been a regular since the network was housed on a few floors at 485 Madison, with studios scattered all over Midtown.

Paley sometimes ran into another broadcasting pioneer at '21', General David Sarnoff, founding father of RCA and NBC. So fond of our food was he that when he was recovering from a mastoid operation in the late 1960s he eschewed the hospital food and called '21' to arrange delivery of both lunch and dinner.

Among stars of both networks who frequented '21' was Jackie Gleason. Although famed as a drinker, "the great one" did not do his serious imbibing with us. He preferred bending the elbow at Toots Shor's bar just down the block. Jackie was the only guy we'd let into '21' whom we knew was drunk. He'd come in for lunch and order a rib steak at table 30 in the rear of the barroom. He was always alone and, I believe, feeling lonely. He invariably asked me to keep him company.

The first time he did so, I replied, "I'll be delighted to join you for a few minutes, Mr. Gleason."

"Hey, pal," he said, "I'm not *Mr.* Gleason. I'm Jackie."

"I appreciate that," I said, "but it's our policy that no customer is ever addressed by anyone who works at '21' by his or her first name. And that policy applies to the owners."

This was true.

"When Sinatra asked me to call him Frank," I said to Mr. Gleason, "I gave him the same lecture."

With a laugh, Gleason replied, "Whatever you say, Pete."

From that point on we were, as he liked to put it, "pals." I not only thought he was the greatest comedian on television, I believed he'd proved himself to be a great actor in his role as Minnesota Fats opposite Paul Newman's Fast Eddy Felson in the movie *The Hustler*. Observing that he always had a bottle of wine with his meal, I decided to treat him to a really fine Burgundy, which at that time cost fifty dollars a bottle. He tried it and enjoyed it, so I told him I'd see that a case of it was reserved for him in the cellar.

The next time he was in for lunch I saw with horror that he had a bottle of Burgundy in a champagne bucket. Rushing to his table, I demanded, "Mr. Gleason, what the hell are you doing? You do not put that magnificent Burgundy *on ice*."

He sat there looking at me with the same wounded expression millions of fans of his hit show *The Honeymooners* saw in the face of Ralph Kramden after Ralph made a fool of himself again in front of his wife, Alice.

On another occasion as I went over to his table I saw that he was staring toward the bar. When I sat beside him he pointed a finger in the same direction and declared, "Pete, I have to have that train. I've got a collection of model trains and a huge layout in my new house in Peekskill. Sell me that one."

I explained that the model locomotive, tender, gondola car, and caboose displayed on the wall behind the bar in a glass case had been presented to the club by the president of a mid-western railroad. "I don't think he'd be pleased the next time he comes in and sees it's not there."

"Well, the hell with him. I gotta have that train."

"I can't give it to you without his permission. When he's here next time, I'll ask him."

"Tell him I don't give a damn what it costs me."

A couple of weeks later when the railway man showed up I kept my word and relayed Gleason's message.

"If he wants it that bad," he said with a cunning smile, "tell Mr. Gleason he can have it, but there is a price. He has to mention the name of my railroad on his TV show."

Informed of this, Gleason said, "I'll do better than that. If he gives me that train I'll mention his railroad every week for a month."

"There's one other problem, Mr. Gleason," I said solemnly.

"What problem?"

"If I remove the train and give it to you there's going to be a big gap on the wall behind the bar."

"So put something up in its place."

"That's easily done, Mr. Gleason, but I think whatever goes there should be something from you."

Sensing I had something in mind, he chuckled. "Okay, Pete. Whadda ya want from me?"

"When I saw you in *The Hustler* you used a special pool cue that came apart and fit into a carrying case. I want that cue and the case."

"Pete, old pal," he said, laughing, "you got it."

Indeed, I did get it. And after the railroad president heard his company's name on Gleason's show not once but four times, he was so thrilled he gave '21' a duplicate of the model train.

Railroads are also represented in the barroom by two huge locomotive bells. Gifts from the president of the Pennsylvania Railroad, they stand on a shelf that separates the middle and front areas of the barroom. They form the backdrop for Michael Douglas and Charlie Sheen in their luncheon scene in the movie *Wall Street* as they sit at table 3, Charlie Sheen confronted with uncooked steak tartare as Douglas's character, Gordon Gekko, eats nothing.

"Lunch," Gekko cynically declares, "is for wimps."

I'm sure that anyone who ever paid the check for lunch at '21' would agree with me that a person who believed such a thing could exist only in a work of fiction.

Ten

THE GO-GO YEARS

Little by little throughout the 1960s, as a new generation discovered sex, drugs, rock and roll, and rebellion against anyone over thirty, the restaurant business in New York found itself challenged. All over the city the great eateries and clubs were losing out to spots where music and dancing were regarded as more important than the offerings on the menu (if there was one).

Among the new "in" spots were Mr. Laff's, partly owned by baseball player Phil Linz; Maxwell's Plum; Friday's; Harlow's, a discotheque; and Arthur, a playground for well-heeled youths of all ages. If you wanted to catch a glimpse of the Andy Warhol crowd you'd find them at Max's Kansas City near Union Square.

The jazzy music of Swing Street was largely a thing of the past, and even the strip joints were passing into oblivion in an onslaught of wrecking balls. By 1971 our longtime next-door neighbor Leon & Eddie's had been shuttered and replaced, temporarily, by Toots Shor's, which had moved up from Fifty-first.

After Toots abandoned the Leon & Eddie's location the building remained vacant. Fifty-second was a clutter of parking lots and boarded-up facades. In short, Swing Street was a shambles, with only '21' in place to remind New Yorkers of what it had been.

With shocking suddenness the Pavillion, Colony, El Morocco, and the Stork Club were also gone. The last was demolished to make way for a vest-pocket park bankrolled by CBS's William S. Paley. For places that remained, business was declining between ten and forty percent a year.

"New York watchers proclaimed it the death of haute cuisine itself," observed authors Michael and Ariane Batterberry. "Within a very short period, an extraordinary number of New York's best restaurants, all French and all of the haute cuisine caliber, had closed their doors."

But not '21'. Happily, we kept going by offering exactly what our customers wanted—good food and drink in a hospitable atmosphere. "But it's luxury dining," said my brother Bob. "Not gourmet dining."

Columnist Mel Heimer called it the magic formula. "The big thing," he said, "is that you are comfortable. The place is reasonably quiet. It is warm in winter and cool in summer. Lighting is dark enough to quiet a hangover and bright enough to read the outlandish prices by. If there is a drunk at the bar, he is a well-behaved drunk. The people are handsome and well-scrubbed, the cocktails are big and enjoyable, and the food fills the hungry man with pleasure. And when you have been clipped in the pocketbook and sent blissfully on your way, you still have that last souvenir with you, the legality of saying to the people you meet later in the day, 'Well, when I was lunching at "21" today. . . .'"

After passing through the iron gate, a customer who came in for lunch, dinner, or just drinks at the bar went down a couple of steps and through the door held open by an outside doorman. Within, he would be greeted by Chuck Anderson, Monte Sideman, Michael Bemer, or Tom Ray. Ahead to the left was the check room and across from it the counter and display case offering cigars, cigarettes, '21' items, and books of leading authors of the day: John Updike, John Le Carré, Richard Condon, Studs Terkel, and Peter Benchley (Nat's son and Robert's grandson).

If the reservation was for one of the rooms on the second floor, a customer could choose the stairway where Hemingway enjoyed his dalliance with Legs Diamond's girlfriend or take an elevator reached by going through the lounge where Brendan Gill had dared John O'Hara to put up or shut up. It's here where customers who'd arrived early for their reservation or were waiting for a lunch, dinner, or drinking companion felt as if they were in a combination men's club and art gallery devoted mostly to Western themes.

Author Marilyn Kaytor described the lobby this way: "Few people see the front of '21' without its hustle, bustle and commotion of people, kisses, and little exchanges of gossip and news between management and patrons. But if one can disregard the porridge of people, he will see a lobby and lounge sporting gray-green, whirly carpeting that butts up against a plaid pattern, the two totally discordant but somehow part of the sporty character of the place. Set off against the carpets are wood-paneled and green walls, leather chairs and sofas, television sets, and a fireplace where logs crackle merrily in wintertime, over which hangs a portrait of John Carl Kriendler. In a predominant corner is a large glass case with boots and a ten-thousand-dollar silver saddle called 'The Bar 21,' once Jack's pride and joy."

Take the stairway or elevator to the second floor and you'd enter an ambiance of quiet conversations in sedate surroundings luxuriously appointed with white table coverings and sparkling silver and china catching the glimmer of crystal chandeliers. Go past the cigar counter and stairway and, depending on your mood, you found either an English public house that Charles Dickens might have recognized or a Dodge City saloon the likes of which had been enjoyed by Wild Bill Hickok and the Earp brothers.

A benefit of operating on two floors was the ease with which we could accommodate a customer who feared the consequences of accidentally running into another patron. Those expressing such concerns were usually husbands in the company of women who were not their wives (and were unlikely ever to be). In these instances fraught with unpleasant potentialities we simply seated the women upstairs and the men in the barroom, then did our best to assure they didn't leave at the same time.

We also showed discretion regarding a sensitive relationship involving Sheila MacRae, who was separated from Gordon, singing star of movies, TV, clubs, and summer theaters. Sheila wanted to keep her affair quiet because she feared the negative effect it might have on Gordon, who wanted to get back with her. Of course, the man she was seeing did not want his wife to find out. Why Sheila couldn't recognize there wasn't going to be a happy ending I have no idea. I felt sorry for her. I liked her and had many pleasant memories of her and Gordon in happier moments in '21' as they zestfully sang along with Mac.

According to Sheila's memoir, *Hollywood Mother of the Year*, she finally recognized the futility of the affair with the man she called her "Jewish Prince" in a chance encounter with him in the rain in front of '21'. He was leaving as she was arriving. I saw her a few minutes later in the lounge. Seeing her crying as she stared at the door in hopes he'd come back, I took her hand and asked, "Sheila, when are you going to give this up? Come on!"

She sadly wrote in her book that running into him outside '21' showed her it could never be completely over between them, just as she'd never gotten over her love for Gordon.

No woman who came to '21' personified the tragic ending more than Jacqueline Kennedy. For a time after she had settled in New York following JFK's assassination she'd come to the club in the company of Frank Sinatra. When she became a Doubleday book editor she had lunch with us two or three times a week for discussions with her Doubleday authors or writers she hoped to sign up. One of her favorite meals consisted of broiled lamb chops. Or she might order turbot poché au court bouillon with sauce mousseline. When she dined with Aristotle Onassis we assured their conversations wouldn't be overheard by the simple device of not seating anyone at tables on each side of theirs.

Among our more garish customers was the bantam-sized author whose book *In Cold Blood* had been the spark which had set off the confrontation between Swifty Lazar and Otto Preminger. Although Truman Capote was by no means a "regular," he frequently arrived with two of the era's most glamorous women, Mrs. William "Babe" Paley and socialite Slim Keith. No event exemplified the triumph of the "pop culture" at the start of the decade more than a ball given by Capote at the Plaza Hotel. Guests were ordered to wear masks and dress in black and white. Of this odd bash, acerbic social commentator Cleveland

Amory said, "This is almost a joke. Fond as I am of Truman, I think we can say that society is not only *kaput*—it is Capote."

Another figure crowned as the royalty of pop culture, who led its adherents to such temples as Studio 54, Cheetah, and Electric Circus and to worship "art" in the shape of Coca-Cola bottles and cans of Campbell's soup, was Andy Warhol—who, as far as I am aware, never set foot in '21'. But a subject of Warhol's work in praising and promoting everything "pop" did. Marilyn Monroe was given a private tour of the club by Bob.

While Monroe, Warhol, Capote, and Jackie Kennedy represented a shift in the nature of celebrity as the 1970s got under way, I had only to look around at the neighborhood to see more permanent changes. Each day as I went to work I was acutely conscious of the revolution taking place in the geography of West Fifty-second Street. The brownstones being demolished were to be replaced by skyscrapers of corporations which didn't exist when Jack and Charlie found a bargain in real estate at No. 21.

Forty years later the land was not only even more valuable, but what stood on it was a thriving business. With Mac at the helm the enterprise was grossing about four and a half million dollars a year. Sidelines such as the 21 Brands venture brought in another two and a half million. The physical assets, including the three buildings, their contents, and the art, were worth many millions more.

This financial tally sheet made '21' an object of appeal for a development subsidiary of the Ogden Corporation and its president, Ralph Ablon. He'd taken over the company from an architect and entrepreneur, Charles Luckman. They'd worked out and shaken hands on that deal in '21'. Expressing an interest in acquiring the club, Ablon offered $12.5 million in an exchange of stock and a guarantee that our family would stay on and run things. It was a tempting offer. Negotiations dragged on for nine months. Then a plunge in the stock market brought a sharp decline in the value of Ogden shares. When the deal fell through our regular customers breathed a sigh of relief.

One writer described '21' in 1970 as an "all-in-the-family operation where nepotism works, with each contributing to the profits by helping to keep alive the mystique that is the most valuable asset of '21'." Movie moguls Jack L. Warner and Samuel Goldwyn, notorious in Hollywood for hiring relatives, regarded '21' as the most successful example of family favoritism since the Wright brothers. This did not mean non–family members could not be part of the club management. We were increasingly aware that not only was '21' more than likely to outlive the Kriendler brothers, it would also probably continue beyond the next generation. Consequently, after the failure of the Ogden sale in September 1969 we augmented the family executive group with a young professional manager. A boyish-looking Oklahoman, Bruce Snyder came to us from the Marriott Corporation's in-flight food service operation and would prove to have a phenomenal memory for customers' names and occupations.

Not long after he arrived on the scene our concerns about assuring that '21' would continue traditions were sadly confirmed. While vacationing in Palm Springs, California, Charlie died. He was sixty-nine.

Of all the tributes then and before concerning Charlie's acumen as a quiet, behind-the-scenes businessman with a keen eye on the books and a sharp lookout for a good idea, I think none was more heartfelt and to the point than Mark Hellinger's whimsical contribution to the 1936 *The Iron Gate*. Noting

Charlie's "sparkling ideas," he wrote, "When '21' opened it was the only restaurant in the world where ladies were compelled to walk up three flights to powder their noses. The climb made them so tired that, when they reached the ground floor again, they were compelled to sit down for another drink. This idea, alone, paid the cost of the joint within a month."

Recognizing that Jack had the natural instincts and talents required of "the man out front," Charlie had been content to keep out of the limelight. But I know that had it not been for the "Charlie" following "Jack" in "Jack and Charlie's" there would not have been a '21'.

Yet '21' carried on. With a daily capacity for serving 466 diners in 1971, we were averaging about fifteen thousand dollars a day in receipts and an annual gross of about four and a half million dollars. A drink at the bar cost $1.65. A hamburger was $14. Dinner for two ran between $30 and $75, plus the tips for a waiter, headwaiter, captain, sommelier, and bartender.

The next year the head of the Dining Room Employees Union Local 1 announced that unless owners of the city's top restaurants agreed to union demands for substantial increases in wages and benefits, chefs, waiters, waitresses, bartenders, busboys, and other workers would strike. The union was seeking a two-year contract containing a ten-dollar-a-week raise for each year of the agreement. For '21' that would amount to a substantial increase in operating costs.

After members of the Restaurant League were unable to agree on a unified position, individual restaurants were free to deal with the union separately. A few settled. Those who did not were struck. During the middle of November there were picketers in front of O. Henry's Steak House, Sardi's, La Cote Basque, and about a dozen other places. When the strike hit

'21' many regular customers volunteered to help out. Among them was writer/producer Arthur Kober. He manned the bar. Socialite Liz Whitney waited on tables. Each day John Edelstein rushed from his executive position with W.R. Grace & Co. to lend a hand at stoves and work side by side with members of the Kriendler family: Bob's wife Florence, Jerry Berns's wife Martha and their daughter Cecily Berns Miller, Sheldon Tannen's wife, Ellen, and Jeff Tannen. Charlie Berns's wife, Molly, supervised the bar area.

Regarding being assigned to cook, John Edelstein confessed amazement. "For some reason they thought I had experience, so I didn't say anything because I thought it would be fun," he said. "We made simple hors d'oeuvres—fresh shrimp, herring, crab meat, prosciutto, and things we just arranged on service plates. Entrees were limited to duckling and filet, and the rest of the menu was asparagus with hollandaise and a dessert of strawberries in liqueur. I learned that really great raw food carries itself. We did not have to hokey it up. I was amazed. But those pots and pans, even empty, weigh a ton. We didn't finish washing them and dishes until the sun came up."

When Aristotle Onassis assumed his seat at his usual table on November 23 he looked at Bob anxiously. "What am I having?"

"Well, we have hamburgers," Bob replied cheerfully, "and we also have kosher hot dogs."

"I'll start with a vodka," said Onassis, "then I'll try the wurst with mustard and a bottle of beer."

The bill was ten dollars.

The next day's coverage of the strike in newspapers across the country featured the Onassis angle. The *Chicago Tribune* gave it the headline ONASSIS HAS KNOCKWURST AT '21'.

The news was even flashed around the world. The *Herald Tribune* international edition headlined:

WHEN ONASSIS

IS HUNGRY,

ONASSIS EATS

Although there was no apparent relationship between the issues of the strike and the newspaper stories that Onassis had been forced to eat such a lowly meal, the walkout was settled that very day.

Two years later, the lowly hot dog was the main course at a party held in the Puncheon Room by Atheneum Publishers. The event was to celebrate the publication of a book about George and Ira Gershwin. The bash was planned by Alice Regensburg of the Lynn Farnol Group. Arriving at the club in anticipation of a truly swanky meal, disappointed *New Yorker* magazine writer Geoffrey Hellman cornered Alice and said, "Only you could plan a party in '21' and serve hot dogs and sauerkraut!"

Book launches had always been held at '21', but none was so meaningful to those of us who worked at the club than a luncheon given by Metro-Goldwyn-Mayer in 1977 for Mary Hemingway. Entitled *How It Was*, her book was a memoir of life with Ernie.

In addition to arranging parties, tending to especially particular palates such as that of Aristotle Onassis, protecting the privacy of celebrities of the 1970s, and supervising the everyday operations of '21', Mac was active in the American Legion and had served as post commander of Air Force Post No. 501. (He'd retired from the air force as a colonel in February 1968.) Other civic and charitable organizations benefiting from Mac's service included Boys' Town of Italy, the George Junior Republic, the Aerospace Foundation, and the Air Force Association, of which he was a director. He also served on the board of Freedom House and continued his friendship with Rex Stout. When he learned that Rex was about to publish the *Nero Wolfe Cookbook* he was delighted and looked forward to the publication, scheduled for August 8, 1973.

Mac never saw it. Undergoing treatment for cancer at Mount Sinai Hospital, he developed pneumonia and died on August 7 at the age of sixty-five. He'd been married and divorced four times and left three sons, John, Christopher, and Maxwell; daughter Jessica; our two surviving sisters, Anna Tannen and Eunice Sercus; Bob; and me.

One of the most telling tributes to Mac had been expressed years before his death by writer Ulric Bell. Bell said, "In war and peace, I have seen Mac apply his burning belief in freedom like a persistent hotfoot. Mac cares not who writes the nation's laws as long as they are written right. Nor does it matter who writes the nation's songs, as long as Mac may sing them over a loaf and a jug. And Mac cares not who fights America's wars as long as he is among the first to fight."

Bob succeeded Mac as president of the firm. At age fifty-nine, married to Florence, with sons Jeffrey and John Carl and a daughter, Karen Nelson, and maintaining a deep interest in Marine Corps activities, he operated from a third-floor office with walls covered with pictures of himself with celebrity customers, including one taken when he'd escorted Marilyn Monroe on her tour of the club.

Prior to Marilyn, another glamorous star of the silver

screen had become one of my favorite customers. But I'd been smitten by Joan Crawford years before the iron gate went up on Fifty-second Street. Ever since I was a high schooler hanging around the Red Head I've been "a leg man." And when I was in college there'd been no more beautiful pair of what gossip columnists called "gams" on the movie screen than those of Joan Crawford. When she started showing up at '21' in the 1930s she did so on the arms of matinee idols, two of whom she married—Douglas Fairbanks Jr. (1929–33) and Franchot Tone (1935–39). Her third husband was another actor, Phillip Terry (1942–46). The fourth and last was Alfred Steele, whom she married in 1956. He was chairman of the board of Pepsi-Cola. When he died in 1959 she joined the business as a boardmember and publicity executive.

Joan's preferred drink at '21' was Smirnoff vodka. Seated at her usual table upstairs, she almost always ordered calves' liver and bacon and a spinach salad, also with bacon. If she were not having lunch or dinner with another Pepsi executive or courting somebody in the advertising game, or on occasion negotiating a deal for one of her occasional returns to the movies, it was my pleasure to be invited to keep her company. Had I not been very happily and devotedly married to Jeannette, I might have dared to see if there could have been more between us than a friendship.

Another movie star with beautiful legs whose screen career was more past than present or future, but who continued to dress up the club in the 1970s, was Ginger Rogers. Her first grand entrance had been in 1930 on the strength of a Broadway hit in George Gershwin's *Girl Crazy*. That success took her out to Hollywood and eventual film immortality as the dancing partner of Fred Astaire. But whenever she returned to New

York she made her way to '21.' In the seventies she'd also made a transition from movie star to the world of commerce as fashion consultant to the JC Penney retail chain. Ginger fancied our chicken hash.

A third actress to go from screens (TV and movies) to a new career in business was Polly Bergen. No matter what else she was having, her order included an ample helping of sauce maison.

Still looking after our customers as maitre d' in 1975 after twenty years was Walter Weiss. Guardian of the front door was a charming Irishman, Harry Lavin. Originally from Sligo, Ireland, Harry had worked briefly for Toots Shor before joining '21' in 1974 as a server of drinks in the lounge. His dream then had been to win promotion to captain in the upstairs rooms. But when an opening came for a greeter, Bob decided that Harry's Celtic charm would be more valuable to the club in that capacity. It proved to be a good fit. Harry not only stayed in the job, but his beguiling manner and gentle diplomacy earned him a place in a roster of employees characterized as "legendary."

Also deserving that accolade was Anthony Pedretti, our executive chef. Sporting a white toque and white double-breasted jacket, he was assisted by associate chef Matharin Beneat and the night chef, Joe Rivera Jr. Their staff was made up of forty-five cooks (sauce, fry, fish, vegetable, broiler, cold meat, and fresh fish), salad and fruit men, and bakers. Anthony's duties also extended to training kitchen personnel.

As Bob explained to an interviewer in 1975, "We take boys who come in and show an aptitude. They may come in a pot walloper, and suddenly they're a vegetable man, then they seep up in the ranks. It's a real thrill when we see one of them ultimately wearing a white hat."

For weekend getaways Bob took Florence and family to what a writer called "the Kriendler-Berns Long Island compound" in Westhampton Beach. It was also where Bob went in April of 1974 to recuperate from open-heart surgery. By August he was feeling good enough to return to presiding over our weekly staff meetings and day-to-day operations of the restaurant while "schmoozing" with customers who included Republican powerhouses Governor Nelson A. Rockefeller, Senator Jacob K. Javits, Henry Kissinger, and, on one occasion, President Gerald R. Ford. Ford was not allowed to depart without having his picture taken with Bob and promising Bob that if he sent it to the White House he'd autograph it. Eager to add the photo to those on his office wall, Bob was in Westhampton on August 15, 1974, when he was stricken with a fatal heart attack.

The funeral service at Temple Emanu-El was attended by more than 1,500 mourners, whom the *New York Times* described as a "mingling of civic leaders, Mr. Kriendler's Marine Corps and Reserve comrades and what many of those present called the '21' crowd." In that number were Julius Hallheimer, who'd beaten the Prohibition raiders in 1930 and continued as our lawyer for forty years before retiring, headwaiter Tino Gavasto, and Emil Diana, who'd been with the club for twenty-eight years. Restaurateurs in attendance were Vincent Sardi, Toots Shor, and P. J. Moriarty. An eight-man Marine Corps Reserve honor guard stood watch, two at a time, beside the flag-draped coffin.

Rabbi Ronald B. Sobel called Bob "preeminently a man of a great, good heart, a man who was host to the great and famous but who also gave of himself totally on behalf of the not-so-great and the unimportant."

Colonel Alexander W. Gentleman, with whom Bob had served on Guam in World War II, called him a man with a gift for friendship who had five great loves: his family, his country, the Marine Corps, Rutgers, and '21'.

The service ended with taps played by a bugler and the Marine Corps hymn as a recessional by the temple organist.

Honorary pallbearers were Senator Javits, Marine Corps Commandant Robert E. Cushman Jr., New York Attorney General Louis Lefkowitz, former Rutgers University president Dr. Mason Gross, Art Buchwald, Earl Wilson, and Louis Sobol. Louis declared, "It is rather too early a passing for a man who was part of an era."

With Jack, Mac, three of our sisters, and now Bob gone, only two of Carl and Sadie Kriendler's children survived—Anna and me.

Eleven

THE "ME" DECADE

A t the start of the 1950s Lucius Beebe had observed that the annals of the Kriendler family's business could be divided into three distinctive eras: its beginnings in the days of Prohibition and the torrid Roaring Twenties, what F. Scott Fitzgerald called "the years of the great tea dance"; between Repeal and the war, when New York public life was taken over by café society; and the postwar "nightclub society" period in which patronage of such expensive premises was dominated neither by fashion nor personal wealth, but by the expense-account executive and his brother in arms, the expense-account publicist. They spent corporate funds for corporate ends in a multinational corporate America that seemed hell-bent on proving that President Calvin Coolidge had hit the nail on the head concerning the nation when he declared, "The business of America is business."

The symbol of the third era of '21', which would continue for the remainder of the century and toward the third millennium, was the "power lunch." Assessing the phenomenon in an article entitled "The Power of '21'" that appeared in the October 5, 1981, issue of *New York* magazine, reporter Richard West judged '21' "the most powerful and famous restaurant in the country, a place of refuge and glory for the rich, the influential, the celebrated."

West also painted a word picture of me at the age of seventy-six as a "connoisseur and an extrovert" obsessed with rooting out whatever I saw as "treasonous to '21' principles." Describing his visit to '21', Mr. West continued, "Pete Kriendler looked splendid coming down the stairs from the dining room to the lobby, a red carnation in the buttonhole of his dark suit."

Reporting on watching me as I saw someone I didn't know on the way out with an old friend, West wrote, "In a gravelly voice that suggested he gargles with carpet tacks he said, 'How are ya? I'm Pete Kriendler and I'm the boss. Did ya enjoy the meal? Was everything all right in the saloon?'"

My next activity, according to West's essay, was to go "on the prowl to assure the ship was in good shape." Entering the barroom, I paused to pay "respects" to "*New Yorker* heavies" Peter Fleischman and George Green, asking the dapper Green if he got the shrimp cocktail without dill, as he'd ordered. I then lamented to another customer the closing of my favorite Italian restaurant, La Scala; gave a wave to someone else; and checked on the condition of two "warming tables" in each section to assure that the Sterno burners were working properly and that service tables had a supply of sauce maison jars, silverware, and napkins.

Under the careful scrutiny of the *New York* writer, I next asked the captain to see if Doubleday chairman John Sargent and his companion, Constance Mellon, were ready for dessert.

This was followed by a request to Walter Weiss to bring a telephone to the table of Gerald Schoenfeld of the Shubert Organization. Hearing a noise, I said, "Walter, tell that busboy we do not slide chairs here. We pick them up."

Noticing that Joseph Kennedy III had been placed at table 28 in the rear of the barroom, West expressed surprise. I explained, "If these young people get full star treatment now, what do they have to look forward to in thirty years?"

Also lunching in the middle bar section that day were Louis Russek of Health-Tax, seated at table 21 under the "Maxwell's Table of Happy Memories" plaque; the movie producer and director Robert Altman at Bogie's table (No. 30); and Frank Polk, at his usual spot at Siberia's No. 53.

"All three sections of the bar were filled, the air charged with the thick smell of tarragon sauce and cigar smoke," continued the *New York* article. "It was a noisy crowd of businessmen, coupon clippers with the air of perpetual leisure, and sleek women with summer-colored skin, slender wrists, and slim legs—all a display of expensive, imported health. Prospective diners and drinkers-only stood two-deep along the mahogany bar, which curves the length of the room, munching Charles Chips pretzels (less salt) from fine silver bowls and sipping $3 ginger ales and more costly Bloody Marys mixed by silver-haired Henry Zbikiewicz, bartender since 1939 (his only job)."

Observed that day as I made my tour of the club were: Otto Preminger at table 3, his bald head long since mended and showing no sign of the spot where Swifty Lazar had smashed a scotch glass on it; Fred de Cordova, producer of Johnny Carson's *Tonight Show*, having replaced financier Felix Rohatyn at table 5; Christina Ferrara DeLorean; Mrs. Donald Trump; Mrs. Douglas MacArthur and Dr. Armand Hammer lunching together; New Jersey governor Brendan Byrne; and New York Cadillac tycoon Victor Potamkin.

This is what Richard West saw after he ascended the green-carpeted stairs to the second-floor dining room: "A large serving room occupies the center of the floor at the top of the stairway, and to the left of the stairs, toward the rear of the building, the small Tapestry (Tables 105 through 114) and Bottle (200 through 211) Rooms, the latter displaying eleven champagne-bottle sizes from a one-fourth bottle split to the giant twenty-bottle Nebuchadnezzar."

These back rooms were generally regarded as undesirable by most of the movers and shakers of the day—akin to Siberia in the barroom—but some businessmen preferred them because of their very seclusion.

In the main front room one found a beamed ceiling and cream-colored walls, dark wainscoting, a collection of Georgian silver plates, pewterware, urns, cups, samovars, plates, and tankards valued at four hundred thousand dollars. Here diners found quiet surroundings; silverware, white linen tablecloths and napkins in place before their arrival; tangerine carnations on the table, red and white ones in the corners. It was a more habitable place for serious business talk, a sanctuary more suit-ed for stratagems than the livelier bar below. "It is a room," West wrote, "that brings to mind Samuel Beckett's line 'Something is taking its course.'"

It may be argued that in the 1980s no man exemplified and embodied Calvin Coolidge's business maxim more than Marvin Davis. He had been coming to '21' since the mid-1940s, brought by his father, Jack Davis, who'd made his money in the Seventh Avenue garment trade. Four months before *New York* magazine assigned Richard West to visit '21', Marvin had bought Twentieth Century Fox. By coincidence West was engaged in research for his article when Marvin came in for lunch.

As Marvin's limousine glided to a stop in front of the club, outside doorman Fred Diel alerted Harry Lavin at the reception desk. Harry passed the word to escort Freddie Porcelli. Notification of Marvin's imminent presence was also conveyed to me and to Sheldon Tannen (executive vice president), who greeted Marvin in the lobby and accompanied him into the barroom, where Walter Weiss guided Marvin to his usual table, No. 15, nearest the kitchen.

Across the way at table 2 was builder William Levitt (of postwar Levittown fame). Next to him was Molly Berns, lunching with Mary McDonough Phillips of *Town and Country* magazine. Felix Rohatyn was awaiting the arrival of Citibank's Walter Wriston. Hilton Hotels' managing director, executive vice president for corporate properties Greg Dillon was seated near singer Morton Downey and his wife, Anne. Jack Paar and his wife, Miriam, were not far away, and directly below a model of an Ashland Oil Company truck suspended from the ceiling sat Orin Atkins, Ashland's boss.

But all of these luminaries were about to be upstaged with the arrival of former president Richard Nixon and wife Pat. This was the second presidential party in three days. Gerald and Betty Ford had come in for a late dinner after attending the musical hit *Amadeus*. President Ford had a hamburger with ketchup and Mrs. Ford ordered hash Calcutta. Like the Fords, Nixon was seated at table 10 with the gold "Richard Milhouse Nixon, President's Table" wall plaque.

One of my favorite customers was financier Paul Mellon. He once told me, "Pete, if you had one-half of one percent of

"21"

the deals made in '21' you might even be richer than you are at this moment." Paul was a Yale man (class of 1928). As a charter member of the Comanche Club he was almost always accompanied by other Yalies. He was also a great philanthropist and an appreciator of fine art who donated masterpieces to museums in the United States and Great Britain.

Other favorites of mine who played important roles in the world of high finance were Felix Rohatyn, who masterminded the bailout of nearly bankrupt New York City in the mid-1970s, and the Rudin brothers, Jack and Louis, who managed most of the major buildings in the city. The most colorful millionaire frequenting '21' was Malcolm Forbes, owner of *Fortune* magazine. A collector of motorcycles, he generally arrived at the club on one and with a crash helmet that made him resemble an astronaut. He'd arrive sporting a leather biker's jacket over his suit and sometimes on top of a tuxedo. He never stopped trying to persuade me to climb on behind him for a spin around the town. My excuse was that I was too busy to leave the club. He was also crazy about hot-air ballooning and proved just as relentless in attempts to entice me to go up in one as he was about turning me into a motorcyclist. I managed to avoid floating into the wild blue yonder on the basis of my obligations to '21'.

As a collector of toys (mostly lead soldiers and trains) Forbes was fascinated by the assortment of models hanging from the barroom ceiling. Fortunately, he never emulated Jackie Gleason in appropriating one of our items for himself. Malcolm was a very good friend to '21' and to me until the day he died.

All of these great men of commerce showed the traits found in all those who become leaders of men, including compassion and empathy for others—and, of course, a facility for making money, not just for themselves but for the people working for them. One infallible measure of such individuals was how they treated the staff of '21'. If a waiter liked someone it wasn't because he was a good tipper. The customer had proved to be a decent and kindly disposed person.

While the country's prosperity under Ronald Reagan remained to be realized, '21' was thriving. Our 1981 receipts of ten million dollars had more than doubled those of 1967 ($4.5 million). Added to that sum was a million in sales of cigars and '21' gifts under the Selected Items banner, and four million garnered by our Irongate Products operation. According to the accounting firm of Laventhol & Horwath, the typical top-ranked New York restaurant could be expected to do an annual business of sixteen thousand dollars per seat. A seat at '21' averaged twenty-five thousand dollars.

Looking out for the books at this time was Jerry Berns. Like his brother Charlie, he was the cautious money man. But Jerry was also busy representing '21' as a member of various national restaurant organizations, on the executive board of the Culinary Institute of America, and overseeing the administration of '21' scholarships aimed at assisting and cultivating talented young men and women who had their eyes and hearts set on careers in the restaurant business. He also joined me in keeping in touch with all aspects of the work of various Kriendler foundations which we had established in the memories of Jack, Mac, and Bob.

As important to us as these other interests were, nothing was as close to our hearts and more vital as ensuring the health and vitality of the cornerstone of the Kriendler-Berns-Tannen families—the '21' club—from morning to night.

What continued to fascinate me was how the character of '21' changed throughout a day. If you thought of it in human terms it could only be described as someone who woke up in mid-morning, put in a busy day, stayed up pretty late, and was never at a loss for lively companionship at any point in that long day. But there was a period in the afternoons after the departure of the "power lunch" crowd when things slowed down enough for me to take a rest or even a refreshing nap before the arrival of the cocktail set and those who wanted dinner.

"By 2:30 the dining room was empty, and only a few remained at the bar," noted Richard West in *New York* magazine. "The bosses had retired to upstairs offices; Walter Weiss had started home to Long Island to nap and change his tux; the second shift in the kitchen had arrived, including the busboy who wraps the lemons in surgical gauze; only the bartenders, Phillip behind the tobacco counter, and Naini Shekhar, one of the greeters, were in place. The restaurant settled in for a brief siesta. Only in the early-morning hours between three and four, after the cleanup crew had left and before the first kitchen worker, would there be another period of inactivity at 21 West 52nd Street."

In these quiet hours it was easy for me to conjure up the spirits of customers and friends who would have marveled as much as I did at the success of the direct descendant of the Red Head, Fronton, and Puncheon; and to sorely miss the two men who'd built a speakeasy into a New York institution and left it to others to perpetuate.

"It is this continuity—unchanging, unaltered, faithful to its code," Richard West told readers of *New York* magazine, "that has made the '21' club the most powerful and famous restaurant in the country. Now in its fifty-first year, it has not

been worn down by obsession but has been tested and strength-
ened by endurance. Like many of its older, loyal patrons, it is
experiencing with undiminished esprit a second life better than
the first."

At the age of seventy-six I found it both thrilling and more
than a little humbling to realize I was "the boss." Because I
seemed to pop up everywhere at once, the employees started
calling me "the Electric Jackrabbit." My seeming omnipresence
wasn't only because I felt an obligation to see that everything
was exactly as our customers expected it to be, but because I was
having a hell of a good time. Yet who wouldn't have felt that
way? Where else would a guy like me find himself having a chat
on the same evening with oil industry wildcatter Michael
Halbouty, former Miami Dolphins partner Earl Smalley, actor
Darren McGavin, Seagram's owner Edgar Bronfman, NBC
president Bob Sarnoff, opera diva Anna Moffo, movie star Cliff
Robertson and his stunningly gorgeous wife Dina Merrill, and
Arlene Francis and her husband, actor Martin Gabel . . . and
then be told by Walter Weiss that Frank Sinatra had just
arrived?

Had Bob Benchley been able to wander in and assume his
spot in the corner, he'd have discovered a lot of changes had
been made to keep '21' up to speed with the times. First, he
would have found that we not only extended credit to customers, but that to obtain it all they had to do was take from
their wallets or purses a small piece of plastic (the credit card
had arrived at '21' in the early 1970s). Then, I'm sure, Bob
would have shaken his head and offered some witty observation
concerning the presence of television sets in the lobby,
installed as replacements for the stock ticker that had afforded
the latest quotations to the money men of Bob's day. And I had

no doubt Bob would have been dismayed to learn that we no longer offered the services of a masseur and a barber to trim his hallmark mustache. The telephone switchboard was also gone.

Evidence of a new era on West Fifty-second Street was found all around us. The physical transformation begun in the 1950s in which old brownstone houses were cleared for the rise of skyscrapers was all but completed. We found ourselves bracketed and dwarfed by towering structures, from the massive silver-toned Tishman Building at 666 Fifth Avenue to the austere and elegant CBS headquarters known as Black Rock at the corner of Sixth Avenue.

An indication of how valuable the properties in the block between those buildings had become could be found in a narrow, oddly shaped lot next to '21' that had been the site of Leon & Eddie's and for a brief period the location of Toots Shor's bar. But because it was narrow and shallow and adjoining properties were not available for expansion, its ownership had changed at least four times. (In 1980 it was taken over briefly as a Reagan For President campaign office.) The value of this plot along the western wall of '21' and the east side of the new E.F. Hutton headquarters had gone from a million dollars in 1976 to $7.5 million. (The land would ultimately be acquired as a home for the Museum of Broadcasting.)

Setting aside the value of '21' as a prosperous restaurant and looking at 21 West Fifty-second Street strictly in terms of an investment in real estate, Jack and Charlie's purchase of the property for $130,000, and the successive additions of 17, 19, and the buildings housing 21 Brands, had been a brilliant move.

Although 21 Brands had been a publicly offered operation with shares sold on the American Stock Exchange, '21' itself had always been privately held as a partnership. As a result of the prosperity of the club itself and the value of the land under it, we were from time to time asked if we'd care to sell. One of the earliest offers to buy had come from Jack Warner, but it had been made in sort of a half-joking way at a time when we weren't interested. And there had been the previously discussed failed offer by the Ogden Corporation in 1969.

Another suitor who came along was a Texas oil billionaire, Enrico di Portanova, who wanted to give the club to his wife as a present. In 1980 he offered $13 million for fifty-one percent of the club and its buildings. Because I have never been fond of the idea of being a minority owner I was not enthusiastic, although the deal would have required the new owner to guarantee that the family would stay on as management. This proposition slipped into limbo and eventually died.

But in 1984 I reexamined my position. With my brothers gone and myself not getting any younger (I was seventy-nine years of age and had been working since 1929), I wondered if the moment had come for me to make a change which would allow me more time with Jeannette, and leisure to take fishing trips and concentrate on other interests (more about these in the next chapter).

There was no lack of parties interested in buying. During the summer of 1984 Donald Trump came forward with an offer. But he wanted a deal in which he would pay out the price over ten or twenty years. We insisted on a five-year arrangement. No deal.

Next to step forward was Marshall Cogan. An entrepreneur and a regular '21' customer, he'd recently lost out on acquiring Sotheby's auction house. He and his partner, Stephen Swid, made an offer of $21 million for the club. Their partnership eventually disbanded, but the deal went through, leaving

Marshall as owner of a club he described as "important an institution in its field as Sotheby's is in the world of art."

I was optimistic regarding Cogan's purchase not only because the deal included consultations involving the Kriendler-
Berns-Tannen family in the operation of '21', but because
Cogan's wife, Maureen, was committed to preserving the
unique qualities of the club, especially regarding the art collection. She brought in an interior designer, Charles Pfister, to
oversee the refurbishing in a manner that would be respectful
of the club's past.

As Marshall Cogan would eventually concede, the transition did not proceed flawlessly. While renovations were going
on, a new management team was put in place. Cogan engaged
Ken Aretsky and Anne Rosenszweig, founders of the successful
nouvelle cuisine restaurant Arcadia, and Alain Sailhac, then
the head chef at Le Cirque. He brought along a saucier named
Michael Lomonaco. This new team decided to abandon the
'21' tradition of serving steak in the upstairs dining room.
Henceforth, if you wanted a steak you'd have to eat in the barroom. The upstairs menu was strictly nouvelle cuisine.

Regular customers were aghast. Many stayed away. A
writer for the *New York Times* noted "frissons of alarm and
apprehension among '21's legions of devotees unlike anything
in memory—as if the Department of the Interior had decided
to jazz up the Lincoln Memorial to put Honest Abe more in
sync with the 1980s."

In his '21' cookbook Michael Lomonaco termed it "a fiasco." Marshall Cogan said, "I made a concerted effort to upgrade
the quality of the food. But I did initially make it too frou-frou."

"Ultimately it was agreed that Rosenszweig would return
to Arcadia," Michael recorded in his book. "Cogan and Aretsky

continued searching for a formula that would both bring in new business and woo back '21's formerly faithful." When Alain Sailhac departed Michael succeeded him.

The work of restoration took two years. The refurbished club opened on May 11, 1987.

After surveying the changes the *New York Times's* restaurant critic, Bryan Miller, observed, "Two things remain immutable at '21': the legendary bar, which has been polished up but essentially unaltered; and prices: lunch runs about $40 to $50 a person, dinner is $65 and up, up, up depending on the wine."

The barroom, he noted, "with its long, arching wooden bar, banquettes under the toy-festooned ceiling, and vintage cartoons and newspaper clippings on the walls, is as virile and vibrant as ever." He found the upstairs dining room offering "the warm and welcoming feeling of a country cabin after a day of skiing. The thick carpet with its '21' insignias, fabric panels above the glowing wood wainscotting, and floor-to-ceiling curtains muffle noise well. Brass chandeliers, leather banquettes, and tables with plenty of elbow room add to the pampering ambiance."

Assessing the food, Miller found Black Angus steak in a hot mustard crust "a dependable winner," the sweetbreads excellent, the butterflied pan-fried shrimp in herb butter "bright and tasty," red snapper atop creamy risotto "an extraordinary match," and the chicken hash "soothing."

It was this '21' that was captured in the 1987 Oliver Stone movie *Wall Street*, with its scene in which Michael Douglas as the ruthless financier Gordon Gekko instructs young insider-trader Charlie Sheen in how to get to and stay at the top in the world of big business. Declaring that lunch is for wimps as they sit at table 3, Douglas looks at Sheen's attire and in a bit of advice sums up the style of doing business in the "me" decade. "Buy a different suit," he says. "You can't come in here like this."

Twelve

THE '21' LEGEND

I began this book by stating that I ended up as a saloon keeper thanks to my big brother. I'm also indebted to Jack for stimulating another satisfying aspect of my life—the interest I shared with him in the art of the West. But when I ventured out there for the first time in the early 1930s, it wasn't to collect paintings.

Considering myself an outdoorsman, I packed my rods and guns and set my heart on fishing and hunting. I wanted to bag a bear. While I had years of angling experience, I was such a novice on the subject of bruins that before I headed out to Wyoming I had to pay a visit to the Bronx Zoo to learn how to recognize one.

As a hunter of wildlife I put myself in the same category as Theodore Roosevelt and his predecessor Grover Cleveland, who expressed the hunting philosophy of both men in *Fishing and Shooting Sketches*. He wrote, "There can be no doubt that certain men are endowed with a sort of inherent and spontaneous instinct which leads them to hunting and fishing indulgence as the most alluring and satisfying of all recreations. I believe it may be safely said that the true hunter or fisherman is born, not made. I believe, too, that those who thus by instinct and birthright belong to the sporting fraternity, are neither cruel, not greedy and wasteful of game and fish they pursue; and I am convinced that there can be no better conservators of the sensible and provident protection of game and fish than those who are enthusiastic in their pursuit, but are regulated and restrained by the sort of chivalric fairness and generosity, felt and recognized by every true sportsman."

I did get my bear, but only one, and it wasn't left where I shot it. My companions and I made several meals of the meat. But a more important experience for me during that initial excursion into the wilderness around Cody, Wyoming, was seeing the rugged beauty of the land and its wildlife. I returned to New York with a lasting appreciation of the splendors of the West that became a passion for the works of artists who captured and preserved it.

I became a student and collector not only of masterpieces by earlier painters such as Frederic Remington, but also of contemporary painters and sculptors. Year after year and piece by piece I was able to assemble some of the finest examples of works dating from the 1950s which captured and confirmed the power of the realities and myths of the Old West.

Of course, Jeannette provided great interest and support for my activities in these areas. She had never been a slacker in doing all she could to boost art and artists of all kinds, and among her favorite philanthropies were the New York City Ballet and the New York City Opera. Both benefited from her own contributions and her tireless work as a fundraiser. Her love of dachshunds also ensured her support for Cornell University's Veterinary School.

Unfortunately, there came a time when Jeannette began to suffer from the effects of the bane of aging women, osteoporosis. At age seventy-seven she also struggled valiantly against diabetes and pulmonary disease. The combination of these afflictions was to overtake her on the morning of December 6, 1991. She collapsed in our living room and was rushed to Mt. Sinai Hospital.

There was nothing that could be done to save her. Because we had no children, there were, other than myself, no immediate survivors. But she is remembered and will be honored in perpetuity through the works of the great artists collected in the Kriendler Gallery of Contemporary Western Art. It was established in both her name and mine as part of the Whitney Gallery of Western Art of the Buffalo Bill Historical Center in Cody, Wyoming.

Of the opening of the H. Peter and Jeannette Kriendler Gallery the Whitney curator, Sarah E. Boehme, said, "It gives us the opportunity to both celebrate and to assess the Buffalo Bill Historical Center's collection and programming. The Kriendler Gallery also will evolve with new acquisitions, scholarly discoveries, and maturing educational mandates. Its inauguration enriches the Historical Center with the creative spirit of the living arts and assures the continuing vitality of the museum."

Included in the collection are such diverse works as Anne Coe's *At the End of Her Rope*, a 1992 painting in acrylic on canvas depicting a cowboy on horseback towing a disabled pink Cadillac with a rope lassoed around its longhorn hood ornament. A more traditional piece of Western art is Fred Fellows's *No Easy Way Out*, a rider on a bucking horse done in bronze.

In addition to being honored by being asked to serve on the board of the Cody museum, I was pleased to accept an invitation to become a member of the Advisory Board of the Remington Art Museum in Ogdensburg, New York.

A delightful benefit of my being a director of the Whitney Gallery in Cody was getting to work with another board member, Wyoming's United States senator Alan Simpson, who retired from the Senate in 1996 to lead seminars at the John F. Kennedy School of Government at Harvard. Before being elected to the Senate in 1978 Al had been a practicing attorney in Cody, assistant attorney general of Wyoming, Cody city attorney, and a congressman (1964–77). Tall and rangy and as bald as a cue ball, he's twenty-six years younger than I (he was born in Cody in 1931), and he's always gotten a kick out of hearing me, the oldest member of the board, refer to him as a youngster. Upon the retirement of Mrs. Henry H. R. Coe, Alan became chairman of the board of the Whitney Gallery in Cody.

A devoted family man, Alan's daughter operated an art shop in Cody, and his two sons were lawyers in the Simpson hometown. Alan is to me such a personification of the "man of the West" depicted in so many of Remington's drawings, paintings, and bronzes that it's easy to picture him loping over rugged terrain on horseback, roping a steer, or crouching beside a campfire on a bitterly cold, star-spangled Wyoming night.

Few political figures I've known have exhibited the humor and wit I have found in Alan. He enjoys spinning wild and woolly tales of his upbringing in Wyoming, including a few scrapes with the law and admissions to having stretched the truth to get out of hot water so often that he quickly earned the nickname "Alibi Al."

Being a saloon keeper, I'm especially fond of a yarn Alan

will repeat at the drop of a hat (ten-gallon or not). He calls it "A Toast to Water." He attributes it to an inebriated politician who mistakenly stumbled into a meeting of the Women's Temperance Union, only to be invited to speak in the expectation that he'd be an example to be cited by the teetotaling ladies in waging their campaign to drive John Barleycorn from the nation.

The following is a transcript of a version Alan presented to a group in Washington, D.C., in 1996, as broadcast by C-SPAN:

A Toast to Water

I have seen it glisten in tiny teardrops on the face of infancy. I have seen it coursing down the cheeks of youth. And I have seen it in rushing torrents down the wrinkled cheeks of age. I have seen it in the blades of grass and leaves of trees, sparkling like tiny diamonds as the morning sun rose in resplendent glory over the eastern hills. I have seen it in the heavens as they shudder and weep in gentle rain and splash in shimmering droplets upon the warm and fertile earth to nurture the tiny tendrils of fruit and grain. I have seen it tumbling down the mountainside in cascades as fleecy as bridal veil with the music of liquid silver filling the vast forest arches with symphonies. And I have seen it in silent rivers rippling over pebbly bottoms and roaring in mad cataracts over precipitous waterfalls in its rush to join the Father of Waters. And I have seen it in the Father of Waters going in majestic sweep to join the ocean. I have seen it in the ocean on whose broad bosom float the battleships of the nations and the commerce of the world. But ladies, as a beverage it's a damn failure!

One thing that was certain about '21' customers was that water was not their preferred drink. As Earl Wilson quipped, the waiters and busboys that surrounded you naturally assumed you were a man of the world, and expected you'd be drinking wine.

Through the years, connoisseurs had noted that the quality of our wine cellar had been consistently excellent and with particular strength in our Burgundies. The average number of bottles in stock was around 25,000 in about five hundred varieties and vintages, from good table wines under twenty dollars to a double magnum of Chateau Lafite Rothschild for $1,400. Since Charlie Berns's venture in starting 21 Brands we had been trailblazers in promoting California wines as equal to the French, and in some instances even better.

Without a doubt, the wine cellar ranked high on the list of very attractive qualities considered by James Sherwood, founder of Sea Container Corporation. Parent company of a worldwide chain of deluxe hotels and restaurants, the firm had achieved enormous success in 1982 by restoring a legendary and luxurious European train, the Venice-Simplon Orient Express. That triumph was emulated in Asia with the launching of an Eastern and Oriental Express running between Singapore and Bangkok and a deluxe river cruise between Mandalay and Pagan in Burma.

Lacking a New York operation, the firm set its sights on acquiring '21'. In a deal which did not directly involve me, it did so in 1997. Among changes instituted was the closing of the upstairs dining rooms for lunch and dinner and making them available only for private and corporate functions. Downstairs, the barroom, now the only part of the club functioning as a public restaurant, was modified by removing a portion of a wall in the east section (Siberia) to provide direct access from the front lounge. This required shortening the bar by a few feet.

A new chef was also hired. Formerly with Bouley and Colors, and for a time at his own restaurant, American Renaissance, Erik Blauberg had a reputation for what a *Times* critic called "flashy food and unusual flavor combinations." In assessing Blauberg's debut at '21' the reviewer noted that at first the transition was "awkward" and that Blauberg "seemed to have difficulty balancing past and present at '21'," but "now appears to have made peace with '21', restoring french fries to the hamburger (they had been banished in favor of pickled vegetables), and adding dishes that are in perfect tune with the room."

The Zagat Survey said, "Although this 'NY landmark' is still criticized as 'clubby' and 'pricey,' under new management it's doing a lot 'to make newcomers feel welcome' with chef Erik Blauberg's 'better than ever' American food, 'famous people-watching' and prix-fixe meals that are 'a wonderful deal'; as always, private parties here are impressive; in short, 'It's back and better than ever.'"

The people-watchers at lunch or dinner were likely to spot the "names" of the nineties: Barbara Walters, Donald Trump, Jean Kennedy Smith, Laurence Tisch, Helen Gurley Brown, Larry King, Walter Cronkite, Tom Brokaw, Phyllis George, George Steinbrenner, Joe Torre, Michael Bloomburg, Michelle Pfeiffer, Rod Stewart, Bill Murray, Senator Al D'Amato, Geraldo Rivera, Dominick Dunne, Ed Koch, and Julia Roberts.

After sampling the menu, *New York Post* writer Braden Keil opined that although '21' was "half-museum" the kitchen is "no dinosaur." He found Erik Blauberg's fare "lighter," adding, "Not only has the restaurant survived since it originally opened as a speakeasy, but it's prevailed as one of the world's most famous eateries."

To assure continued success, the new manager, Bryan McGuire, didn't overlook the value of publicity and the fact that there's no better way to grab the attention of the press than by bringing in celebrities. And it's nice if you can come up with an angle. In 1998 this took the form of a monthly series of breakfasts with guest speakers telling what they expected in the new millennium. First to do so was ex-governor Mario Cuomo. Subsequent guests included Alair Townsend, publisher of *Crain's New York Business*; George Plimpton; Jay McInerney; and Anthony Haden-Guest. A "Baseball in the New Millennium" event featured ex-Yankee pitcher Jim Bouton, who blasted a proposal to build a new Yankee Stadium in Manhattan as an idea that would only be for the benefit of Yankees owner George Steinbrenner. He added, "I can't fathom the Yankees playing anywhere else but the Bronx." Perhaps fortunately, George had not been invited to the breakfast.

Another "celebrity-watcher" a customer could have ogled in the summer of 1998 was literary agent Lucianne Goldberg, who'd advised Linda Tripp to tape-record telephone conversations with Monica Lewinsky, thereby setting off the scandal which threatened to bring down the Clinton presidency. Goldberg had come to '21' to talk with CBS-TV's *60 Minutes* producer, Don Hewitt.

While renovations were being made in the barroom in August 1997, the club was closed and I was in Cody, Wyoming, for a visit to the Buffalo Bill Historical Center and a meeting of the board of the Whitney gallery.

No longer involved in '21' and unemployed for the first time in my life, I did my best to keep busy. Part of my day was spent in catching up on the news in the *Times* and with my investments through phone calls to brokers. There were occasional lunches at '21', often with Frank Polk in Siberia. On my birthday and other special days I was treated to dinner by my '21' secretary, Judith Channell, and my grandniece Jan Constantine, senior vice president and general counsel with publishing magnate Rupert Murdoch's News America. There were concerts and operas to go to in the evening, or television programs to see. With the Metropolitan Museum of Art directly across Fifth Avenue from my home, there was never a lack of exhibitions to take in. And on some sunny afternoons I just parked myself on a bench in front of the museum to watch the girls go by.

Come March, I continued an annual ritual of going down to Florida and the spring training camp of the Dodgers, my favorite baseball team since their Brooklyn years when I became a friend of the owner. I'd remained pals with Walter O'Malley even though he'd taken the team to Los Angeles. At some point in the relationship I was actually hired by the family as a "consultant" for a yearly fee of twenty-one dollars. And each spring or summer I traveled to Cody. I usually stayed for a month and enjoyed it, but I was always happy to get back to New York.

On my return from Cody in 1997 I learned I'd been chosen by the Museum of the City of New York to receive one of its "Our Town Treasures" awards. I found myself in stellar company. The other recipients were not only distinguished New Yorkers, but old friends and '21' regulars: Brooke Astor, Phyllis

"21"

Cerf Wagner, Kitty Carlisle Hart, Louis Auchincloss, and Gordon Parks. In addition to saying flattering things about me the program notes referred to '21' as "a New York City icon."

When you hear yourself being called a treasure, and a saloon where you've spent your entire adult life described as an icon, you realize it might be a good idea to take a moment to have a look at yourself. Therefore, I began exploring the possibility of occupying suddenly abundant spare time by writing a book about my '21' experiences.

The last time I'd reviewed my life in that context had been about twenty years earlier when I talked to Marilyn Kaytor as she was doing research for '21': The Life and Times of New York's Favorite Club, published in 1975. I had also had a chat with chef Michael Lomonaco while he was preparing his '21' Cookbook, which was published in 1996.

Around the time I was mulling over the notion of doing a book of my own I was interviewed by the British Broadcasting Corporation as part of a TV documentary on the subject of Prohibition. That experience stoked the fires of my resolve to record the part my family had played in that saga.

Whether anyone might be interested in reading about me was a legitimate question. Yet I had no doubt that someone would show an interest in the '21' story. Through the years the club has drawn a good deal of attention from magazine writers. In addition to the movies already mentioned, the club has also been the setting for scenes in novels. Yale man Erich Segal's Doctors has a character who's been invited to dine at someone else's expense. Told to give his appetite "free rein," he unhesitatingly says, "Okay then, how about The 21 Club?" In Rubout *at the Onyx*, a detective yarn set mostly along Swing Street in the 1930s (and authored by my collaborator on this book), clarinet-playing private eye Harry MacNeil misses seeing low-level gangster Joey Seldes gunned down at the bar of the Onyx Club because Harry is "up the street at Jack and Charlie's '21'." When Lolly Longbridge plans a scavenger hunt in Judith Krantz's *Mistral's Daughter*, one of the items on Lolly's list of things to be collected is "one waiter's jacket from Jack and Charlie's." And in Ian Fleming's James Bond thriller *Diamonds Are Forever* Agent 007 is taken to '21' by Tiffany Case. "You know what they say about this place?" she says. "All you can eat for three hundred bucks."

Colorful and romantic as these customers are, fiction could never truly imitate life in '21' or take notice that '21' was on its way to becoming a legend in its own time. That evolution was, I suppose, like growing old; you don't understand what's going on until it's staring you in the face. One moment I was a teenager loafing at the bar of the Red Head and nursing a soft drink and hoping to dance with a girl and the next thing I knew I was the boss of a legend by the name of '21'.

Years and years ago in either the Red Head, Fronton, Puncheon or at the bar in '21', one of the newspapermen—it could've been Hellinger, Hemingway, Broun, or Benchley—said a rule of journalism is that when truth becomes legend, to hell with the truth; print the legend.

In considering writing about Jack, Charlie, Mac, Bob, Jerry, Sheldon, and all the others whose hard work and dedication went into creating and sustaining '21'—and in recalling tales of our customers—I hadn't been able to point to a moment when I might have looked around '21' and realized I was part of a legend. All I saw was a swell place to get an honest drink and a good meal in the company of people who were fun to be with.

So how and why did '21' become legendary?

Marilyn Kaytor wrote, "'21' is a very special place; not a bar, not a restaurant, but a great jolly drinking and dining establishment with an aura of self-assurance and an intimate masculine flavor that sets it apart from other gin mills into almost the private club category, yet it doesn't suffer from the parochialism of a private club. It is home to those in need of sensitive shelter."

She concluded, "A barroom becomes loved, if it does, because of the stamp of its owners. It is the mood of a place more than the drinks that captures the public's fancy."

That '21' grew into legend was for all these reasons, but it could not have become an icon without customers. Lucius Beebe had recognized that in 1952. "Legend gathers thickly about restaurants," he wrote, "but never more so than around one frequented by the great and the picturesque."

How much more picturesque can you get than Dorothy Parker leaving '21' one afternoon long, long ago, and Clare Booth Luce stepping aside for her and saying, "Age before beauty," to which Dorothy retorted, "Pearls before swine."

Did that moment of delicious cattiness really happen, and in '21'? Was it actually in the '21' lobby that Bob Benchley said, "I must get out of this wet coat and into a dry martini?" Did Bob *ever* say that? Is it true that Humphrey Bogart told an autograph seeker in front of '21' to commit insecticide? Who can tell for sure? Who cares? Does it matter? Not a damn bit.

The essence of the '21' legend may be found in the long-time customer who was leaving the country and was given one of our hallmark red-and-white checkered tablecloths as a memento. For the rest of his life, on nostalgic occasions, he'd take it from a drawer and spread it atop a table and sit there looking at it and remembering good times and fine companions.

Another spoke of the "charming variety" of the people he'd met in '21': moody, hard-drinking writers brooding about life; beautiful, fur-draped women, each with a particular and distinctive charm; sparkling Hollywood celebrities; the well-heeled, freewheeling, jet-propelled extroverts. They all added up to what he called "an institution" and others preferred to call a legend.

Deciding to forge ahead with writing a book about myself in which the main character would be '21', I contacted a friend in the William Morris Agency. He put me in touch with a vice president in the literary department, Mel Berger.

After listening to my pitch, Mel said, "I know just the guy to work with you. I'll give you his number and you can take him to lunch at '21' and you can see if you two hit it off."

On Tuesday, July 8, 1997, which also just happened to be my ninety-second birthday, I sat down for lunch at my customary table in Siberia (against the east wall in the corner by the long bar) with Frank Polk and H. Paul Jeffers, the fellow who was to become my collaborator on these memoirs. While we talked, we were interrupted by the presentation of a cake with candles ablaze, applause, and a robust rendition of "Happy Birthday" by the waiters, captains, bartenders, busboys, and customers.

With a tape recorder running as we feasted on the cake, Paul asked, "Can you sum up the life and times of Peter Kriendler and '21' in a few words?"

With my mind alive with memories, I understood that there hadn't been *one* moment when '21' became a legend, nor had it become one for any single reason. Had it been that simple there would have been nothing worth writing about. So how could I sum up the life and times of '21' and my part in them in a few words?

What I said was, "Every day was New Year's Eve."

INDEX